D0450700

NOT SO QUIET . . .

NOT SO QUIET...
Stepdaughters of War

HELEN ZENNA SMITH

AFTERWORD BY JANE MARCUS

THE FEMINIST PRESS
at The City University of New York
New York

Not So Quiet . . . was first published in Great Britain by
Albert E. Marriot in 1930
© 1930 by Helen Zenna Smith
Afterword © 1989 by Jane Marcus
All rights reserved.

Published 1989 by The Feminist Press at The City University of
New York, 365 Fifth Avenue, Suite 5406, New York, NY 10016.
www.feministpress.org

Printed in the U.S. A.
10 09 08 07 06   11 10 9 8 7

Library of Congress Cataloging-in-Publication Data
Smith, Helen Zenna, 1896–1985.
    Not So Quiet.

    Reprint. Originally published: London : A.E. Marriott,
1930.
    1. World War, 1914–1918 — Fiction. I. Title.
PR6031.R45N6 1988   823'.912   88-31072
ISBN-10: 0-935312-97-8, ISBN-10: 0-935312-82-X (pbk.)
ISBN-13: 978-0-935312-82-9 (pbk.)

The Feminist Press gratefully acknowledges Barbara Hardy for
recommending the republication of *Not So Quiet* . . . for a new
generation of readers.

This publication is made possible, in part, by public funds from
the New York State Council on the Arts.

Cover art: *A V.A.D. Motor Driver* by Gilbert Rogers. Reproduced
by permission of the Imperial War Museum

" . . . *each in his separate star,*
Shall draw the thing as he sees it
For the God of Things as they are."

(Extract from confidential sealed
paper given to every V.A.D.
on embarkation for service in
France during the Great War.)

NOT SO QUIET . . .

CHAPTER I

WE have just wakened from our first decent sleep for weeks—eight glorious dreamless hours of utter exhaustion. The guns are still booming in the distance as energetically as when we fell on our camp beds without the formality of removing our uniforms, shoes, gaiters or underclothing. We have not had our garments off for nine days, but there has been an unexpected lull this afternoon; no evacuations, only one funeral, and very few punishments, though we feel the usual midnight whistle will break our run of luck any time now. That gives us ten minutes to dress and stand by ambulances ready for convoy duty. In the meantime we snuggle neck-high in our flea-bags and munch slabs of chocolate and stale biscuits. We have slept like logs through the evening meal—all except Tosh, who never misses a food-call on principle. It is her turn to make the Bovril. We gloatingly watch her light the little spirit lamp. We are hungry, but we are used to hunger. We are always hungry in varying degrees—hungry, starving, or ravenous. The canteen food is vile at its best; at its worst it defies description—except from Tosh. We have existed mostly on our own Bovril, biscuits, and slab chocolate since arriving in France, and when all is said and done it is a colourless, discouraging diet for young women of twenty-three—which our six ages average—who are doing men's work. Tosh is the only one who can systematically eat the canteen tack without vomiting or coming out in food boils; but she has a stomach as strong as a horse's. Also, she has been out longer than the rest of us and is more hardened. At first her inside used to revolt as ours still does, but she thinks that in another month or so she could eat what the food resembles without turning a hair.

The girl in the next bed, known as " The B.F.," objects to this remark on the grounds of coarseness, but Tosh only grins. The rest take no notice. A short while back we should have shrunk into ourselves with undisguised horror at the simile, but our minds, in addition to our digestions, are becoming acclimatised. Sordid comparisons are in the picture here where life has so suddenly become sordid. We wish they would both dry up and let us doze on our biscuits until the whistle actually blows. Besides, we know The B.F.'s pro-

NOT SO QUIET . . .

tests are merely for refinement's sake. Tosh the sinner is not of the common herd. She is the niece of an earl. That, in The B.F.'s eyes, covers a multitude of Anglo-Saxon franknesses.

I watch Tosh lazily. She is wandering around in the flickering candlelight dressed in a soiled woollen undervest and a voluminous pair of navy blue bloomers, chain-smoking yellow perils at a furious rate. There is something vaguely comforting in the Amazonian height and breadth of Tosh. She has the hips of a matron—intensified by the four pairs of thick combinations she always wears for warmth, a mind like a sewer (her own definition), the courage of a giant, the vocabulary of a Smithfield butcher, and the round, wind-reddened face of a dairymaid. She says she picked up her repertoire of language from the stable lads—her father is a well-known sportsman—and there is no reason to doubt her word. Nevertheless, Tosh is the idol of the entire convoy, not only of this room. I have adored her since the first night I arrived, that ghastly first night I was shoved on to an ambulance and told to meet my first convoy of wounded. I had never driven by night before, even in England. My nerves were all on edge, and the first ghastly glimpse of blood and shattered men sent me completely to pieces. We backed our ambulances in a long row. Tosh was next in line to me. She watched me climb down, saw me, half-fainting, retching my heart out against the bonnet of my own bus, slipped from her driving seat, seized me and shook sense into me. " Pull yourself together, you bloody West Kensington lady with your bloody West Kensington tricks. You're loaded. Get back before Commandant spots you. You're holding up the line. Get back."

I got back. I drove till dawn to and fro—station, Number Five Hospital—Number Five Hospital, station . . . sick, numb, frozen-fingered, frozen-hearted . . . station, Number Five Hospital— Number Five Hospital, station. . . .

It ended, just as I thought it would never end. Back again at the depot I collapsed with my head on the steering wheel. Tosh helped me down, forced steaming cocoa into me. . . . " Pretty bloody kick-off, Smithy. But wait till you get gas cases or, worse, liquid-fire. . . ."

I whimpered like a puppy. . . . I couldn't go on. . . . I was a coward. . . . I couldn't face those stretchers of moaning men again . . . men torn and bleeding and raving. . . .

Tosh laughed a funny, queer laugh. " And the admiring family at home who are basking in your reflected glory ? ' My girl's doing her bit—driving an ambulance very near the line. . . .' " She laughed again. " Will they let you off, Smithy ?

Not likely! You'll never have the pluck to crawl home and admit you're ordinary flesh and blood. Can't you hear them? 'Well, back *already*? You didn't stay *long*, did you?' No, Smithy, you're one of England's Splendid Daughters, proud to do their bit for the dear old flag, and one of England's Splendid Daughters you'll stay until you crock up or find some other decent excuse to go home covered in glory. It takes nerve to carry on here, but it takes twice as much to go home to flag-crazy mothers and fathers. . . ."

I watch her now running a comb through her hair, softly damning and blasting the knots. Generous hair, Tosh's, as generous as the rest of her, thick, long, red as a sunset in Devon when not grime- and grease-blackened. As I stare she parts the strands over her right ear, peers anxiously into the square of looking-glass, and emits a string of swear-words before turning to The Bug.

" Lend me your scissors, Bug."

The Bug silently hands them over, lights a cigarette, and passes me the paper packet.

" Everyone read this paper? " asks Tosh.

Everyone has. Tosh spreads the newspaper on the floor near her bed and kneels down, brandishing the scissors.

The B.F. cries out in alarm. "You're not going to cut off your hair, Tosh? Your *lovely* hair."

" Why should I be a free lodging-house for waifs and strays ? " Tosh laughs hoarsely at her own crude wit. She has, when amused, the big porky, jolly laugh of a fat publican.

" Oh, Tosh, how *can* you ? Short hair's terribly unfeminine. I wouldn't cut off my hair for anything."

" No, you vain little scut, you'd rather crawl."

Snip, snip, snip go the scissors. Snip, snip, snip. The long, red strands fall into the much-scanned crumpled newspaper. I crane my neck. *Have* I read it ? Is it the *Daily Mail* or the *Daily Express* ? If it's the *Mail* I have read it, but if it's the *Express* there's something I haven't quite finished. . . .

A red curl of Tosh's hair hides the top of the page. I can't see. Perhaps a post will come to-morrow bringing fresh newspapers ; we haven't had any letters, or, better still, parcels, for six days.

Snip, snip, snip. . . .

" No wonder I've scratched my head off—no wonder I couldn't sleep ! " Tosh points triumphantly to the paper. We interestedly follow the direction of her fingers and go on munching our ginger biscuits. A few weeks ago we should have vomited. But after cleaning the inside of an ambulance it would take more than a few lice to make our gorges rise.

" A bloody platoon," says Tosh.

Snip, snip, snip. . . .

" I'll bet you're all as alive-o, if you only carried out a smashing attack," chuckles Tosh.

I catch the eye of The Bug and we both grimace— we know Tosh is very near the truth, for we have both been itching furiously for days past. Small-tooth combing, though a temporary check, has no lasting effect. We get them from the " sitters "— the cases well enough to sit beside us in front on the ambulances. Straight from the field dressing stations, before that straight from the trenches, who can wonder the sitters are alive with vermin ?

Snip, snip, snip. . . .

Tosh's hair is half off, giving her a curiously lop-sided effect. I wish I had her courage, but a mental vision of Mother restrains me. Poor Mother, she would die of horror if I came home on leave with my hair cut short like a man's. She wouldn't understand the filth and beastliness after my cheery letters home. Only dreadful blue-stocking females cut their hair. Besides, Mother has always been so proud of my hair—why, I cannot imagine. It is not beautiful hair. It is long, but thin and mouse-coloured. Nondescript. Like its owner. Like its owner's name, Helen Smith. Helen Z. Smith. How jealously I preserve the secret

15

of that Z., that ludicrous Z. bestowed on me by my mother. Z. was the heroine of a book mother read the month before I arrived on earth. She wanted me to grow up like Z. Z. was the paragon of beauty, virtue, and womanliness. Mother has been sadly disappointed over the first ; I am still the second, but the third—well, Z. was never an ambulance driver somewhere in France. I am very dubious about the third.

Snip, snip, snip. . . .

No, I had better not emulate Tosh. It would definitely put the tin helmet on the womanliness. It would also spoil Mother's pet story of myself and my sister Trix—of how, a wee fair head and a wee dark head, lately released from the tortures of curl-papers, we used to walk demurely to Sunday school while Mother waved from the front gate. Since Father grew rich and promoted us to Wimbledon Common, Mother omits the reference to the front gate—it isn't done on Wimbledon Common to wave from the front gate—but she still bores everyone who will listen (and a lot who won't) with the story of the two wee curly heads. With Trix a V.A.D. and me ambulance driving, I can see those wee curly heads working overtime, while Mother drops a sentimental tear on the socks she is knitting for my second-loot brother, her " hero boy."

Snip, snip, snip. . . .

"You'll look awfully unsexed, Tosh," warns
The B.F.

"Unsexed? Me? With the breasts of a nursing
mother?" Tosh winks behind The B.F.'s back.
The poor B.F. gasps and goes scarlet. Tosh is
revolutionising her ideas of the British aristocracy
in private life more and more each day.

Snip, snip, snip. . . .

We go on munching our biscuits and smoking our
gaspers. Directly the kettle boils there will be hot
Bovril, something to warm us before starting out—
thin, miserable stuff, for the bottle is nearly empty
and there are six of us, but enough to send a glow
through our bodies. We think of it with mouth-
watering anticipation and watch Tosh marshalling
the lively contents of the newspaper more towards
the centre with a pen-holder.

"What an R.T.O. was lost when I became an
ambulance driver," says Tosh.

That goes down well with us, even The B.F.
Inwardly we are proud to think our stomachs no
longer heave up and down at the sight of a louse.
After all, a few vermin more or less make little
difference. Our flea-bags are full of them, in spite
of Keatings and Lysol, and our bodies a mass of
tiny red bites with the tops scratched off. We are
too hard worked to spare the necessary time to keep

17

clean, and that is the trouble. It is four weeks since we had a bath all over, nine days since we had a big wash—we haven't had time. We dare not hot-bath in case we have to go out immediately after-wards into the snow. The last girl who did it is now in hospital with double pneumonia and not expected to live.

Tosh finishes her barbering. She shakes her head like a shaggy dog. I see to my satisfaction that the paper is the *Mail* and not the *Express*. I have read it, after all. Tosh crumples it into a ball, takes the enamelled chamber from under her camp-bed, and proceeds to make a bonfire inside it. It smokes at first, but after a few seconds begins to crackle merrily.

"Wholesale slaughter," says Tosh. "Well, it's the fashion in our circles, *n'est-ce pas?* Anyone got a fag?"

She takes another sheet of paper and small-combs her short locks, shaking the results into the emer-gency incinerator. We all do this when we get a chance and our heads become too unbearable. If Commandant knew there would be ructions and punishments galore. "Mrs. Bitch," as Tosh has christened Commandant, is punishment-mad. She punishes us by giving us extra work to do in our time off (when we have any). Usually it is extra orderly duty, though recently she distinguished herself by sending me out with a dustpan and small brush into the snow-covered path where the ambulances stand to sweep up the bits of paper, cigarette-ends, and rubbish that were lying in the snow. I had committed the awful offence of warming my hands near the canteen fire, because they were too frozen to go on cleaning my engine, and Commandant caught me.

"What are you doing here?" she inquired majestically. "You are supposed to be ambulance-cleaning, I *thought*."

I explained about my frozen fingers.

"Oh!" said Mrs. Bitch, with a sweet smile. "Then perhaps you haven't enough work to do to keep your fingers warm. Perhaps a little extra work will help."

That is how I became a scavenger. Commandant is dreadfully efficient. Like most dreadfully efficient women, she is universally loathed. Even The B.F. has got as far as calling her "Mrs. You-Know-Itch!"

"I feel pounds lighter," says Tosh. "If only I could soak and soak and soak in a real bath."

Our thoughts fly to bathrooms : big, white-tiled bathrooms with gleaming silver taps and glass-enclosed showers, bathrooms with rubber floors and square-checked bathmats, bathrooms fitted with

19

thick glass shelves loaded with jar upon jar of scented bath salts, white, green, mauve—different colours and different perfumes, lilac, verbena, carnation, lily of the valley. We see ourselves, steeped to the neck in over-hot, over-scented water ; in our hands are clasped enormous, springy sponges foaming with delicious soapsuds, expensive soap-suds—only the most expensive will suffice—sandal-wood, scented oatmeal, odiferous violet. Massage brushes lie to hand, long-handled narrow brushes with quaint, bulbous bristles of hollow rubber that catch the middle of the back just where the arms are too short to reach. . . . We scrub and scrub and scrub until we are clean and pink and tingling and glowing, we lie in a pleasant semi-coma until the water begins to cool, but emerging has no terrors. Electric fires glow softly ; before them are spread incredibly huge bath-sheets, soft, lavender-scented, monogrammed, waiting to caress our dripping bodies, to smother them in voluptuous warmth. Now we are dry ; we pepper our newly-born selves with talcum powder. " June Roses " fills the air with its fragrance, daintily argues with the scent of the bath water, triumphs. . . .

" Half a pint of icy water between six of us," says Tosh. " Oh Hell, there's a war on, they tell me."

We munch stolidly.

My cigarettes have given out. Tosh gets the cups, wipes them with a handkerchief and divides the contents of the Bovril carefully.

" If there isn't a parcel soon with a new supply we go out empty to-morrow," says Tosh.

Skinny wakens with a yawn, exhibiting a hideous vulcanite plate in her lower jaw. Skinny is smart and tolerably good-looking in uniform, but when she first awakens she reminds one uneasily of a corpse. Her face is yellow with the skin stretched tightly across the high cheekbones and there are queer bags under her eyes. Tosh says the bags mean kidney trouble. Certainly Skinny is out of her flea-bag every quarter of an hour—an awful nuisance when we are nervy and easily awakened. She isn't very quiet about it, either. When Skinny is asleep her rather large mouth pinches up tightly and greyly, and she is irresistibly like a photograph a gardener of ours showed me once of his mother, taken in the coffin after death.

Skinny glances at her wrist-watch and grabs the biscuit tin. " You've cut your hair off," she remarks to Tosh.

Tosh gives her a quick glance and turns her back. She loathes Skinny, and never misses an opportunity of snubbing her—not the good-natured ragging to which she treats The B.F., but the kind of snub that makes those present wish they had never been born. It is Skinny's own fault. She will talk to Tosh. Tosh has asked her straight out not to, but she will persist. Tosh wants Commandant to move Skinny to one of the two-bed or three-bed cubicles —there are often vacancies when the girls go sick— but Commandant knows Tosh wants it, and therefore Skinny will remain with us to the bitter end.

"You look like a Shakespearian page, Tosh, or Rosalind," continues Skinny.

Tosh goes on stirring the Bovril.

"Something fascinatingly boyish," says Skinny.

Tosh swings round. "Boyish my bottom," she snaps. "Take your Bovril and shut up. I hate being lousy ; I don't care a curse what I look like."

There is a silence. Tosh stirs the Bovril fiercely and passes it round. In the fifth bed Etta Potato snores peacefully through everything. Her real name is Etta Potter, but someone dubbed her Etta Potato the day she came out, and Etta Potato she will be for the duration. She is a good-natured soul, phlegmatic, law-abiding, and totally devoid of nerves or imagination. She could sleep on a clothes-line suspended by pegs from the ears, and wake as good-tempered as though she had rested in a soft feather bed.

"Bovril ! "

The Bug thrusts a biscuit into the parted lips of Etta Potato and she wakes, smiles amiably, and begins to chew without inquiry. The Bug is the most interesting member of our communal life— to me. Chiefly because she is a mystery. We know about the others : The B.F.'s father is a motor manufacturer ; Etta Potato is a virgin war widow : her husband went straight from the registry office to the trenches and was killed a week later ; Tosh has been in the picture papers so often she hasn't a shred of private life left ; Skinny is the only child of a big pot at the War Office ; while I am the nondescript daughter of a nondescript father who made money, sold his business, retired, and is spending the rest of his life in a big house on Wimbledon Common trying to forget the word " jam." (How father must hate the " plum-and-apple " jokes that are flying around !). But of The Bug we know nothing. She is quite tiny, wiry, tragic-eyed and dark, with a bitter mouth and a disconcerting trick of saying nothing at all that irritates Commandant to the point of insanity. She is quite the most silent girl in company I have ever met, but sometimes when we are alone—a rare thing in this communal bedroom—she talks on and on in a flat, monotonous voice as though she hated the world and was thinking her hatred out loud. Her name, The Bug, originated from the quaint, round-shouldered way she hunches up behind the steering-wheel.

"What was supper like, Tosh?" asks Etta Potato.

Tosh tells her in one graphic word, and The B.F. clutches her bosom dramatically and cries: "Tosh!" Tosh christened her The B.F., but we are quite convinced that, although flattered at being on nickname level with the niece of an earl, she hasn't the vaguest notion that the cryptic letters signify anything other than her own initials—Bertina Farmer.

The B.F. is quite liked. She is fearfully "refeened and neece," but we forgive her that: she is such a harmless ass. Her definition of a true lady is one who is ignorant of the simplest domestic details to the point of imbecility. She insisted on helplessly inquiring the first day she came over *however* one knew when water had reached boiling point. The servants at home had always boiled the family water, she said. She was very shocked at Tosh's coarse comment on this form of economy in the home.

The B.F. is like a Harrison Fisher girl on a magazine cover, and is frankly disappointed with the War. The War Office has not quite played the game sending her here. She had an idea being out in France was a kind of perpetual picnic minus the

24

restrictions of home life. She saw herself in a depot, the cynosure of innumerable admiring male eyes. It seems such a waste of a well-cut uniform to be in a place where the men are too wounded or too harassed to regard women other than cogs in the great machinery, and the women are too worn out to care whether they do or not. She intends to transfer to the base at the earliest opportunity. " For," she said the other day, " surely you can do your bit just as patriotically in an amusing place where there are amusing officers ! "

(The B.F. is very fond of talking about " doing her bit." She would go down terribly well with my parents.)

Tosh gravely advised her not to overdo " doing her bit " with the amusing officers, in case she was not so amused in the end.

The B.F. is pretty and soft and rather plump. She was comically like a ruffled doll as she drew herself up. " I can tell by your face, Tosh, you're being obscene, but I do *not* see the point."

" Oh, you'll see *that* if you overdo ' doing your bit,' " laughed Tosh. " Won't she, girls ? "

" Do you know what she means ? " inquired The B.F. piteously.

We did.

A few weeks ago we should not have known.

The Bovril is good. We want more, but there is

25

none. Tosh empties the chamber of charred paper out of the window, letting in a blast of icy air. The wind is rising, moaning round the convoy like a thousand angry witches. We shiver. Is it going to snow again? It may grow warmer if it snows. It can't grow any colder. It has been freezing hard for days. We break the ice in the water-jug in the mornings and waken with our hot-water bottles frozen to a solid lump. We snuggle deeper into our flea-bags and tell one another we really must get up. The Bug wants to change her underclothing and Etta Potato wants to wash to the waist to save doing it in the morning. She looks intensely relieved when informed the water jug is nearly empty, that there is just enough water for a hasty sponge of the face and hands. Her " big wash " must wait, indefinitely, until she plucks up courage to carry the hot water from the outhouse across the open yard, through the snow, into the bedroom. The Bug decides after all not to change into fresh underwear; her old ones are warm, and there is no sense in changing into clean, cold things until she washes her body thoroughly. We all agree. The Bug is grateful for our approval. She will show her gratitude in the usual manner, by pointing out the danger of bathing on some cold night when we feel slack. Skinny pensively ponders if there is time to write to her bosom friend, Ellie, in Brighton, but makes no attempt to move. We are glad, for she will read aloud what she has written, and we all detest Ellie, the bosom friend in Brighton. We don't know her personally, but that makes no difference.

Tosh puts on her underskirt, a second pair of woollen stockings, thick shoes and gaiters, and rolls her body, cocoon-wise, in a khaki scarf of extraordinary length before donning her uniform. She tries on her cap. It is several sizes too large now, owing to her depleted hair. We all lazily proffer advice. A safety-pin and a reef in the back of the cap is easily the most popular and workable. The B.F. produces the safety-pin. Tosh pins her cap and tries it on. The safety-pin is not strong enough —it flies apart and jabs her in the back of the neck.

"St. Peter's holy trousers!" ejaculates Tosh.

We roar with laughter.

"Tosh!" reproves the B.F. "Your blasphemy!"

"What? You don't call that blasphemous?" Tosh is genuinely surprised. "If you really want to hear some blasphemy. . . ."

The very last thing The B.F. wants. She interrupts hastily. "You can say what you like, Tosh, but it is blasphemous to talk about St. Peter having trousers. . . ."

NOT SO QUIET . . .

"Holy ones," says Tosh. "I did make them holy, B.F."

"*Any* kind," insists The B.F. "It's blasphemous to say he's got any kind at all."

"B.F.! Don't tell me there are no trousers in heaven. Don't tell me the men go trotting about showing all they've . . ."

"Tosh!" The B.F. turns crimson and the rest of us fall about. Then, the joke over, we as suddenly grow quiet again, waiting for the whistle. The only sound in the room is the crackle-crackle of the newspaper Tosh is stuffing into her cap. In the silence the guns grow ominous and audible. More ominous than when last we listened to their eternal rumble-rumble. They are always louder at night when the day noises have ceased. There has never been a lull in their muffled thunder night or day for the last fortnight. It is seldom they worry us ; we are too dead beat as a rule to notice them. Usually we fit them into the backs of our subconscious minds and forget them. They are like the pianoforte accompaniment to a gramophone record of Melba or Caruso—there, but never listened to until the voice ceases.

Booma-boom-booma-boom-boommm!

"I've lost a hairpin," says Etta Potato. "No, false alarm."

She smiles. Placid Etta Potato. Her chief

28

worry in life is the fear of losing her hairpins. They are many and large, stout iron affairs with the black enamel worn completely away, and Etta Potato can be traced by them as effectively as the hare in a paper-chase. During a recent air-raid, when her ambulance—fortunately empty—was knocked into a ditch by the impact of a bomb which fell in the next field, Etta Potato was found under the bonnet hunting for one of the lost hairpins. I watch her now carefully hairpinning her smooth, brown bun, and I see her in about sixty years hence—placid, scarcely lined and imperturbable, still fastening a smooth bun with hairpins. The bun will be white, but the hairpins will probably be the same.

Booma-boom-booma-boom-boommm !

" God, I hate those bloody guns," mutters Tosh, and this time The B.F. is silent. We stare ahead. We hate and dread the days following on the guns when they boom without interval. Trainloads of broken human beings : half-mad men pleading to be put out of their misery ; torn and bleeding and crazed men pitifully obeying orders like a herd of senseless cattle, dumbly, pitifully straggling in the wrong direction, as senseless as a flock of senseless sheep obeying a senseless leader, herded back into line by the orderly, the kind sheep-dog with a " Now then, boys, this way. That's the ticket, boys," instead of a bark ; men with faces bleeding through their hasty bandages ; men with vacant eyes and mouths hanging foolishly apart dropping saliva and slime ; men with minds mercifully gone ; men only too sane, eyes horror-filled with blood and pain. . . .

My last letter home opens before me, photograph clear, sent in response to innumerable complaints concerning the brevity of my crossed-out field postcards : "*It is such fun out here, and of course I'm loving every minute of it ; it's so splendid to be really in it. . . .*"

The only kind of letter home they expect, the only kind they want, the only kind they will have. Tell them that you hate it, tell them that you fear it, that you are as terror-stricken as you were when they left you alone in the dark in that big, quiet house on Wimbledon Common, you who had been accustomed to the cheery trams and rumbling motor-buses of Shepherd's Bush—tell them that all the ideals and beliefs you ever had have crashed about your gun-deafened ears—that you don't believe in God or them or the infallibility of England or anything but bloody war and wounds and foul smells and smutty stories and smoke and bombs and lice and filth and noise, noise, noise—that you live in a world of cold sick fear, a dirty world of darkness and despair—that you want to crawl

ignominiously home away from these painful writh-
ing things that once were men, these shattered,
tortured faces that dumbly demand what it's
all about in Christ's name—that you want to find
somewhere where life is quiet and beautiful and
lovely as it was before the world turned khaki
and blood-coloured—that you want to creep
into a refuge where there is love instead of
hate. . . .

Tell them these things ; and they will reply on
pale mauve deckle-edged paper calling you a
silly hysterical little girl—" You always were inclined
to exaggerate, darling "—and enclose a patent
carbolised body belt ; " the very latest thing for
active service, dear, in case you encounter a stray
' bitey ' " (that's what you used to call a louse
yourself, hundreds of years ago ; refined, weren't
you ?), an iron tonic, some more aspirin tablets.
" Stick it, darling ; go on doing your bit, because
England is proud of her brave daughters, so very
proud. . . ."

England is proud of her brave daughters.

Almost as proud as Father and Mother.

" It's so splendid to be really in it. . . ."

The only kind of letter they want. Father can
take it to his club and swank : " I've got two girls
out in France now, and a son in training. He'll
be ordered out any minute, he says. Ah ! One

of my girls pretty well in the firing line ; not allowed to say, of course—Censor and all that—address Somewhere in France "—swelling himself—" doing her bit, you know, doing her bit. Just on twenty-one. Plucky? Yes, but loves it. An English-woman to her finger-tips—wouldn't keep out of it—proud to do her bit for the old flag "—blowing his nose emotionally—" proud to do her bit, God bless her. . . ."

And Mother, head of more committees than any-one else on Wimbledon Common, fiercely competing with Mrs. Evans-Mawnington in recruiting. Mrs. Evans-Mawnington and Mother like the angles at the base of an isosceles triangle : maddeningly equal to one another. Mrs. Evans-Mawnington has a son ; so has Mother. The angles are equal. Mrs. Evans-Mawnington is head of the same number of committees as Mother. The angles are equal again. But Mrs. Evans-Mawnington has no daughters, which is where Mother scores. Her angle is two daughters up on Mrs. Evans-Mawning-ton's angle—oh ! decidedly two daughters up. She expects soon to out-committee Mrs. Evans-Mawnington on the strength of her two daughters. She will make Mrs. Evans-Mawnington's angle so small Euclid himself would never recognise it. " So brave of you, Mrs. Smith, to have given your children, so noble. . . ." Mother triumphantly smirking across the room at the disgruntled Mrs. Evans-Mawnington, who has no daughters : " We must all do our bit, mustn't we ?   Abnormal times. I had a letter to-day from my Nellie, so cheery, so full of spirit, not at all the kind of life she's been accustomed to—such a sheltered life she's always had—it's a trifle rough out there, but she wouldn't come home for anything."—Wiping away a tear.—" When I think of her wee fair head walking along with the wee dark head of my little Trix—she's in a hospital in France— both of them doing their bit . . . we must all do our bit. . . . I am wearing myself to a shadow, but they shall never say Mother didn't do her bit, too ; if they are in it, Mother shall be in it too. . . ."

Mrs. Evans - Mawnington scowling, furious-mouthed, jealous . . . Mother smug, saccharine-sweet . . . shelves of mangled bodies . . . filthy smells of gangrenous wounds . . . shell-ragged, shell-shocked men . . . men shrieking like wild beasts inside the ambulance until they drown the sound of the engine . . . *" Nellie loves to be really in it "*—no God to pray to because you know there isn't a God—how shall I carry on ? . . . *" Proud to do her bit for the old flag."* Oh, Christ ! Oh, Christ ! . . . I'm only twenty-one and nobody cares because I've been pitchforked into hell, nobody cares because I'm going mad, mad, mad ; nobody cares because I'm afraid I've no guts, I'm white-livered. . . . "*We must all do our bit.*" . . . They've made me a heroine, one of England's Splendid Women, and I'm shaking with fright, I can't hold the wheel . . . one of England's splendid heroines . . . how easy to drive the bus clean over the hill into the valley below . . . an accident. . . . " She died for King and Country." . . . Mother in deep mourning, head of another committee, enrolling recruits at top speed . . . one daughter dead on active service equal to how many daughters alive Somewhere in France ? . . . Shrieks of torn bodies . . . old men safe in England snubbing slackers. " By Gad ! if I were a few years younger, by Gad ! " . . . Flappers presenting white feathers to men who don't want to be maimed or killed . . . ever-knitting women safe from the blood and the mud, women who can still pray to their smug God, the God who is on our side, the God who hates the enemy because He is on our side . . . women who don't have to stare into the black night and hum a revue tune—" If you were the only girl in the world "—to drown the wild-beast noises of men gone mad with pain . . . one of England's heroines . . . a failure, a failure . . . a coward, a weak, suburban coward . . . screams of men growing louder and louder, maddened men, louder, louder, louder, shrieking down the song and the engine. . . .

The whistle blows.

" Out of it, *mes petites harlots*," says Tosh.

We scramble from our flea-bags.

CHAPTER II

THREE ack emma.

I am the last ambulance home . . . which means no hot cocoa. My luck has been dead out this convoy. The others struck it fairly easy, but I started off badly. I got Number Thirteen Hospital at the station gate—not only the farthest one out of camp, but the one on top of the hill with a rough, detestable, badly-winding road, dotted with irregular heaps of snow-covered stones hard enough to negotiate by daylight, but hell to drive up at the crawl with a load of wounded on a pitch black night in a hurricane of wind, . . . when the slightest jar may mean death to a man inside. We all loathe drawing Number Thirteen, and an audible sigh of relief always goes up from a driver when the sergeant on duty gives her any other number.

It would be my luck to get it on a night when the roads are so ice-polished the wheels seem to be skating—no grip at all—and the wind is blowing a gale. It nearly turned the old bus turtle as we unexpectedly caught the full force at the summit on my first trip. Next journey I was too fed up to care. This was not my lucky night with a vengeance. I was carrying a spotted fever case, which meant that after I had been unloaded in the front entrance of Number Thirteen I had to have the ambulance disinfected and myself sprayed until I smelt like a newly-scrubbed public lavatory. This precaution always seems to me a little late, considering that spotted fever cases are put in indiscriminately with five or six non-infectious sitters and stretchers for the journey to the hospital, which is not to be wondered at, considering the fiendish rush at the station when a big convoy arrives.

Disinfecting over, I dimmed headlights and drove downhill at a terrific pace to make up lost time. But my luck was again out. Commandant saw me drive in the yard. Where had I been ? What did I mean by slacking in this disgraceful manner ? Spotted-fever case ? Oh. (Slightly disconcerted, but by no means squashed.) No excuse. I should have been back a quarter of an hour ago. Get reloaded at once. Enough time has been wasted, without wasting more in idle conversation. (A thing I had been longing to point out, but lacked the necessary guts, like the wretched funk I am.) Freezing outwardly but inwardly boiling, I backed the bus to the train again, to be reloaded with another spotted-fever stretcher, which meant the

37

whole rotten routine again. The language I used at this back-hander would have left Tosh among the also-rans.

Crawl, crawl, crawl up the hill. . . . The men are mercifully quiet. Too exhausted to groan very audibly, poor wretches. . . . Number Thirteen at last . . . unloaded, back to the disinfecting section. . . . " Hullo, again ? You seem to like us to-night " in response to my pleas . . . a little quicker this time, or not so thorough, . . . I neither know nor care. Down the hill at a hell of a rate, the old bus skidding and shaking. I shall be over the hill if I don't slow up. . . . I don't care. I am past caring about my personal safety. Once the ambulance is empty I can let her rip, and to hell with the consequences. The station yard at last. . . . Have I escaped Commandant ?

Alas, I have not ! She was waiting for me. Obviously on the warpath. Something had upset her apple-cart. She was out for victims, and I am the victim she would rather nab than anyone in the convoy. It is a most extraordinary thing that whenever I do anything right, there is no sign of Mrs. Bitch. But let me do the slightest thing wrong, and she materialises like a Jack-in-the-box from nowhere. She drives an ambulance herself, but, being Commandant, she is able to choose the nearest and easiest hospitals in order to supervise the convoy. I am not blaming her for this. If I were in her place, I would choose the cushiest runs. What is the use of being Commandant if you can't?

Not late again? Another spotted fever case? Number Thirteen very far out? She is allowing for all these things. I had better report for punishment in the morning at 10.30. I would be cleaning my ambulance at 10.30? Ten o'clock then. She could have done Number Thirteen in half the time. Less. How—unless she had flown there and back —one does not ask. Nothing is impossible to a superwoman. Tosh says Mrs. Bitch must give God the inferiority complex twice daily. He took seven days to make the world, according to Genesis. Mrs. Bitch could have done it in half the time. She can do anything in half the time it takes anyone else.

One of these days I will murder her slowly and reverently and very painfully. I will take lots of time over it—unless I meet her coming up the hill with dim lights, denoting an empty ambulance, in which case I will crash her bus head-on and take the risk of my own skidding into the valley afterwards.

Twice more to Number Thirteen. A man vomiting the whole of the last trip. Never ceased for a second, poor fellow. We clean our own ambulances, so I knew what that would mean in the morning.

He died as the stretcher-bearers lifted him out. I was glad. . . . Out of hell at last.

Again to the station, to be told by the sergeant I could go home to headquarters : the train was unloaded. I was, he added, unnecessarily, the last out by a good half-hour.

Back at last. I pull into the ambulance line, switch my engine off, crawl down, stiff and creaking in every joint, bang my chilled hands together to restore the circulation, switch my lights off, and tramp into the mess-room. The fire dead . . . of course. Everyone gone. Roll-call over. Clump, clump, clump. . . . The door opens. Commandant pokes her head in. She gives me a baleful glare. The roll-book is in her hand. " H. Z. SMITH," she barks. " Present," I retort, springing smartly to attention. She bangs the door without saying goodnight. Silly bitch ! Clump, clump, clump. . . . I wish she would drop dead in her tracks. I childishly poke out my tongue at the receding steps on the bare boards and inspect the cocoa jugs, hoping someone has had the decency to leave a spoonful in one. No luck. Empty, as I anticipated. Every night the cook makes a certain number of jugs of cocoa, from which the drivers are supposed to take a ration . . . one cup each. But as there is never enough to go round, the last poor half-dozen swine have to go to bed frozen to the marrow, after two to five hours' duty in the bitter cold. It is no joke on these rough French roads . . . sometimes snowing, sometimes windy, and sometimes raining. Both the snow and the rain drip down your collar and wet you to the skin. But the wind cuts your face to pieces until your lips bleed. It is difficult to say which is worst. And then to bed without a hot drink on top of it. It would be easy enough to make a few extra jugs in order to allow everyone to have a second cup, if necessary. But no, Commandant's rules once made are as unalterable as the orbits of the heavenly planets. Her arithmetic, though opposed to ordinary reckoning, is unanswerable. If she says thirty cups of cocoa will go into forty ambulance drivers . . . they go, and no argument.

I could, of course, make cocoa in my bedroom if I liked. . . . Surprisingly, there is no rule forbidding this up to date. But it means fetching water from the pantry . . . incidentally going outside for it across the snow-covered yard, carrying it to the bedroom, digging out the cocoa and sugar from under Tosh's bed . . . and I am too dog-tired. Besides, I suddenly remember we have run out of provisions. I wish I had a cigarette. But I have run out of those too. I turn the mess-room lights off.

The bedroom is in darkness. Tosh and the others

are already asleep. Where are the matches?
From across the corridor I hear whispers and stifled
giggles. Someone is awake there, though the light
is extinguished too. The last drivers in before me,
I suppose. What can they find to amuse them in
this life, I wonder resentfully. Where are the
matches? I stumble over a shoe in the darkness,
and Tosh mutters, " For Christ's sake keep quiet,
can't you? " I angrily demand how in hell I
can keep quiet when she leaves her shoes in the
middle of the room and hides the matches . . . find
them as I am speaking, and light a candle, shielding
the glare from the sleepers with a magazine. . . .
All dead to the world. Not a sign of a cigarette,
either. Hidden them, knowing I'd run out.
Suspicious beasts. Do they think I'd condescend
to swipe their rotten fags, even if they left them
strewn all over the place?

Go on, . . . sleep, all of you. Snore away,
. . . blast you all. I wish to God I had a room
of my own, where I could have a little peace now
and again, without having to listen to you grunting
and snoring like pigs. Sleep, sleep, sleep, . . .
that's all you think of. Never mind if I'm cold
and hungry and without a smoke.

I hate them for sleeping so soundly. That means
they are warm. One can't sleep unless one is
warm. God, it is freezing in here! No water in

the kettle. No hot bottle. Damn them for swiping all the water. How can I pluck up courage to undress in this icy room? . . . Shall I strip to the skin, or shall I dig into my flea-bag as I am, merely removing my uniform, shoes and gaiters? . . . Etta Potato gives a grunt and turns over. Damn her for being asleep. Damn them all for being asleep. Damn them for drinking my cocoa. Damn them for swiping all the hot water . . . they might have left me enough for a bottle. They knew I was doing Number Thirteen. Selfish beasts, all of them. Snore, snore, snore. . . . A sudden rage takes possession of me. My lips tremble. Tears burn the back of my throat. I nearly take the magazine away from the candle to let the light shine full in their faces. . . .

I will not undress fully. Supposing another convoy is signalled. Supposing that hellish whistle blows just as I have stripped to the pyjamas. If I undress completely, it is ten to one I shall be late for roll-call at 7.30. No . . . I will remove my uniform and keep the rest on, shoes and stockings, too. Fuggy . . . but what does it matter providing I unfreeze and get to sleep. My teeth are chattering. My fingers are blue. A chilblain has burst on a knuckle. And no water for a hot-water bottle. I stare. . . . What is that under Tosh's pillow? A half-smoked cigarette? It is. I commandeer it

43

stealthily with an unholy joy. Saving it for the morning, was she? I smirk malevolently. I light it at the candle. Drink my cocoa, and snore, warm and snug, while I am freezing, will they? Use up all the water and leave me none for a hot bottle, will they? . . .

Booma-boom-booma-boom-boommm!

The guns are going it with a vengeance. No sleep for the men in the trenches to-night. Poor wretches, are they as cold and unhappy and home-sick as I am? I can hardly believe it possible. A distant glow on the sky-line shows clearly through the window, yellow and warm, like London from the outskirts. . . . The Front. Now and again there is a distant explosion, the flash quite visible, the explosion quite audible and distinguishable above the guns. A mine or a bomb attack. More killed . . . more wounded . . . more convoys. More hell . . . more bloody, bloody hell.

The cigarette is finished, . . . the butt carefully secreted. To-morrow I shall deny all knowledge of it. As I am about to blow out the candle, I make the discovery that Skinny is not in her bed. Probably in the w.c. again, poor devil, for the night. The canteen food either does that or has the reverse effect. The luminous hands of my watch say 3.15. I worm my body into the flea-bag. It is surprisingly warm. My feet touch something, . . . some-

NOT SO QUIET . . .

thing hot. A hot-water bottle? They have made a hot-water bottle for me. My friends! They have not forgotten me. This touch of kindliness finishes me completely. The tears roll down my cheeks. I feel a rotter . . . a beast. I have been calling them everything vile, and all the time they have done this for me. Cold, miserable, worn-out themselves, they thought of me doing Number Thirteen, and I repaid them by cursing them and swiping Tosh's last cigarette. . . . Her last. What a cad I am. To-morrow I shall present her with every single one mother sends me, if there is a mail. Comforted, I dry my tears. I am beginning to thaw. Soon I shall doze off. God bless the man who invented hot-water bottles. Or was it a woman? . . . I don't know. But God bless whoever it was. A statue should be erected to him (or her) . . . a large hot-water bottle. Far more amusing than the silly-faced statesmen in stone trousers. . . .

A suppressed giggle comes from across the corridor. Telling dirty stories, I suppose. The laugh does not irritate me this time. I am too gloriously drowsy. The grateful warmth steals over my aching limbs. . . .

.   .   .   .   .

" Roll-call. Wake up ! "

Tosh's voice. But I was already awake. That whistle would rouse the dead . . . no chance of further sleep while it shrills forth the triumphant news that sleep is at an end. I spring from bed. The others are furiously dressing. I begin. We do not speak. How I envy Tosh her short hair. My own is full of knots. Our hot breath pants from us in little jets of steam. It is colder than ever. The snow is falling outside, but it has not warmed the atmosphere one degree. What is the time? Seven twenty-six. Four minutes to go. " Where the hell is that cigarette ? " Tosh mutters. I pretend not to hear. Seven twenty-seven. Three minutes.

When this war is over . . . how like the first line of a comic song that is . . . if ever it is over, and I am safely back in Blighty, the sound of an ordinary police whistle will always travel me back faster than Aladdin's magic carpet, to this bare bedroom with Tosh, The Bug, Skinny, The B.F. and Etta Potato. For a second I shall spring to alert wakefulness, then, realising I am no longer a uniformed automaton, I shall run like a rabbit . . . in the opposite direction, as far from the loathly arrogant summons as I can possibly run, nor shall I stop my headlong flight while the sound is even faintly audible. But if I travel swift as a lightning flash, I shall not be able to leave behind the hatred that will possess me to my dying day of Commandant's police whistle.

46

Commandant's police whistle is ruining my pre-War disposition entirely. It rouses everything vile within me. Not long ago I was a gentle pliable creature of no particular virtues or vices, my temper was even, my nature amiable, and my emotions practically non-existent. Now I am a sullen, smouldering thing, liable to burst Vesuvius fashion into a flaming fire of rage without the slightest warning. Commandant's police whistle. . . .

If I am bathing or attending to my body with carbolic ointment or soothing lotion . . . it orders me to stop. If I am writing a hasty letter, or glancing at a newspaper . . . it shrieks its mocking summons. Whatever I am doing it gives me no peace. But worst of all, whenever I am asleep . . . it wakens me, and gloats and glories in the action. If only I could ram it down Commandant's throat, I could die happy in the knowledge that I had not lived in vain.

We are dressed . . . fully. We give each other a short survey. Skinny has a wrinkled stocking, and Tosh's tie is hanging out. My neck is dirty, but it is too late to remedy that. Etta Potato pulls my collar higher. That camouflages it excellently. Commandant insists that we are carefully and neatly dressed for 7.30 roll-call, . . . white shirts, ties, smoothly-dressed hair, brushed uncrumpled uniforms . . . even though we may have been driving till

5 a.m. In that case we may return after roll-call, and sleep until 9, but as this means missing breakfast altogether, we can only do it when our private provisions permit. Woe betide a kind friend sneaking a cup of tea from the mess-room for a driver who has a headache and feels too ill to stay up for 8 o'clock breakfast.

We have tried not dressing fully for roll-call. For a whole glorious week our room roll-called in pyjamas tucked cleverly beneath uniforms, after which we returned to our flea-bags till 9, and breakfasted comfortably on tea and potted meat. But we were discovered and made an example of. Commandant delights in making examples. Now we are severely inspected during roll-call, to ensure that our morning toilet is complete.

" All ready ! "

We arrive just in time. Commandant has been up since dawn, by all accounts. She would have made a good wife for Napoleon. He didn't need any sleep, either. The room is packed with heavy-eyed pasty-faced girls with weary drooping mouths and dejected expressions. They are ill for want of sleep. Some of them look on the verge of collapse. A girl who arrived three days ago is coughing badly, . . . she caught a chill on the boat. But Commandant will work her till she drops. I cast an experienced glance over her. Within three

48

weeks she will be back in Blighty—marked unfit.
Lucky devil. I envy her. I wish I wasn't con-
stitutionally strong. But although I get an occasional
dose of food poisoning, my health is good. Even
being wet to the skin doesn't seem to harm me, and
when the roof leaks and my canvas bed is soaked
through, I wake up without anything worse than
a sniffy nose. The girl coughs so badly that
Commandant has to wait until the paroxysm is
over, but she is merely annoyed, not concerned, at
the interruption. Like all efficient machines, she
has no humanity. There are no such things as
coughs, colds, chills, headaches, or stomach-aches
in this convoy. Commandant regards any illness
not requiring actual hospital treatment as mere
feminine affectation. They say she is a married
woman with daughters of her own. . . . I cannot
believe it. No woman who has suffered the pangs
of childbirth could have so little understanding
of pain in other women's daughters. Should one
acquire a temp., the doctor is called in . . . it may
be something infectious. Should he order you to
bed, Commandant obeys him—to the letter. The
Bug was ordered to bed with a chill last week.
" Stay in bed for the afternoon," said the doctor.
And The Bug stayed. But Commandant turfed
her out immediately the afternoon had passed. The
doctor had said nothing about the evening. So

49

The Bug drove for five hours in the pouring rain,
and next day went into hospital with a temp. of
103. She was there till last Monday. If she could
have wangled it, she would still be there.

Roll-call is over. Having been in bed before
5 a.m., there is no going back till 9. We crowd
round the fire. It is my day to do cook's room.
There are many fatigues I detest, but cleaning
cook's room gets my back up more than anything.
Why should I clean it? Why cannot she clean her
own as we all do? She has about quarter the work
we have. She is a fat, common, lazy, impertinent
slut who leaves little dusty rings of hair littered
about for us to collect. She fills the chamber to
overflowing with dirty slops, bits of torn letters,
and any other rubbish she can find. Her room reeks
of stale sweat, for she sleeps with the window
hermetically sealed. It astounds me why the
powers-that-be at the London headquarters stipulate
that refined women of decent education are essential
for this ambulance work. Why should they want
this class to do the work of strong navvies on the
cars, in addition to the work of scullery maids under
conditions no professional scullery-maid would
tolerate for a day? Possibly this is because this is
the only class that suffers in silence, that scorns to
carry tales. We are such cowards. We dare not
face being called " cowards " and " slackers,"

which we certainly shall be if we complain. What did we think we came out to France for ? . . . A holiday ? Don't we realise there is a war on ? . . . So we say nothing. Poor fools, we deserve all we get.

We would, perhaps, feel less badly about cook if she were a good cook. But she is not. She is the worst cook it is possible to imagine in one's worst nightmare moments. Not only is the food badly cooked, but it is actually dirty. One is liable to find hair-combings in the greasy gravy ; bits of plate-leavings from the day before and an odd hairpin. The principal dinner dish is a sort of disgusting soup-stew made of meat that hangs over a drain until it is cut up . . . sinister-looking joints of some strange animal—what, we cannot decide. We often go outside in groups to examine it . . . carefully holding our noses meanwhile . . . but we cannot determine its origin. It is certainly not beef or mutton. No wonder we have all had food poisoning. No wonder we have so many dysentery cases. No wonder our smallest cuts fester and have to be treated in hospital. I grazed my thumb cleaning the fireplace the other day, and went septic immediately. The hospital orderlies say they would never stand our rations. They have Army rations, of course.

The canteen is, like the rest of the quarters,

a bare-boarded room with no floor covering. It is the duty of the drivers to keep the fire going all day. The drivers clean the mess-room. In fact, they do the housework of the whole quarters, in addition to driving doctors and sisters to and from the station, doing "evacuations," funerals, and convoys. The ambulance drivers have no fixed hours. They can be called out any one of the twenty-four. As each driver comes in she writes her name on a list on the notice-board, and when the names preceding hers have been crossed out, her turn for duty comes again. This is during the day, of course. At night we all turn out *en masse* for convoy work. We have no fixed rest times after driving all night, and consider ourselves lucky to get two consecutive hours' sleep during the afternoon. We are supposed to have an afternoon off weekly ; . . . I have never had mine once. For, apart from our set duties, there are Commandant's punishment duties.

" If only I could go back to bed ! "

Tosh stirs the fire with her toe and watches the kitchen door gloomily. Breakfast is a minute late.

" You got Thirteen last night, didn't you ? "

" And spotted-fever *twice*," I add, firmly, not to be cheated of my full share of woe.

There is a concerted murmur of sympathy, and I immediately feel better. It is amazing what a little sympathy can effect. The story of Mrs. Bitch's bullying draws forth another murmur. " Poor old Smithy, what a rotten shame. . . ." Really, life isn't so bad. I feel almost human by the time breakfast arrives.

We gather round the canteen table, chattering, our tongues loosened by the hot tea. The table is a long, American-cloth-covered affair supported on trestles. One can buy post cards of the canteen, in which smiling white-capped V.A.D.'s stand by waiting on the drivers. But we think they must have been photographer's models hired for the occasion. We have never seen them in our time. Also the bowl of flowers that graces the centre . . . that must have been hired, too. There have been no flowers in the memory of the " oldest inhabitant," a driver called " Chutney." Against the wall stands a piano, which we each get soaked " one shilling-weekly-for-the-use-of," and which we have never yet seen opened, much less heard played. A lot of time we have for playing pianos. That weekly shilling has caused more indignation in the convoy than the invasion of Belgium caused the Belgians.

Breakfast is worse than ever. The bread is hard . . . what there is of it ; and the margarine smells of . . . I hesitate for a comparison, and Tosh supplies it unhesitatingly. It is carried unanimously. Still, the tea is wet and hot, and for a wonder plentiful. It will run to a cup and a quarter each. We cheer up. After all, we are young and easily cheered up. The latest war story goes the rounds of the table. Something General Joffre is supposed to have said when first he saw the Scottish kilt. . . . Of course he didn't say it, but it is fun to pretend he did. "*Pour la guerre ce n'est pas bon, mais pour l'amour c'est magnifique !*" We are immensely tickled.

And there may be a mail to-day. We tell one another there is sure to be. We have all written home for supplies. Tosh for Bovril and Huntley and Palmer's Best Assorted and potted meat. Me for Bovril and ginger biscuits. We have a heated argument as to the rival merits of Best Assorted and ginger. Ginger wins easily. Ginger warms you up, sustains you. . . .

Edwards is engaged. We give her a cheer for giving us a thrill. Tosh accuses her of being in the f.w., and having to get married. Edwards denies this hotly. Then more by luck than good management, says Tosh, with a grin. Edwards hits Tosh in the eye with a piece of hard bread. We implore details. Is it the Aussie ? The one who sends her those chocolate biscuits every mail ? It is. We approve. We like the Aussie's chocolate biscuits. After the War they will live in Sydney. The Aussie doesn't know he is engaged yet. He proposed last mail, but Edwards only wrote yesterday and accepted him. He has lost a leg in the War, but Edwards is glad because the trenches won't get him again.

" No man of mine will ever go to any war again," says Edwards. " I know too much. Let the people who make the wars fight them. I would rather see a child of mine dead than see him a soldier."

" I don't think that's very patriotic, dear," says The B.F.

" You wouldn't," replies Edwards. " You're the type that loses her son in the War and erects a tablet in the village church. . . . ' A mother's proud memory.' Proud ? Because her son has been murdered after murdering some other mother's sons ? "

" It isn't murder to kill your enemies in wartime, darling," protests The B.F. complacently.

" Enemies ? ˙Our enemies aren't the Germans. Our enemies are the politicians we pay to keep us out of war and who are too damned inefficient to do their jobs properly. After two thousand years of civilisation, this folly happens. It is time women took a hand. The men are failures . . . this war shows that. Women will be the ones to stop war, you'll see. If they can't do anything else, they can refuse to bring children into the world to be maimed and murdered when they grow big enough.

55

Once women buckled on their men's swords. Once they believed in that 'death-or-glory-boys' jingo. But this time they're in it themselves. They're seeing for themselves. . . . And the pretty romance has gone. War is dirty. There's no glory in it. Vomit and blood. Look at us. We came out here puffed out with patriotism. There isn't one of us who wouldn't go back to-morrow. The glory of the War . . . my God ! . . ."

"Oh, darling, we are doing our bit," says The B.F.

"B.F.," says Edwards, "you're the most dangerous type of fool there is. Someone ought to collect women like you in a big hall and drop a bomb . . . wipe you out . . . before you can do any more damage . . . a whacking big one. You're a true chip of the old block . . . the pig-headed, sentimental, brainless old block that got us out here . . . patriotic speeches . . . 'fighting for world freedom.' . . . I don't know what we're fighting for . . . who does ? But it isn't for world freedom. Nothing so pretty."

"We had to fight. We are in the right, aren't we ? " The B.F. flushes pettishly. "The Church says so, dear."

"God is on our side ! " Edwards bangs the table. "They even drag poor God into it. Priests upholding war from the pulpit, the blasphemous . . ."

56

The argument goes on. My thoughts wander. I am glad I am not Edwards. She will never be able to forget these days and nights of war and horror. All her life she will have the reminder with her in the Australian husband with one leg. Limp, limp, limp. . . .

When I marry it will be someone whose straightness and strength will erase from my mind these mangled things I drive night after night.

" All the same, I don't think you're very patriotic, dear," says The B.F.

" Oh, pass the ruddy Maggie-Ann. What's the use? The closed mind, . . . you can't cope with it. The Book of Common Prayer, . . . Kensington High Street, . . . the Union Jack, . . . and Debrett. What's the use? "

At 10 a.m. I report to Commandant for punishment. I listen to her harangue in silence. Once I used to argue with her. But it only means more punishment. I am to take tea-orderly to-day and clean Commandant's car in addition to my own. I wonder what she would do if I suddenly sprang at her and dug my fingers into her throat, her strong, red, thick throat that is never sore, that laughs scornfully at germs, that needs no wrapping up even when the snow is whirling, blinding and smothering. . . .

I go without reply. She calls me back.

" Have you nothing to say, Smith ? "

" I don't understand, Commandant. What do you expect me to say ? *Thank you very much?* " I retort, unguardedly. Fool . . . fool. . . . I could kick myself. She has been egging me on to answer back. Fool . . . fool. . . .

" Insolence ! " Her cold grey eyes narrow. She compresses her thin lips. . . . " You had better clean the w.c. as well. Perhaps that will teach you discipline. Stand to attention while I am addressing you, please."

One of these days I shall lose control. . . .

CHAPTER III

CLEANING an ambulance is the foulest and most disgusting job it is possible to imagine. We are unanimous on this point. Even yet we hardened old-timers cannot manage it without " catting " on exceptionally bad mornings. We do not mind cleaning the engines, doing repairs and keeping the outsides presentable—it is dealing with the insides we hate.

The stench that comes out as we open the doors each morning nearly knocks us down. Pools of stale vomit from the poor wretches we have carried the night before, corners the sitters have turned into temporary lavatories for all purposes, blood and mud and vermin and the stale stench of stinking trench feet and gangrenous wounds. Poor souls, they cannot help it. No one blames them. Half the time they are unconscious of what they are doing, wracked with pain and jolted about on the rough roads, for, try as we may—and the cases all agree that women drivers are ten times more thoughtful than the men drivers—we cannot altogether evade the snow-covered stones and potholes.

How we dread the morning clean-out of the

insides of our cars, we gently-bred, educated women they insist on so rigidly for this work that apparently cannot be done by women incapable of speaking English with a public-school accent !

" Our ambulance women take entire control of their cars, doing all running repairs and all cleaning."

This appeared in a signed article by one of our head officials in London, forwarded to me by Mother last week. It was entitled " Our Splendid Women." I wondered then how many people comfortably reading it over the breakfast table realized what that " all cleaning " entailed. None, I should imagine ; much less the writer of the muck. Certainly we ourselves had no idea before we got here.

I wonder afresh as I don my overalls and rubber boots. I know what to expect this morning, remembering that poor wretched soul I carried on my last trek to Number Thirteen, who will be buried by one of us to-day.

I am nearly sick on the spot at the sight greeting me, but I have no time for squeamishness. I have Commandant's bus in addition to my own to get through.

The snow is coming down pretty heavily now, the waterproof sheet over my bonnet is full, and the red cross over the front of the driving seat totally obscured by a white pall. Blue-nosed, blue-overalled drivers in knee-high waterproof boots are diligently carrying buckets of water and getting out cloths in readiness for the great attack. The smell of disinfectant is everywhere. No one speaks much. It is a wretched morning and the less one talks the sooner one will be out of these whirling flakes.

The inside of my ambulance is at last cleared of its filth. I swill it with water. More water. Now with disinfectant. I examine it minutely. Commandant's 11 to 12 inspection is no idle formality. She goes over every square inch of each ambulance, inside and out, the engines are revved up, the tyre pressures tested, everything. With all her faults, she knows her job. If only she had a little heart, she would be an ideal woman for this sort of work. Why is it that women in authority almost invariably fall victims to megalomania?

Now for the engine. I start up after ten minutes' hard work, for the engine is stone-cold. Something is wrong. A choked carburettor? I clean it. No better. She doesn't seem to be getting the petrol quickly enough. A dirty feed? Or a plug? I test the plugs. They are O.K. It must be the petrol pipe. It is. I listen. She is running sweetly enough now.

Tyres are all right, thank heaven. Perhaps a little more air in the offside rear? Done.

Ten thirty-five. How time is flying! I shall never get the Commandant's ambulance ready for eleven o'clock inspection. I polish the outside of mine hurriedly. A lot of good it is washing and polishing in this weather; by the time we have turned round at the bottom of the lane we will be splashed all over. But Commandant insists on it being done—wet, fine, mud, sleet, or snow.

Ten forty. Can I do it? I make a bee-line for Commandant's bus. First in the line, of course. Who would dare swipe her place? Heroes have earned the V.C. for less daring than that brave deed would require. I open the doors. Oh God!— gangrene. My stomach heaves up and down. I run behind the ambulance, where the others cannot see.

Ten forty-five. Five precious minutes wasted. I creep back, furious with myself. I ought to be accustomed to gangrene by now. With clenched teeth I set to work, swilling, scrubbing, disinfecting. I cannot see, and nothing on this earth will ever make me see, why the hospital orderlies cannot clean the insides of the ambulances while the women drivers sleep after their gruelling night-work.

Sleep? When shall I ever sleep again? In at 3.15, up at 7.30—four and a quarter hours—all I shall get to-day—all the others are likely to get to-day. With luck we may snatch an hour or so before the midnight convoy.

Ten fifty-five. I am safe if her engine is in good running order. I manage a jug of boiling water for the radiator. She starts fairly easily. She sounds pretty good to me. A hasty polish.

Eleven o'clock. Done it. I am sweating all over. My chilblains are smarting where the disinfectant has got into the cracks, but I don't care. Here comes Commandant, punctual to the tick, hoping for victims.

Inspection over. I have escaped with a caution. Being a snowy day, she will overlook the two small spots I have omitted to clean off the bonnet.

To our rooms to change back into uniforms. No post in yet. That means eating the canteen filth to-day. We shall probably be poisoned, but we are so starving after our work in the snow we are prepared to eat anything.

Commandant's whistle blows.

" Potter ! "

Etta Potato runs. Two sisters to be met and taken to Number One. Poor old Etta Potato—the train will be hours late and she will miss dinner, such as it is. She cannot possibly get back in time. Any driver out on duty during mealtimes simply misses the meal. No one dreams of saving it for her.

The whistle blows again.

" Smith ! "

My turn.

" I thought I told you to clean the w.c. ? "

I was going to do that after dinner, I explain. Commandant does not believe me. I had forgotten. Don't lie to her, please. Tea-orderly to-morrow as well as to-day will perhaps assist my memory in future.

I change back into overalls, get a pail, and stagger to the w.c. These are the occasions on which I rejoice that we have only one w.c. for forty-five people. I lock the door. A constant stream of people try the handle and implore admission. I refuse. They plead urgency. I am left completely cold. The Bug arrives. I cannot let my own room down. She can come in if she gives me a cigarette. She agrees.

I surreptitiously light up while she goes inside, one eye on the end of the corridor, ready to douse light if Commandant appears. Smoking on duty will probably mean being hanged, drawn and quartered, in the mood she is in to-day. The Bug emerges and I lock myself in again.

The w.c. is scrubbed, fresh newspaper cut, the seat polished, the pan scoured, the chain pulled on the cigarette butt. I take the pail to the outhouse. I meet Tosh coming in, and she asks me what I have been doing. I tell her, cleaning the w.c.

" You ladies with influence," gibes Tosh.

Dinner is nearly over by the time I have changed. One mouthful and I finish. The soup-stew literally stinks.

" Dead dog," says Tosh.

I bag a hunk of bread and an infinitesimal piece of margarine and munch.

Being tea-orderly has its compensations on a foul day like this. I am not sorry to be kept busy in the canteen setting cups and saucers and cutting bread. At least there is a fire there, although it means waiting on forty odd impatient drivers from 3 till 6.30, carrying their dirty dishes to and from the kitchen, filling cups and tea-urns and so on. Cook condescends to make the tea, but there she finishes. It is a fatiguing business when one has had no sleep, and usually one bitterly envies the others, snatching a few minutes' rest between jobs. But this afternoon there is very little rest. There are eleven funerals from different hospitals and a record number of evacuations. An evacuation is the jolliest job of all—the cases who are well enough to stand the long journey to Blighty. It is a joy to hear them singing. Sometimes we join in and forget the empty hospital beds so soon to be filled up by the next pain-wracked convoy. Unhappily, a record number of evacuations means a record number of convoys. We know what to expect to-night.

The Bug bursts in full of news. There *is* a mail in. It is being sorted now. Someone told her two hours ago. Two hours? That means the first batch may be delivered any time now. . . .

An hour passes. One by one the drivers come in, frozen, add their names to the bottom of the list, and demand refreshment. As fast as one name is signed Commandant has the top name out again. That whistle is driving us mad this afternoon. A sister to be met here, another funeral, another evacuation, a parcel of medicine from the station to such and such a hospital, bustle, bustle, bustle. I fall over myself to get the girls fed before they are sent out again. A fresh arrival brings a rumour of two extra convoys—one at eight o'clock and one at ten. We groan. Is it merely a canteen rumour or has it a foundation?

It is nearly dark now, and the wind is rising. Snow is whirling against the window. A blizzard would not surprise us. And still the mail does not arrive. Someone complains that the tea is stone-cold. It is not my fault. If I have asked that lazy beast of a cook once to keep the tea hot, I have asked her a dozen times. The girl does not believe me. I advise her to tackle cook herself. She retorts that it is my business, not hers. Is she tea-orderly or am I? I retort suitably—and in the middle of the argument the mail arrives, a big batch of letters

66

and a huge bag of parcels. The letters are taken to Commandant's room to be sorted. Heaven knows when they will be out. It is a queer thing that, though efficient beyond words at everything else, Commandant seems to take a delight in seeing how slowly she can sort the mail. It is the only thing she cannot do twice as quickly as anyone else. I have known her keep letters back till next afternoon, producing them just as the recipient had dismally decided everyone had forgotten her at home. But I am not terribly interested in letters. As tea-orderly it is my job to sort the parcels.

I spread them on the bare boards. The crowd nearly knocks me over in its eagerness. There are two dozen or more. One for Tosh, two for me. I leave the others to sort out their own and fly to the w.c. with my spoil. The first, Bovril—three large bottles, two tins of ginger biscuits, slabs of chocolate to eat with them, a hundred cigarettes. Cheers ! Poor Mother, she doesn't know I smoke. She thinks I give them to the wounded Tommies ; that is why she keeps me so liberally supplied. I open the second parcel. Handkerchiefs, smelling-salts, Keating's, a lavender bag, a writing-pad, a cake of carbolic soap, and my fifth carbolised body-belt. From my godmother, Aunt Ellen. I rush to the bedroom and fill my suitcase. Back to the canteen, where more drivers are clamouring for tea. I give cook a piece of my mind because it is cold and washy, and she threatens to report me to the Commandant. I tell her to report and be damned to her. The room is filled. Everyone is laughing and jolly and expectant. Edwards is nearest Commandant's office. We tease her good-naturedly about the Aussie. Some wit dramatically recites his supposed love-letter—" My own sweetheart darling : how can I live longer without thee. . . ." Wholesale trading is going on, body-belts for Bovril, biscuits for cigarettes, hairpins for saccharine. . . .

Half-past five. And still Commandant has not sorted the letters.

.   .   .   .   .

At six o'clock the room is practically empty. Those who are hungry for letters have given up in despair and gone to lie down. The ten o'clock convoy may turn out a certainty, although the eight o'clock one is off. Five new drivers arrive straight out from England. They look half-dead. They have had a drive of about seventy miles in the snow in an ambulance on top of a filthy crossing to Boulogne. They are completely exhausted. The tea is finished, too. I am about to inquire of cook when Commandant comes in. She eyes the new-comers severely and, without any greeting, turns to me.

" Smith, show these drivers to the vacant beds and see they report to me in five minutes."

What a welcome ! No wonder the poor things look depressed. She leaves her door open. I simply dare not ask about the tea.

There is a label on each camp bed with their names. Two of them are friends.

" Can't we share the two-bed cubicle ? " they ask. " We stipulated we were not to be separated and they promised."

I shake my head. They insist on asking Commandant. I advise them not to, but they will not listen. I know exactly what will happen.

" I'm dying for a cup of tea," says one, " and then I'm going to have a sleep."

Poor deluded fool. She has no idea she will be sent straight out on an ambulance to learn the various localities of the different hospitals, to take over her own ambulance at midnight. She is lucky if she gets a cup of hot tea first. It all depends whether Commandant has closed her door and I can bully cook.

" We go out with an experienced driver for a month on her ambulance for probation, don't we ? " asks one. " I suppose we'll start to-morrow ? I hope so, I'm awfully keen."

" I'll see if I can get you some tea," I reply evasively.

Too late.   The whistle blows.

" Smith ! "

" Commandant is waiting.   Will you come this way ? "

They file into the room.   Commandant tells me to go.   I depart thankfully to the kitchen for tea. I have no desire to listen.   I know exactly what is going on.   I know the scene and the dialogue word for word.

COMMANDANT : I have your names here, but I will go over them now to verify them.   (*Does so.*) Now you will put on your overcoats and gloves and each accompany one of the old drivers, who will show you the camp and the various hospitals.   You will memorise these carefully, in order to be able to take your own ambulance at midnight when the convoy arrives.

An awful silence, during which the drivers gulp and eye one another.   Then one, a courageous fool who rushes in where angels fear to tread and who will pay for it every day of her life until she gets back to Blighty, steps forward.

THE FOOL : Excuse me, Commandant, you don't mean we take over an ambulance by *ourselves* at midnight ?

COMMANDANT : Certainly.   Why not ?

THE FOOL : But I understand it's a large,

straggly camp with dozens and dozens of hospitals dotted all over the place.

COMMANDANT : Each one is numbered. You are going out now to learn the numbers and the locations.

THE FOOL : But none of us has ever driven an ambulance in the dark before.

COMMANDANT : Then how dare you come out here as experienced drivers ?

THE FOOL : We didn't ask to come, Commandant. We had our orders to catch a certain train and report here. But we were distinctly told we would be on probation for a month, to drive beside another girl and learn the ropes.

COMMANDANT (*with a sneer*) : Oh ! You thought you had come out to slack, did you ?

THE FOOL : Oh no. Not to slack. We came out to work, and we wouldn't shirk if we had the chance. It isn't a question of slacking. It's a question of competence. I don't feel competent to take an ambulance out in a snowstorm in the dark for the first time on these rough roads in a strange place I don't know. I don't think it's fair to the wounded men.

COMMANDANT (*playing her trump card*) : Oh ! Perhaps you'd better go back to England, then.

THE FOOL (*hastily*) : Oh, no. Please ! It's only

71

because I haven't any idea what it means driving an ambulance of wounded in the dark. . . .

COMMANDANT (*sweetly*) : Then you'll be able to tell us what it's like at midnight to-night.

(CURTAIN.)

The door opens. The five newcomers emerge, drooping visibly. Commandant blows her whistle and scans the list. She selects the first four names, and turns to me. " You have finished tea-orderly, Smith. Take one of these new drivers. Preston, go with Smith."

A fair, fragile-looking girl of about eighteen turns apologetically to me. I try to look pleasant. It is not her fault.

" Yes, Commandant," I reply.

Preston follows me out.

．　　　．　　　．　　　．　　　．

The snow is thick now. My engine, having been off all the afternoon, is stone-cold. It takes nearly twenty minutes to get going. I am so cold my fingers refuse to grip the wheel. Preston gets up beside me.

" Station first," I tell her.

How am I going to point out landmarks when they are all snow-obscured ? The black tree-stump on the left that leads to Number Eight, the shell-hole that indicates the turning to Number Five, and so on. Familiar as the landscape is to me, it takes

NOT SO QUIET . . .

me all my time to keep my bearings. We go on and on in silence till the station is reached. We couldn't converse, even if we felt chatty. The snow gets in our mouths every time we open them.

"In this gate—you can follow the others, so you'll be all right. We back here into a straight line ; I'll show you the trick of that. You've got to toe the plimsoll or you'll throw the line out of gear, and Commandant will be down on you."

"She's rather hard, isn't she ? " asks Preston. "I mean—very efficient, isn't she ? "

"Which of you said you were nervous of night-driving ? You ? " I ignore the timid criticism.

"Yes." Preston looks surprised. "Who told you ? "

"No one. I guessed. After you are loaded you make for the gate. The orderlies tell you your load at the train—so many stretchers and so many sitters. You tell the sergeant ' Six stretchers and three sitters '—or whatever it is. Then he tells you the number of the hospital."

"I hope I find the right hospital in the dark," says Preston. "Do you think—— "

"I think you'd better faint when you get back and stay unconscious until Commandant gets the doctor. Then you can learn the ropes by daylight to-morrow." I am not joking. I always advise new-comers to do this. But only one out of every dozen has the sense to swing the lead. Newcomers are too conscientious for the first couple of weeks. After that they wangle whatever they can in the way of bed, like the rest of us. The callous way Commandant risks the lives of wounded men by placing them in charge of a nervous beginner who is as liable to drive them over the hill into the valley below as anywhere else makes my blood boil.

" Oh, I couldn't do that," says Preston. " I—— "

" You must do your bit," I interrupt sarcastically.

" I came out for that, didn't I ? " she asks simply.

Poor bloody fool. I savagely tread on the gas and tear up the hill.

CHAPTER IV

IT is after ten when we get back. I am so numb I cannot feel my feet. Preston is almost in hysterics. She will be no use at all for this work. She is one of those vague flustered creatures with no driving sense at all. How she passed her test is beyond me. Probably got 100 per cent. for theoretical driving, and scraped through on the practical. All the theory in the world will not help you when you are stuck in a snow-drift.

I was bad enough when I began, but at least I can drive. Preston never will. If Commandant were at all approachable I would go to her and point out the danger she runs by trusting an ambulance load of wounded to Preston; but I have not been sent out to make a report. . . . Merely to enact the rôle of human road map. Commandant would resent any criticism of a newcomer's driving. This girl has been twice round the camp . . . I am only supposed to take her once. But so worried am I at the possibility of the wounded men being ditched in the snow . . . or worse . . . I have exceeded my duty. The result is she has not located one hospital correctly.

I have shown her the man-traps, the corner where if you do not slow down you are likely to crash, the hill with the double bend at the bottom, . . . but she is utterly bewildered. I hope she gets into a snow-drift on her way to the station and sticks there for the night—as a girl did last week. It will be a blessing if she does. I thankfully leave her in the mess-room with her companions, waiting for Commandant to allocate their respective ambulances. All I want is a hot drink, a fag, a hot-water bottle, and an hour's stew in my flea-bag.

The others are asleep. Will the kettle never boil? There are four letters on my camp-bed, . . . one from my sister Trix, one from mother, one in a handwriting I do not recognise, and one from Aunt Helen. They can wait until I am warm and cosy under my blankets.

At last the kettle steams. Bovril, . . . a large, strong, boiling cup. I fill my hot-water bottle with the rest of the water. I tear my shoes and gaiters off. I cannot feel my toes. I snuggle into my flea-bag. The heat burns through my woollen soles. It will probably start my chilblains itching . . . but I don't care. Oh, grateful, grateful, warmth. Were I a poet, I would not waste my time on moons and lovers and shining eyes . . . I would compose sonnets innumerable extolling the beauties of warmth ; I would compose crushing stanzas denouncing snow and ice.

Hateful snow and ice. . . . It is incredible that for years I have tried to induce my people to do Switzerland for the winter sports. I would not go now. Wild horses would never drag me anywhere near a cold country again. Sleighing ? . . . Horrible ! Ski-ing ? . . . Worse ! Skating ? . . . Worse and worse ! I never wish even to drink an ice-cream soda or eat an ice-cream sundae again. For me, from now on, tropical suns and punkahs and palm-decked islands, gay with red poinsettia flowers . . . sun-kissed yellow beaches . . . indigo-blue seas tipped by warm, gentle wavelets . . . sun . . . sun . . . sun. . . .

I light a cigarette.

Mother's letter first.

Committees . . . committees . . . committees . . . recruiting meetings. She has seventeen more recruits than Mrs. Evans-Mawnington up to date. Would I like a new body belt ? She has a fearful cold in the head, but is " carrying on " (inverted commas) just the same. " Business as usual," she writes playfully (also inverted commas). Father writing soon. . . . My brother Bertie expects to go to France soon. He is mad to go, . . . he won't be satisfied till he gets to the trenches. . . . She doesn't fancy the idea, but, of course, she is

77

proud to think her son wants to do his duty to his country, to fight for the Dear Old Flag. The cat has had three kittens, . . . three dear fluffy balls of fur, . . . Mons, Wipers and Liège, . . . rather sweet, don't I think? And the way the dog washes them is too charming. . . . Mrs. Evans-Mawnington boasting that Roy Evans-Mawnington is coming home on his last leave before going out to the trenches. Simply awful if Roy got out before Bertie. There'd be no holding Mrs. Evans-Mawnington . . . she'd be simply *impossible*. . . . I will look after myself, won't I? Don't go out in the cold after nightfall with my delicate chest, take my cod-liver oil regularly . . . and be sure to tell Commandant that Aunt Helen was at school with her sister. Aunt Helen says she must be a charming woman if she resembles her sister. . . . Darling, I don't know how proud mother is of me and Trix and Bertie. My three heroes, she calls us, and it does so annoy Mrs. Evans-Mawnington, who has only Roy to give to the country. . . . So-and-so-and-so-and-so, my affectionate mother, whose little daughter is . . .

" Doing her bit." I turn the page. Yes, I am quite right !

The strange handwriting belongs to Roy Evans-Mawnington. I know Roy well, but he has never written to me before. Good old Roy . . . jolly decent of him to write. He was at Oxford when I came out, . . . nice boy, nice clean blue-eyed ordinary English public-school boy. Not particularly intelligent or brainy . . . but just nice. A line to let me know he expects to be out in France by the time this reaches me. . . . Thought I'd be interested. Admired the photograph of me in uniform in Mother's drawing-room, and if I have a Stepney. . . . What sort of a time am I having? . . . Lots of admirers? Don't let us one-pippers down by getting mixed up with a brass hat, will I? . . . Writing to Trix, too, but rather hear from me really. . . . I look jolly smart in uniform. Suits me rather. . . . Don't forget that spare photograph. He has a fairly decent one of himself taken in khaki the day he got his one pip, if I would like it. . . . Jolly glad he's going out. Top-hole to be really in it. Sick of slacking at home, and drilling and route marching. . . .

Poor Roy.

Aunt Helen's contribution is almost a replica of mother's. Committees . . . committees . . . committees . . . recruiting meetings. Don't forget to tell the Commandant she was at school with her sister Ada. Given a big sum to the Red Cross . . . also, so *pleased* with my patriotism and noble example to all girls of my age. She thinks it her duty to tell me she's made a will in my favour. . . . (As

she will probably outlive me by half a century, this
does not thrill me as it ought.   The best description
of Aunt Helen is that no one has ever dared to
call her Nellie—those kind of people do not die
young.)   What do I think—Annie Orpen is sure
Fräulein at school is a *spy !* When they played " God
Save the King " the other day, they all watched
Fräulein, and she was *seconds* late standing to
attention ! *Quite, quite* reluctant, . . . so Annie
says.   Isn't it appalling to have the enemy in our
midst in this bare-faced fashion ? . . . So hard to
get butter . . . housekeeping is a dreadful trial.
Altogether the War is a dreadful calamity. . . .
Send if I want anything.   By the way, my mother
tells her Trix described someone as a " damn
wash-out " in her last letter home.   She is shocked
beyond words . . . hopes I will never forget myself,
and use such *strong, vulgar* expletives. It is for women
in France to have a womanly, refining, softening
effect on the troops.   After all, a refining influence
means a great deal in war-time, doesn't it ? . . .
She is writing a strong protest to Trix, and is mine
affly.

I have kept the best wine last.   I tear open Trix's
letter with real anticipation.   A fat six-paged letter
in Trix's tiny handwriting.   News . . . news . . .
news. . . . Dear Trix.   She and I have always
been together until now.   There is fifteen months'

difference between our ages, . . . but we might be twins, we are so inseparable. We have every taste in common ; we have attended the same schools ; we know each other's most intimate secrets ; we go everywhere together. If she had not been too young we would have come here together. I am thankful for that fifteen months' difference in our ages. Had Commandant treated Trix as she treats me I should have let myself go the first few days. . . . Of that I am certain.

> " No. 4 Washing-Up Alley,
>> " Workustohellandback Hospital,
>>> " B.E.F., France.
>> " (God knows the date . . . I don't.)

" DEAR SIS,

" If you write me a cheery, brown-haired-lass - in - khaki - doing-her-bit-for-her-country letter again, I'll go mad and bite someone. I get quite enough of that muck from home. We have a lorry driver here who was in your shop about four months ago . . . Nipper Dale. She knows you and she says you have got as thin as a rail. She says your shop is one of the worst in France. It's notorious everywhere. She says it's merry hell. She says there are only about thirty girls out of a hundred who have stuck it longer than six weeks or so. Is this true ? Let me know, and if it is, you've jolly well got to transfer.

" Here it isn't too bad. Our hours are awful. We never get any time off and the sisters treat us like lumps of dirt. They simply loathe the V.A.D.'s, and seem determined to make us sorry we ever enlisted. Still, we survive. It would take more than a few sisters to quell me. I wash up dishes from morn to dewy eve. Snitch and I share a wash-house . . . note above address . . . so it's not too bad. You've no idea how many dirty dishes there are in the world, Sis. I am bounded on the north by plates, on the south by bowls, on the east by cups, and on the west by saucers. If all the dirty dishes I have washed up were placed end-to-end they'd reach to the moon. When I am not washing up dishes, I take in meals on little wagons on wheels to the wards. My entrance is the signal for all the beds to chuck bits of paper and tooth-brushes at me. They have no respect for my uniform. The sisters get furious. I shall be taken off breakfasts soon, I have no doubt. The convalescents come out and dry up for us sometimes ; some of them are topping. I do a bit of flirting in between plates. Snitch is a good sort. A man she was a bit keen on from her village was brought in wounded the other day. Snitch was terribly thrilled, and asked Matron if she could go and see him.

" Now, Matron isn't a bad old stick at all ; a bit

Stone Age in her outlook, but not a bad old bird. We all like her, but she has one bee in her Sister Dora cap, and that's w.c.'s. ' Certainly, my child,' she said to Snitch, ' you can go and sit with your friend ; but you must not be idle. Take this.' So she hands poor old Snitch a big wad of tissue paper and a pair of scissors, ' While you are talking to your friend,' says Matron, ' you can cut squares of paper for the w.c. I will give you some string, and every hundred sheets you can string them ready to hang up.' Wasn't it a howl ? Matron was quite annoyed when Snitch refused point-blank. She said it was false modesty. But poor old Snitch was furious. Aids to romance . . . what ? Fancy cutting squares of lav. paper while talking to the wounded hero you're a bit gone on ? The story has gone the rounds, and the patients are calling poor old Snitch Lavatory Liz. They keep on bringing her parcels of tissue paper to the wash-house, and bits of string and scissors. Snitch will never live it down. She hasn't seen the hero yet. She won't give in and Matron won't. Besides, she's afraid the story will have got to his ears, and she's afraid to face him. If it was me I should shout with laughter, but poor old Snitch is afflicted with blushing modesty.

"Have you heard from home ? They make me sick with the awful bottoms they write about doing our duty, etc. I think it's funny. The other day mother called me her English-hearted heroine. A bit soft, I thought. She always was a bit mushy, but this war seems to be finishing her off. How you and I have been able to survive mother all these years I'm blessed if I know. Anyhow, there's one heroine who wouldn't have been so keen if she had known she was coming to France to spend from 6.30 a.m. to after 9 p.m. up to the elbows in greasy water in a bath of steam. Still, I suppose it's preferable to cleaning Matron's bicycle every day for six months, as I did in England during my training. Why the dickens they dress you up in a pretty cap and make you think you're going to smooth the patient's fevered brow beats me hollow. If they told you the truth you could take it or leave it ; and if you took it, as you probably would, you wouldn't feel they had let you down. They seem to think a V.A.D. is never tired, or that she ever wants any sleep. I've never heard a dog spoken to as some of the pukka nurses speak to us. They are scared stiff we'll pinch their jobs after the War, of course ; but they needn't worry. None of us in Washing-Up Alley ever want to smell iodiform again. All I ask is home and breakfast-in-bed for the rest of my life. I've had all the excitement I want. Being a V.A.D. is an overrated pastime.

"Still, I am not complaining, after what Dale

told me about your shop. I think I'm jolly lucky. She says if she'd stayed there any longer, she'd have gone mad, what with men dying in the ambulances under your very eyes and no sleep. She says is Mrs. Bitch still ruling the roost? and if she is may God have mercy on your soul, but she hopes to hear she died in horrible agony. So let me know, and write soon, darling old Sis.

" Your loving

" TRIX."

Dear Trix. I chuckle to myself at the story of Snitch and the lavatory paper. Dear Trix. Thank God she has struck a soft job under a matron who is not all efficiency and no heart. I chuckle again. I feel almost happy. A letter from Trix is as stimulating as a glass of bubbly. Dear Trix. I know sisters who detest one another, but Trix and I are not that kind. I do not exaggerate when I say I would die for her. She is closer to me than anyone on earth. I am happy to think she is so far from me. Nothing will induce me to tell her the truth about here. Merry hell? . . . Hell, granted, but merry. . . .

Dear Trix. . . . Dear old Trix. . . .

. . . . .

I am in my soft low bed at home, with its rose-pink satin eiderdown, its cosy ribbon-edged blankets and its sweet lavender-scented sheets. My head rests on a downy hand-embroidered pillow. I awaken gently, gradually. I gaze at the pink-flushed walls. Mother wanted them ivory-white, but I insisted on the pinky tone for warmth ; I have always been glad of that. The tiny enamelled clock on my bed-table says 9. Sarah is opening the door.

" Ah, you're awake, Miss Nelly. Your Ma said not to disturb you if you were sleeping, but let you rest after your theatre."

I smile and sit up, propping my head with the tiny, oval, rose-satin cushion Sarah passes me. She places my breakfast-tray where I can get it without effort. It is rose wicker, edged with a transparent glass bottom, . . . the very latest thing in breakfast trays, . . . and the china is rose-coloured and iridescent. I will have everything to match, and they pander to me shamefully. There are tiny snippets of toast on my tray, a boiled egg, marmalade, little rolls of fresh butter. Sarah draws the curtains, hands me my dainty chiffon-lined Shetland dressing-jacket—the one Trix made for Christmas, and adorned with ribbon roses the exact colour of my eiderdown. The sleeves are long and flowing to prevent me from catching a chill in the sleeveless nightdress that mother thinks is so fast. Sarah hands me the morning paper, switches on the electric fire, . . . " Coldish this morning, Miss Nelly, and your ma says you've to rest until lunch if you feel tired, not being in bed till nearly twelve."

A shrill piercing scream.

Merciful God, what was that ? I sit up with a stifled cry. I stare round the bare room, bewildered. Where am I ? Who are these strangers, these half-dressed strangers ?

" Get a move on, Smithy. You'll be late away."

Commandant's whistle.

The midnight convoy signal.

I have been dreaming.

.   .   .   .   .

The convoy is late. We are all lined up waiting —even the five newcomers are at last toeing the line—but the long crawling length of train does not round the bend. Little groups of stretcher-bearers stand about shivering and cursing the delay. Some of them warm their hands at our radiators. Two of them are in high spirits. They have been drinking. Commandant is eyeing them. She will report them before the night is much older. It is seldom the stretcher-bearers take to drink, but one can quite understand their giving way. There are times when I would drug myself with spirits, if I could lay hands on any. . . . Anything to shut out the horrors of these convoys.

Some of the girls begin to tramp about the station yard. I am too numb to get down. I suppose I still possess feet, though I cannot feel them. The wind has dropped slightly, but it seems to get colder and colder. Oh, this cold of France. I have never experienced anything remotely resembling it. It works through one's clothing, into one's flesh and bones. It is not satisfied till it is firmly ingrained in one's internal regions, from whence it never really moves.

It has been freezing hard for over a week now. The bare trees in the road are loaded with icicles, . . . tall trees, ugly and gaunt and gallows-like till the whiteness veiled them—transforming them into objects of weird beauty.

Etta Potato and The Bug want me to come down. They are having a walking race with Tosh for cigarettes—the winner to collect one each from the losers. Won't I join in? I refuse, . . . I am too numb to move. Off they start across the snow-covered yard. Tosh wins easily. Their laughter rings out as she extorts her winnings there and then. All of a sudden their laughter ceases. They fly back to their posts. The convoy must be sighted. I crane my neck. Yes. The stretcher-bearers stop smoking and line up along the platform. Ambulance doors are opened in readiness. All is bustle. Everyone on the alert. Cogs in the great machinery. I can hear the noise of the train distinctly now, . . . sound travels a long way in the snow in these death-still early morning hours before the dawn. Louder and louder.

If the War goes on and on and on and I stay out here for the duration, I shall never be able to meet a train-load of casualties without the same ghastly nausea stealing over me as on that first never-to-be-forgotten night. Most of the drivers grow hardened after the first week. They fortify themselves with thoughts of how they are helping to alleviate the sufferings of wretched men, and find consolation in so thinking. But I cannot. I am not the type that breeds warriors. I am the type that should have stayed at home, that shrinks from blood and filth, and is completely devoid of pluck. In other words, I am a coward. . . . A rank coward. I have no guts. It takes every ounce of will-power I possess to stick to my post when I see the train rounding the bend. I choke my sickness back into my throat, and grip the wheel, and tell myself it is all a horrible nightmare . . . soon I shall awaken in my satin-covered bed on Wimbledon Common . . . what I can picture with such awful vividness doesn't really exist. . . .

I have schooled myself to stop fainting at the sight of blood. I have schooled myself not to vomit at the smell of wounds and stale blood, but view these sad bodies with professional calm I shall never be able to. I may be helping to alleviate the sufferings of wretched men, but commonsense rises up and insists that the necessity should never have arisen. I become savage at the futility. A war to end war, my mother writes. Never. In twenty years it will repeat itself. And twenty years after that. Again and again, as long as we breed women like my mother and Mrs. Evans-Mawnington. And we are breeding them. Etta Potato and The B.F.— two out of a roomful of six. Mother and Mrs. Evans-Mawnington all over again.

Oh, come with me, Mother and Mrs. Evans-Mawnington. Let me show you the exhibits straight from the battlefield. This will be something original to tell your committees, while they knit their endless miles of khaki scarves, . . . something to spout from the platform at your recruiting meetings. Come with me. Stand just there.

Here we have the convoy gliding into the station now, slowly, so slowly. In a minute it will disgorge its sorry cargo. My ambulance doors are open, waiting to receive. See, the train has stopped. Through the occasionally drawn blinds you will observe the trays slotted into the sides of the train. Look closely, Mother and Mrs. Evans-Mawnington, and you shall see what you shall see. Those trays each contain something that was once a whole man . . . the heroes who have done their bit for King and country . . . the heroes who marched blithely through the streets of London Town singing " Tipperary," while you cheered and waved your flags hysterically. They are not singing now, you will observe. Shut your ears, Mother and Mrs. Evans-Mawnington, lest their groans and heart-rending cries linger as long in your memory as in the memory of the daughter you sent out to help win the War.

See the stretcher-bearers lifting the trays one by one, slotting them deftly into my ambulance. Out of the way quickly, Mother and Mrs. Evans-Mawnington—lift your silken skirts aside . . . a man is spewing blood, the moving has upset him, finished him. . . . He will die on the way to hospital if he doesn't die before the ambulance is loaded. I know. . . . All this is old history to me. Sorry this has happened. It isn't pretty to see a hero spewing up his life's blood in public, is it ? Much more romantic to see him in the picture papers being awarded the V.C., even if he is minus a limb or two. A most unfortunate occurrence !

That man strapped down ? That raving, blaspheming creature screaming filthy words you don't know the meaning of . . . words your daughter uses in everyday conversation, a habit she has contracted from vulgar contact of this kind. Oh, merely gone

91

mad, Mother and Mrs. Evans-Mawnington. He
may have seen a headless body running on and on,
with blood spurting from the trunk. The crackle
of the frost-stiff dead men packing the duck-boards
watertight may have gradually undermined his
reason. There are many things the sitters tell me
on our long night rides that could have done this.

No, not shell-shock. The shell-shock cases take
it more quietly as a rule, unless they are suddenly
startled. Let me find you an example. Ah, the
man they are bringing out now. The one staring
straight ahead at nothing . . . twitching, twitching,
twitching, each limb working in a different direction, like a Jumping Jack worked by a jerking string.
Look at him, both of you. Bloody awful, isn't it,
Mother and Mrs. Evans-Mawnington? That's
shell-shock. If you dropped your handbag on the
platform, he would start to rave as madly as the
other. What? You won't try the experiment?
You can't watch him? Why not? *Why not?* I
have to, every night. Why the hell can't you do it
for once? Damn your eyes.

Forgive me, Mother and Mrs. Evans-Mawnington.
That was not the kind of language a nicely-brought-
up young lady from Wimbledon Common uses. I
forget myself. We will begin again.

See the man they are fitting into the bottom
slot. He is coughing badly. No, not pneumonia.

Not tuberculosis. Nothing so picturesque. Gently, gently, stretcher-bearers . . . he is about done. He is coughing up clots of pinky-green filth. Only his lungs, Mother and Mrs. Evans-Mawnington. He is coughing well to-night. That is gas. You've heard of gas, haven't you? It burns and shrivels the lungs to . . . to the mess you see on the ambulance floor there. He's about the age of Bertie, Mother. Not unlike Bertie, either, with his gentle brown eyes and fair curly hair. Bertie would look up pleadingly like that in between coughing up his lungs. . . . The son you have so generously given to the War. The son you are so eager to send out to the trenches before Roy Evans-Mawnington, in case Mrs. Evans-Mawnington scores over you at the next recruiting meeting. . . . " I have given my only son."

Cough, cough, little fair-haired boy. Perhaps somewhere your mother is thinking of you . . . boasting of the life she has so nobly given . . . the life you thought was your own, but which is hers to squander as she thinks fit. " My boy is not a slacker, thank God." Cough away, little boy, cough away. What does it matter, providing your mother doesn't have to face the shame of her son's cowardice?

These are sitters. The man they are hoisting up beside me, and the two who sit in the ambulance. Blighty cases . . . broken arms and trench feet . . . mere trifles. The smell? Disgusting, isn't it?

Sweaty socks and feet swollen to twice their size . . .
purple, blue, red . . . big black blisters filled with
yellow matter. Quite a colour-scheme, isn't it?
Have I made you vomit? I must again ask pardon.
My conversation is daily growing less refined.
Spew and vomit and sweat . . . I had forgotten these
words are not used in the best drawing-rooms on
Wimbledon Common.

But I am wasting time. I must go in a minute.
I am nearly loaded. The stretcher they are putting
on one side? Oh, a most ordinary exhibit, . . . the
groaning man to whom the smallest jolt is red hell
. . . a mere bellyful of shrapnel. They are holding
him over till the next journey. He is not as urgent
as the helpless thing there, that trunk without arms
and legs, the remnants of a human being, incapable
even of pleading to be put out of his misery because
his jaw has been half shot away. . . . No, don't meet
his eyes, they are too alive. Something of their
malevolence might remain with you all the rest of
your days, . . . those sock-filled, committee-crowded
days of yours.

Gaze on the heroes who have so nobly upheld
your traditions, Mother and Mrs. Evans-Mawnington. Take a good look at them. . . . The heroes you
will sentimentalise over until peace is declared, and
allow to starve for ever and ever, amen, afterwards.
Don't go. Spare a glance for my last stretcher, . . .

that gibbering, unbelievable, unbandaged thing, a wagging lump of raw flesh on a neck, that was a face a short time ago, Mother and Mrs. Evans-Mawnington. Now it might be anything . . . a lump of liver, raw bleeding liver, that's what it resembles more than anything else, doesn't it? We can't tell its age, but the whimpering moan sounds young, somehow. Like the fretful whimpers of a sick little child . . . a tortured little child . . . puzzled whimpers. Who is he? For all you know, Mrs. Evans-Mawnington, he is your Roy. He might be anyone at all, so why not your Roy? One shapeless lump of raw liver is like another shapeless lump of raw liver. What do you say? Why don't they cover him up with bandages? How the hell do I know? I have often wondered myself, . . . but they don't. Why do you turn away? That's only liquid fire. You've heard of liquid fire? Oh, yes. I remember your letter. . . . " *I hear we've started to use liquid fire, too. That will teach those Germans. I hope we use lots and lots of it.*" Yes, you wrote that. You were glad some new fiendish torture had been invented by the chemists who are running this war. You were delighted to think some German mother's son was going to have the skin stripped from his poor face by liquid fire. . . . Just as some equally patriotic German mother rejoiced when she first heard the sons of Englishwomen were to be burnt and tortured by the very newest war gadget out of the laboratory.

Don't go, Mother and Mrs. Evans-Mawnington, . . . don't go. I am loaded, but there are over thirty ambulances not filled up. Walk down the line. Don't go, unless you want me to excuse you while you retch your insides out as I so often do. There are stretchers and stretchers you haven't seen yet. . . . Men with hopeless dying eyes who don't want to die . . . men with hopeless living eyes who don't want to live. Wait, wait, I have so much, so much to show you before you return to your committees and your recruiting meetings, before you add to your bag of recruits . . . those young recruits you enroll so proudly with your patriotic speeches, your red, white and blue rosettes, your white feathers, your insults, your lies . . . any bloody lie to secure a fresh victim.

What? You cannot stick it any longer? You are going? I didn't think you'd stay. But I've got to stay, haven't I? . . . I've got to stay. You've got me out here, and you'll keep me out here. You've got me haloed. I am one of the Splendid Young Women who are winning the War. . . .

" Loaded. Six stretchers and three sitters ! "

I am away. I slow up at the station gate. The sergeant is waiting with his pencil and list.

I repeat, " Six stretchers and three sitters."

" Number Eight."

He ticks off my ambulance. I pass out of the yard.

.   .   .   .   .

Number Eight. A lucky number ! A long way out, but a good level road, comparatively few pot-holes and stone heaps.

Crawl, crawl, crawl.

Along we creep at a snail's pace . . . a huge dark crawling blot on the dead-white road.

Crawl, crawl, crawl.

The sitter leans back motionless. Exhausted, or asleep, after the long journey. His arm is in splints, his head bandaged, and his left foot swaddled in a clumsy trench slipper. He leans back in the darkness, his face as invisible as though a brick wall were separating us. The wind cuts like a knife. He must be numbed through, for he has no overcoat and his sleeve is ripped up. He has draped the Army blanket cloak-wise over his shoulders, leaving his legs to the mercy of the freezing night. It is snowing again. Big snow-flakes that hiss as they catch the radiator. I tell the sitter he will find a cigarette and matches in the pocket of my coat nearest him. I have placed them there purposely . . . my bait to make him

97

talk. I want him to talk. He does not reply.
I want him to talk. If I can get a sitter to talk it
helps to drown the cries from inside. I discovered
that some time ago. I repeat my offer, a trifle
louder this time. But he makes no reply. He is
done. Too done to smoke even. No luck for me
to-night.

Crawl, crawl, crawl.

How smoothly she runs, this great lumbering
blot. How slowly. To look at her you'd never
think it possible to run an ambulance of this size
so slowly. . . .

Crawl, crawl, crawl.

Did I hear a scream from inside? I must fix
my mind on something. . . . What? I know—my
coming-out dance. My first grown-up dance frock,
a shining frock of sequins and white georgette,
high-waisted down to my toes. . . . *Did I hear a
scream?* . . . Made over a petticoat . . . *don't let
them start screaming* . . . a petticoat of satin. Satin
slippers to match, not tiny—my feet were always
largish ; so were my hands. . . . *Was that a scream
from inside?* . . . Such a trouble Mother had getting
white gloves my size to go above the elbow. . . .
Was it a scream? . . . My hair up for the first time
. . . *oh, God, a scream this time* . . . my hair up in
little rolls at the back . . . *another scream—the
madman has started, the madman has started. I was*

98

afraid of him. He'll start them all screaming. . . . Thirty-one little rolls like fat little sausages. A professional hairdresser came in and did them—took nearly two hours to do them while Trix and Mother watched, and Sarah came in to peep. *Don't let him start the others ; don't let him start the others. . . .* Thirty-one little sausages of hair, piled one on top of the other, and all the hair my own too, copied from a picture post card of Phyllis Dare or Lily Elsie. Now, which one was it ? . . . *The shell-shocked man has joined in. The madman has set the shell-shocked man howling like a mad dog. . . .* Lily Elsie, I think it was. . . . *What are they doing to one another in there ?*

" Let me out. Let me out."

The madman is calling that. Lily Elsie, I think it was. Lily Elsie. . . .

" Stop screaming. You're not the only one going through bloody hell."

A different voice that one. That must be one of the sitters. . . . Satin slippers with buckles on the toes —little pearl buckles shaped like a crescent. Aunt Helen or Trix gave me those.

" Shut up screaming, or I'll knock hell out of you with my crutch, you bastard. Shut up screaming."

What was that crash ? They're fighting inside. They're fighting inside. . . . Scream, scream, scream. . . .

" I'm dying.   Oh, Jesus, he's murdered me.   I'm dying."

What are they doing ?   Are they murdering one another in there ?   I ought to stop the ambulance ; I ought to get out and see.   I ought to stop them. . . . I ought.   A driver the other night stopped her ambulance, and a man had gone mad and was beating a helpless stretcher case about the head. But she overpowered him and strapped him down again. Tosh, that was.   But Tosh is brave.   I couldn't do it.   I must go on. . . .

They are all screaming now.   Moaning and shrieking and howling like wild animals. . . . All alone with an ambulance of raving men miles from anywhere in the pitch blackness, . . . raving madmen yelling and screaming.   I shall go mad myself. . . .

Go and see . . . go and see . . . go and see.

I will not.   I cannot . . . my heart is pounding like a sledge-hammer.   My feet and hands are frozen, but the sweat is pouring down my back in rivulets.   I have looked before, and I dare not look again.   What good can I do ?   The man who spewed blood will be lying there dead, . . . his glassy eyes fixed on the door of the ambulance, staring accusingly at me as I peep in, . . . cold dead eyes, blaming me when I am not to blame. . . . The madman will curse me, scream vile curses at me, scream and try to tear himself from the straps that hold him down, . . . if he has not torn himself away already. He will try to tear himself from his straps to choke the life from me. The shell-shocked man will yammer and twitch and jerk and mouth. The man with the face like raw liver will moan. . . . I will not go and see. I will not go and see.

Crawl, crawl, crawl.

Number Eight, where are you? Have I missed you in the monotony of this snow-covered road. I have been travelling for hours. Am I travelling too slowly? Am I being over-careful? Could I accelerate ever so slightly . . . cover the distance more quickly? I will do it. A fresh scream from someone as I jolt over a stone . . . I've hurt someone. I slow down again.

Scream, scream, scream. Three different sets of screams now—the shriek of the madman, the senseless, wolfish, monotonous howl of the shell-shock case, and now a shrill sharp yell like a bright pointed knife blade being jabbed into my brain. One, two, three, four, . . . staccato yells. Which one is that? Not the little fair-haired boy. He is too busy choking to death to shriek. Another one has joined in . . . inferno. They are striking one another again . . . hell let loose. Go and see, go and see. . . .

I will not go and see.   I will not go and see.

Crawl, crawl, crawl.

The sitter sleeps through it all.   A pool of snow has fallen in his lap.   We have missed Number Eight. I must have missed the turning in the snow.   The black tree-stump on the left that leads to Number Eight . . . snow-obscured.   I must have missed the turning in the snow.

Crawl, crawl, crawl.

The screams have died down, but a dreadful moaning takes their place.   Oo-oo-oh . . . oo-oo-oh . . . dirge-like, regular, it rises above the sound of the engine and floats out into the night. Oo-oo-oh . . . oo-oo-oh . . . it is heart-breaking in its despair.   I have heard a man moan like that before.   The last moans of a man who will soon cease moaning for ever.   Oo-oo-oh . . . the hopelessness, the loneliness.   Tears tear at my heart . . . awful tears that rack me, but must not rise to my eyes, for they will freeze on my cheeks and stick my eyelids together until I cannot see to drive. Even the solace of pitying tears is denied me.

Crawl, crawl, crawl.

I have given up all hope of reaching Number Eight by now.   I will go on until there is a place to turn.

Crawl, crawl, crawl.

The moans have ceased.   I strain my ears.   The

madman is shouting again, . . . a hoarse vitupera-
tive monologue. I cannot catch his words. I do
not want to catch his words. But I strain to catch
them just the same. He will start the others
again. . . .

Crawl, crawl, crawl.

If only I could find a place to turn. The road
seems to grow narrower. How many journeys
shall I make to-night? Was it a big convoy?
I didn't notice at the station, . . . I always forget
to notice. Perhaps I shall have shrapnels next
time . . . shrapnels, too exhausted from loss of
blood to scream. A sitter who will talk and smoke.
. . . The madman is screaming again . . . he
will start the others.

Crawl, crawl, crawl.

Is that a light? No . . . yes! Number Eight!
The big canvas marquee gleaming dully in the
darkness . . . the front entrance flaps already parted
. . . white-capped nurses waiting in the doorway.
They can see my lights. The orderlies are standing
by. . . . Number Eight . . . Number Eight. . . . I
am there at last. The tears are rolling down my
cheeks . . . let them. Let the tears freeze my eyelids
together now . . . let them freeze my eyelids. . . . It
doesn't matter now . . . nothing matters now. . . .

CHAPTER V

THE B.F. is leaving for England in the morning. She says she is ill, but the truth is she is too bored to stick it any longer. We are having a farewell party, to the great annoyance of those who are trying to sleep in the adjacent cubicles. We have drawn our beds closely together and have spread a large sheet of brown paper on which repose our joint contributions—biscuits, a few ounces of real butter, two tins of sardines, twenty-three cigarettes, a jam-pot of potted meat, a stale seed cake, and, last but by no means least, two bottles of *vin rouge* which we are drinking out of cups borrowed from the canteen. It tastes, candidly, rather like red ink, but we are not fussy. It is contraband, of course. If Commandant discovered it in our room . . . but why worry? it is worth the risk. It is wet and warming and will run to three cups each, and we toast the daring of Tosh, who is responsible for its presence. On arriving at the station this forenoon she discovered the train would be two to three hours late —a mere trifle here—took a chance, dashed into the town some miles away—out of bounds except to special permits—secured the wine, and managed to return in time to pick up her two hospital sisters.

The butter we owe to The B.F., who has been saving it since last mail day ; the sardines are from Etta Potato ; the potted meat from Skinny ; The Bug has given the biscuits, while the stale cake is my contribution to the feast.

We are all a trifle hilarious, partly because of the *vin rouge*, and partly because the thaw is beginning, which makes it several degrees warmer already. We sit, feet in flea-bags, laughing and deriding the protests from those who want to slumber. The provisions disappear quickly. The potted meat is home-made and goes down amazingly well with sweet biscuits. Tosh invents a savoury, " Sardines *à la* B.F."—slices of cake with mashed sardines in between. It is surprisingly good.

" It's time we toasted The B.F." Tosh glances at her wrist-watch. " I expect we ought to let those poor long-suffering wretches sleep before the midnight convoy."

" I should say so," agrees a voice from next door.

" No," we cry selfishly. " It isn't every night we have a farewell party. We don't want to go to sleep. Let's have some speeches. We'll all make speeches. Etta Potato first."

" Etta Potato ! Etta Potato ! "

" Shut up," yells the voice.

" Bottoms," retorts Tosh, rudely ; " large ones, like Commandant's." And the voice says, " Disgusting " ; to which Tosh replies, " I agree, but why question the Creator's handiwork ? " and the voice subsides with a giggle.

" Come on, Etta Potato."

" There will never be a better B.F. in this convoy," declaims Etta Potato with unintentional wit. We shriek with joy.

" Now the Bug."

The Bug smiles. " I wish The B.F. all the luck that she can't help having. She will always fall on her feet. She is the type life loves. Life will give her its best gifts generously, with both hands. She has youth, money, beauty. I envy her all of those, but most of all I envy her genuine love of conventional things—the little things of life that make for happiness. Good luck, B.F., and happiness. The B.F.'s of this world are to be envied."

We applaud, but we are puzzled at The Bug's tone. Tosh shoots her an inquiring glance, but The B.F. smiles rather vacantly and says, " Thank you, dear, so sweet of you."

We cry for Tosh.

" Tosh ! Speech ! "

" Shut up, you noisy hounds. . . ."

" Ladies and those sluts next door with flapping ears . . ."

106

" Tosh, *darling*. . . ."

" This sad, sad parting would never have happened had a simple English girl been able to have—I mean do her bit in France," declaims Tosh. " For five months she has laboured unceasingly. Admit it, all of you. Never has driver been so worked up. She could have started off in top on any frosty night on the self-starter. To no purpose. My sisters, I ask you, is it her fault there are no stray bits in the area ? Despairing, bursting with love . . ."

Tosh pauses dramatically.

" . . . of country . . ."

We yell with joy.

" . . . The wench is forced back to England. In the face of this, does France deserve her reputation ? I say, ' No.' Does France merit the pornographic snigger the very mention of her name earns from those who have never crossed the Channel ? "

" No ! " we shout. " No, no ! "

" I agree. The B.F. has killed that illusion for ever. So she returns to London, where, judging by a rumour that a certain hotel is proposing to erect a memorial tablet to the brave Englishwomen who have fallen there during these early days of the War, one feels she will do her bit not once, but many times. Of such stuff are the women of England made. The pioneer spirit that populates our colonies. As

NOT SO QUIET . . .

Mahomet had to go to the mountain that refused to come to him, so does The B.F. go all out for the bit that would not come to her. Ladies, raise your teacups . . . The B.F."

Convulsed with laughter, we drink the toast to the accompaniment of catcalls from the adjacent rooms. The B.F. nods. Though aware Tosh is pulling her leg, she has no idea to what extent.

" Speech ! The B.F. Speech ! "

" Girls," says The B.F. ; " honestly, I think it's topping of you. Of course, I'm sorry to go, but, honestly, work is dreadful and my hands are simply vile, and no sleep either. I adore being here and helping our brave lads in khaki . . ."

" Oh, Gawd ! " from Tosh, *sotto voce*.

" But I feel I have done my bit, and rest assured I'll do it in England, as Tosh says."

" Unaccustomed as I am to public speaking," murmurs Tosh.

" Go to sleep," shouts a voice.

" I say, Skinny and Smithy haven't made speeches."

" May you always be able to tell Mother everything you do, B.F. Chin-chin." I lift my cup hastily. I detest making speeches.

" Now, Skinny," insists The B.F.

Tosh deliberately withdraws from the party by turning her back and opening a magazine. The insult is deliberate, as deliberate as earlier when she refused to sample Skinny's potted meat. Skinny ignored the first slight, but now, possibly owing to the unaccustomed *vin rouge*, she sits up and stares in a hostile fashion at Tosh's back. I feel uneasy.

" Let's all go to sleep," I suggest.

" Yes," from outside.

" No, Skinny must make a speech first," insists The B.F.

Tosh lights a cigarette and begins to read.

" Go on, Skinny."

" No, Tosh doesn't want me to," replies Skinny nastily. " She resents me being here at all. Pity I'm in the damned room, isn't it ? "

" Shut up, Skinny ; don't be an ass."

" I won't shut up. Why should I ? I've as much right here. I can speak as well as her. This is my room as well as Tosh's, isn't it ? "

" Oh, for Christ's sake," mutters Tosh.

The sound of her voice infuriates Skinny. She leans forward, yellow and corpseish in the candle-light. She is in a direct line with The B.F., whose pink-and-white prettiness throws her into hideous contrast. " If you had your way I wouldn't be here at all, would I ? You've already asked Commandant to move me, haven't you ? "

" Don't be absurd, Skinny. You asked Commandant yourself to move you into a two-bedder

109

with Frost," says The B.F. " I was there ; I walked in when Commandant was saying ' No.' Frost was there, too."

This is news to us. Tosh has asked Commandant ; she made no secret of it ; but Skinny. . . .

The Bug catches my eye.

" So would you want to go if you had rotten things thought about you." Skinny begins weeping hysterically. " I hate people with dirty minds."

" Shut up, Skinny." The Bug puts her hand on Skinny's shoulder, but Skinny pushes her away roughly.

" You keep away from me or she'll be saying rotten things about you too. You want to be careful with a mind like hers."

Tosh turns the magazine page elaborately. I hastily collect the wine bottles and hide them. The others conceal the cups. If the noise brings Commandant on the scene we don't want to be caught with the incriminating evidence. The B.F. is very distressed. She is rather like a puzzled Persian kitten. There is an ominous quiet from the adjacent cubicles. No one is demanding silence now : they are much too thrilled by the unexpected entertainment.

" You're spoiling my party, Skinny," pleads The B.F.

" I don't care," shouts Skinny angrily. " You

don't know what she said to me last week. She thinks I'm a something."

Tosh lights a fresh cigarette from her old butt and goes on reading.

" And I say she's a horrible, bad-minded liar, if she thinks things like that about me. And she does think them or she wouldn't have insinuated what she did to me last week."

" Be quiet, dear," wails The B.F. " We don't want Mrs. You-Know-Itch up here. I'm sure Tosh doesn't think horrid things about you."

" Then why doesn't she deny it ? Why doesn't she deny it ? " sobs Skinny.

Tosh says nothing, though we all wait expectantly.

" You see ? You see ? You don't know what she said to me last week. If you knew. . . ."

She begins to sob violently, terribly. We stare at each other in helpless uncomfortable silence. There is a pause.

" Well, what *did* Tosh say ? " asks The B.F.

We have been dying to ask that question, but have not dared. The silence is intense. The guns in the distance, Skinny's painful, grotesque sobs, and everyone listening. We can almost see the straining ears in the adjacent cubicles. Skinny is working herself up to a pitch of violent hysteria. Her tears are falling on the bare floor like rain, making splashes on the boards. It fills us with a sort of shame instead of pity ; it is so primitive and unrestrained. Someone implores her to control herself, that everyone is listening, but she is beyond control.

" I expect she called you a flirt," says The B.F. complacently. " She often calls me that, but I don't behave like a silly ass over it."

" No," sobs Skinny, " that's just what she *didn't* call me."

She begins to sob again, long, frenzied, drawn-out sobs. Tosh goes on smoking. The Bug and I avoid each other's glance elaborately. The B.F. laughs her little affected laugh.

" You silly old thing, Skinny. With all the men being killed off there have to be some superfluous women in the world. And you're an awfully good driver, darling, and terribly useful. All the same, I do think it rather unkind of you, Tosh, to rub it into poor old Skinny that she hasn't any admirers, really I do, and I think you ought to tell Skinny you're sorry ; it's only fair."

Tosh throws the magazine on the floor. " Good night, everybody."

She curls into her flea-bag. The gesture finishes Skinny completely. She screams. " There, I told you, I told you, I told you." She screams again. Commandant obviously has not returned from Number One Hospital, where she is visiting her great friend the matron. Let us hope she will stay there until the storm is over. All at once Skinny springs from her bed and rushes at Tosh, beating her about the head with clenched bare fists. It is ghastly. Like a street-woman brawling in public. She uses vile language, not like Tosh's good-natured swear-words that always sound characteristic of Tosh and therefore exactly " right," but low, shameful, foul somehow. I want to hide my head under the Army blankets ; instead I help the others tear her away. She appears on the verge of an apoplectic fit, almost foaming at the mouth. The B.F. wrings her hands and asks if she will go for Commandant. Skinny struggles, panting, shouting, " Yes, and I'll tell you who else she thinks things about, too. I'll tell you . . ."

Tosh lies motionless, eyes closed, to all outward appearances asleep.

" Yes, I'll tell you who else . . ."

We have not noticed the door of our room open. Frost from the opposite cubicle comes in, takes Skinny by the arm and pushes her outside.

" I'll calm her down," she whispers, and goes.

" Thank heaven," sighs The Bug.

As the door closes Tosh laughs, a hard laugh that is like a blow. No one says any more. The party is definitely over. Etta Potato blows the candle out.

·   ·   ·   ·   ·

Beyond the hill where lies Number Thirteen
Hospital is a twin hill topped by a queer-shaped
ancient tree that never buds into leaf nor yet rots,
according to local lore. The hill is called the Hill
of the Witch's Hand, and the tree is responsible
for the strange name by reason of the gnarled trunk
that gives the curious illusion of a gigantic palm,
and of the five malformed branches that stretch
like fingers into the valley below, where is the
military cemetery.

Square, undecorated, unfoliaged, with its muddy
earth mounds and regular rows of plain crosses,
the cemetery is as hideous as the war that has
called it into being. No gentle resting-place for a
world-weary head is this bleak track of upheaved
earth fenced with wooden stakes—rather a swift
place to hide men who have violently and dreadfully
died. And over this bleak burial ground stretches
the Witch's Hand, hollow-palmed, sinister, greedy.
Strangely symbolic of war. Reaching out and
demanding. Demanding . . . never denied. Demanding . . . never content.

I fix my eyes on this evil black tree as I change
down for the steep climb. The white glove that
has so graciously hidden it for the last few weeks
has disappeared, and to my fancy the recent load
of heavy snow has bent the five fingers to the centre,
making them more claw-like and avaricious than

before. The Hand will have its fill of victims to-day. This is a sad record in the history of the convoy— the longest list of funerals since the beginning. I have already passed three ambulances coming from the cemetery since I began the ascent, and another has just rounded the brow. They are all tearing back for their next load of dead. There is much burying to be done before night falls.

My funeral is from Number Thirteen, and I am a quarter of an hour late on account of a puncture. The doors of the little corrugated-tin mortuary are open. The orderlies are impatiently awaiting my arrival. They extinguish their cigarettes and dive inside as I turn the corner that leads to the dead-house. Hardly have I pulled up than they have hoisted the first plain deal flag-covered coffin on their shoulders and are loading up. The corporal stands by giving orders. He complains aggrievedly to me at intervals that what with one thing and another he's had no dinner to-day . . . everything simply chronic . . . men dying like flies . . . they'll be running out of coffins before the week's out . . . and no dinner to crown all. One of the strings that holds the Union Jack to a coffin has been carelessly tied. The flag slips into the mud.

"Now, then, Eminway," he chides, severely, "what are you a-doing of?"

He runs into the mortuary for a fresh flag. The

coffin carriers sink to their ankles in mud, squelching in and out. I sit staring straight ahead. The Witch's Hand reaches out ghoulishly in the wind as the corporal ties a clean Union Jack on the coffin to the accompaniment of a running commentary on Eminway's shortcomings.

I am very tired to-day, mentally as well as bodily. I have been conveying these flag-covered boxes for months now to the ugly little cemetery that scars the valley, and I see no end. I have lost count of the number of times I have been a supernumerary in the last scene of the great war drama that opens daily in a recruiting office and drops its final curtain amid no applause on a plain deal coffin draped with a Union Jack, to the tune of " The Last Post " from an orchestra of two. The last picturesque tableau in the masquerade. Countless young lives ending prematurely as numbers in a row of muddy earth mounds in a bare tract of hastily fenced-off ground. Victims of youth's eternal lure—the lure of what may be waiting just round the corner.

Fine youth, eager youth, trusting youth. Five plain deal boxes of standard measurement. What has life in store for us, the occupants were wondering but a short while ago ? Now they are about to be made numbers in a row of muddy earth mounds in a bare tract of hastily fenced-off ground. Fortunate perhaps in that they died, for once belief is shattered it is better to die. We young ones doomed to live on without belief in anything human or divine again are the ones to be pitied.

" O.K. All away."

The corporal signals that I am loaded. The padre is already at the cemetery, also the buglers. Now he hopes he can have a bite, or I'll be coming back to fetch him next trip. All this he tells me, very tickled at his little joke, as I back the ambulance for the crawl into the valley.

The mud is a foot deep. We turn the corner, the orderlies squelching solemnly alongside, cursing amiably each time they strike an extra deep puddle. Overhead is a blue sky streaked with long scurrying clouds ; the wind is rough, but lacks the cutting quality of the past weeks, the winter sun shines weakly, and there is an indefinable something in the air that whips the blood and heartens the flagging spirit. Perhaps it will end soon. Who knows ? Sad indeed to be hidden from sight for ever to-day in the ever-growing cemetery shadowed by the Witch's Hand. It is a day for life, not death. A day for striding the Sussex Downs with a joyful barking dog. A day to return home happily tired at sunset to a leaping fire of friendly logs. But not a day to be made a number in a row of muddy earth mounds in a bare tract of hastily fenced-off ground. When I am buried

I would wish it to be a grey day of desperately sad wind and slanting rain, a day when to leave this earth behind would be a gladsome thing—and this I think I could not do willingly on a brisk day of windy winter sunshine.

The padre meets us at the cemetery entrance. I clamber down. I examine my tyres anxiously. I have come a little too far in. No joke sticking in the mud near the cemetery gates. Once before . . .

The orderlies advise me to risk it. I decide to follow their advice. I stand to attention as the coffins are carried inside. Near the graves the buglers are waiting. They are tired and bored. The five graves are side by side in the centre of a row. The mud is awful. Twice I go in over my ankles as I walk down the avenue of black crosses. A coffin is placed near each yawning cavity. The padre clears his throat, an orderly deftly unties each Union Jack and adds it to the neat little heap. Creak, creak, the coffins are lowered while we stand to attention. A hitch occurs and the orderlies whisper among themselves.

The padre begins the service. I glance at the khaki-clad men. Their mouths are tightly set—grim, disillusioned mouths for mere boys of eighteen or nineteen. Hard-lipped, unseeing, they stare upwards at the Witch's Hand. I shiver. It is not my imagination; the snow has bent it over. It reaches down evilly, the claws snatching at us as we stand defenceless, as though to squeeze the youth from us until we are dry and lifeless.

The padre drones on—I do not hear his words. At last he finishes. He makes a gesture. We bow our heads. Under my lashes I take a last peep at the five deal boxes and sigh. The five dead will sleep soundly enough in their muddy beds to-night. When I raise my head a few seconds later the buglers have their bugles in readiness to their lips. The taller one nods imperceptibly to the other. " The Last Post " fills the valley ; the notes are caught by the hills and flung back. Once more the curtain rings down on the drama that can already boast one of the longest runs on record. When will the final performances be announced ?

The padre stands lost in a reverie, tapping his finger against the book he carries. Seconds pass. One of the buglers blows down the mouthpiece of his instrument to dislodge something, the other fidgets uneasily on one leg. At last an orderly gives a loud significant cough. This rouses the padre. He starts and moves away. His shoulders are drooping. He looks very weary. We follow him. The service has taken barely five minutes from the lowering of the coffins.

The orderlies examine my wheels. They have not sunk further into the morass, as I had feared.

I offer the padre a lift, but he points without speech to another ambulance slowly crawling down the hill. His mouth is set in lines of infinite weariness as we watch. This is an imposing funeral compared with mine. There are six officers and several nurses. A dead V.A.D., I remember suddenly. A gust of wind shakes the Witch's Hand until the fingers tremble with horrible eagerness. I turn my back quickly and start the engine. There is something human and reassuringly earth-earthy in its vibration.

The orderlies throw the Union Jacks aboard. One of them clambers up beside me and lights a cigarette directly we have passed the incoming procession. He tells me he wants his tea—it was fish for dinner and he never could stand fish. From inside comes the noise of the others chatting and laughing. We dash up the hill as fast as the engine will travel. On the way we pass two more ambulances descending into the valley. " My Gawd, we're winning the war," remarks the man beside me, sarcastically. I drop my passengers at the turning leading to Number Thirteen mortuary. They go down the lane marching and whistling " Tipperary." They will be in good time for tea. I discover I want my own badly.

.   .   .   .   .

Tosh meets me at the mess-room door and draws

120

me aside. Commandant wants me. There is a notice on the board to that effect. We have long suspected there was a " policeman " in our midst —now we are certain. Last night's scene has leaked out. Someone has carried tales to Commandant. She wants to pump me. Tosh has been through the third degree for an hour.

" She got nothing out of me," says Tosh, " but The Bug, caught napping, admitted that Frost calmed Skinny down in the finish. So she's in it now. In Commandant's room with Skinny."

" What about Etta Potato ? "

" She isn't back yet, but I'll catch her. Not that she knows anything to tell. Mrs. Bitch is well on the warpath ; she thinks there's something at the back of all this. So go easy."

" I'll go easy." I set my lips obstinately. I am no policeman for Commandant. She will get nothing out of me. I gulp down a cup of tea. I am in exactly the right mood when I enter the office a few minutes later.

Skinny and Frost are sobbing hard. Frost is a thin, weak, spineless creature called " The Chinless Wonder " by those who take the trouble to dislike her. It always amazes me how such a stupid-looking girl can drive better than anyone I have ever met. She is a marvel with a car. Now she is red-eyed and red-nosed, a revolting spectacle.

Skinny is weeping for effect ; I note that at a glance. A ruse to evade Commandant's questionings. Well, Commandant will not make me weep. She can punish me till she is green in the face, but she will not dissolve me into tears. Neither will she make me talk. I become quite reckless. It will be interesting to see how much punishment I can get and still survive.

" What do you know of last night's disgraceful episode, Smith ? " she begins without any preliminaries.

" Nothing."

" Nothing ? You were there."

" I was asleep."

" That is a lie. You were assisting at a farewell celebration for a failure who was leaving—Farmer."

I say nothing.

" Breaking rules like small children."

I would like to ask what can she expect if she treats us like small children, but I will not give her any opening.

" You also had two bottles of strong drink."

I smile at the flattering tribute to the *vin rouge*.

" It is no laughing matter, Smith. Is it true ? "

I make no reply.

" Very well, tea-orderly all next week. Now perhaps you will answer my questions."

I make no answer.

" You realise you risk being sent back to England in disgrace for insubordination if you refuse to obey my orders ? "

The threat leaves me cold. She will not send me back. I only wish she would. She will punish and make our lives a misery, but she will not send us back. Drivers who stick it because if they went home they would be bullied by their people into coming out again—perhaps into something even worse—are few and far between in this convoy where they come and go like tourists on lightning trips. Six drivers out of every ten. We call them " The Seeing-Francers " !

" What did Toshington say to make Skinner attack her ? "

The expected query is unexpected, somehow. I go scarlet. I can feel the blood dyeing my neck, my face, even my hands. Commandant's eyes bore me like gimlets.

" I—I don't know." My tone lacks conviction even to myself, although I am technically telling strict truth. I do not know what Tosh said to Skinny, but Commandant will never believe me. I can surmise what I choose, but I definitely do not know. " I—I was half-asleep."

" You were the one to drag Skinner from Toshington when she vulgarly attacked her. You were not half-asleep."

I become calm again.

"Skinner must have had some terrific provocation. What was it ?"

" I am as ignorant as you are, Commandant."

" That is a lie. What was it ?"

" I do not know, Commandant."

" You do."

" I was half-asleep."

And there I stick. She cross-examines me until I nearly scream. Now and again she switches over to Skinny, who takes refuge in tears. Frost weeps continuously. Commandant finally dismisses me. I have acquired a month's punishment duties, but I could not get through them in that time if there were forty-eight hours to a day. Nevertheless, my head though bloody is unbowed. I feel I have got more than a little of my own back. I sink exhausted on my bed.

Tosh has the kettle boiling. She makes some tea. Revived, I tell the horrible details. Etta Potato has not arrived in yet, but Tosh has left a note on the board. We speculate as to the identity of the policeman. Tosh threatens awful retribution if she can trace the source of the leakage. Whom does Commandant favour most ? We cannot think. She treats everyone with impartial hellishness, excepting perhaps myself. . . .

It is very difficult.

A silence falls.

"We're wrong, Tosh," I break out at last. "We ought to tell Commandant. Carrying tales is rotten, but there are some tales that ought to be carried . . . and you can carry that honour business too far. . . ."

"No." Tosh frowns. "I was a fool to let Skinny know I knew in the first place. Personal dislike's a queer thing. I've always loathed that girl, and I let out at her just because I loathed her. Her morals don't affect me one way or the other. You couldn't shock me if you tried. I should have shut my mouth ; none of my business at all. Anyhow, let Commandant find out for herself. She rather fancies herself as a detective—remember old Thrumms ? Pushed home at two hours' notice for being caught in an ambulance with a man ? The man wasn't pushed home, of course, but the row—remember it ? Well, that would be a gentle ruffle of wind compared with this one. No . . . let Commandant do her own dirty work. If she'd had two ounces of sense she'd have twigged Skinny months ago ; blasted fools these females they put in charge—all bust and no brains. Why should I get mixed in it ? No, I'm too wide a bird. Commandant is dying to sack Skinny, ever since she found Skinny sneaking back from the heavy convoys before final permission was given at the station ;

only she daren't sack her because Skinny Senior is a big pot at the W.O., and he'd make trouble and perhaps lose Commandant the fattest job she's ever had. Oh, she'd love a good excuse to sack Skinny, simply love it . . . well, I'm not being the scapegoat and providing it. Immorality, what a chance! Doesn't it make you sick? Slack as much as you can, drive your bus as cruelly as you like, crash your gears to hell, muck your engine till it's in the mechanic's hands half its time, jolt the guts out of your wounded, shirk as much as you can without actively coming up against the powers-that-be— and you won't be sent home. But one hint of im- morality and back you go to England in disgrace as fast as the packet can take you. As if morality mattered two hoots when it comes to convoying wounded men. Personally, if I were choosing women to drive heavy ambulances their moral characters wouldn't worry me. It would be " Are you a first-class driver? " not " Are you a first- class virgin? " The biggest harlot or the biggest saint . . . what the hell does it matter as long as they put up a decent performance behind the steering wheel and can keep their engines clean? You can't get up to much immorality with dying men, can you? They give me a pain at headquarters the way they've all got morality on the brain. Thrumms the sinner was like an angel with an ambulance of

126

wounded ; our saintly B.F. has started more
hæmorrhages than any ambulance driver of her size
and weight in the whole British Expeditionary
Force, I should think. . . ."

She walks up and down, smoking furiously.

The door bangs open.

" I say, what a storm in a tea-cup," gasps Etta
Potato. " Commandant is certain there's something
fearfully sinister behind all this, Tosh. She grabbed
me as I got in and started questioning me, and when
I told her all you'd done was to taunt Skinny for
not being able to attract men . . ."

" You didn't tell her that. . . ."

" Yes, why not ? That's what it's all about,
isn't it ? "

Tosh and I look blankly at one another.

" Gawd's teeth," ejaculates Tosh.

" Well, she wants you at once," says Etta Potato.

Commandant's whistle blows.

Tosh goes out slowly.

.   .   .   .   .

An hour later we sit huddled round the canteen
fire—Tosh, The B.F., The Bug, Etta Potato and
myself. We have been forbidden to go upstairs
until Skinny has packed. She and Frost are leaving
for Boulogne to-night.

" Sacked for refusing to obey orders," says Tosh
for the umpteenth time. " Commandant was

determined to get Skinny out and she's got her out. Without my assistance, though."

" I think it *was* with your assistance," says The B.F. " Aren't you sorry now, Tosh ? "

" No, she was a dam' bad driver and I'd push any dam' bad driver out if I had a chance," retorted Tosh. " I regret the row, certainly. Commandant absolutely refused to believe anything. ' I am not imbecile enough to believe Skinner would attack Toshington for insinuating that she couldn't attract men '—those were her exact words. ' No girl attacks another for merely being catty, and Toshington is not the catty type.' "

" Well, candidly, darling, I did think it rather catty," says The B.F. " After all, it's not Skinny's fault if she's plain."

The Bug and I avoid one another's glance elaborately.

" Well, Commandant gave them a last chance to tell her what I had said," continues Tosh. " They remained dumb. She asked me again what my exact words were. I said I had forgotten. ' Very well,' said Commandant, ' I order you to tell me.' They again gave an impersonation of two dumb oysters, and that settled it. The old devil's eyes fairly shot triumph. She sacked them on the spot for refusing to obey orders. She said she would not have insubordination in her ranks.

Told them to catch the night train. I'm sorry about Frost," adds Tosh regretfully. " Never knew a girl change gear like Frost. Absolute genius on a car."

" But why didn't she sack you too ? " asks Etta Potato.

Tosh winks at me. " Cunning old devil. ' You've got a faulty memory, Toshington,' she says when they've gone. ' I hope it continues faulty when this particular episode is discussed in the convoy. You may go.' I don't mind admitting it took the wind out of the good ship Toshington's sails for a few brief moments."

" I wonder what Commandant meant by that ? " asks The B.F.

" I shall go on wondering all my life," says Tosh.

The Bug and I look at one another for a long moment. Silently we are asking how much or how little Commandant guesses.

CHAPTER VI

We are worried about The Bug—Tosh and I. The air raids have begun again with the moon. There has been one every night this week. We are all going under for lack of sleep, but The Bug is worse than anyone. The work has trebled ; they are toiling at top speed in the camps to get the men away to the base to make way for the hundreds of wounded pouring in from the field hospitals, but Commandant has not yet grasped that even machines will wear out if they are not rested occasionally. She still rigidly insists on the petty punishments that make our lives hell—and The Bug gets more punishments than any of us. We are short-handed, too. Three girls are in hospital with dysentery, five with septicæmia, and two with measles, which leaves ten ambulances out of action until ten new drivers come—and it is becoming increasingly difficult to get drivers. Rumours of our treatment, not only in this convoy but in other depots, have quelled the ardour of the volunteers at home. Senseless fanatics like Commandant are to blame. She will not see the idiocy of her autocratic policy. Fifty per cent. of us are unfit for duty, but are carrying on because there is no other way out, and The Bug is worse than anybody. She is in a sad state. She is mere skin and bone and has taken to fits of screaming after the midnight convoys. If we try to rouse her from the semi-coma into which she falls she gets violent. It is lack of rest, topped by an encounter with a stretcher case who ripped his bandages away and had practically no face. Last week even Tosh got the wind up and brought Commandant. The Bug was sitting up screaming about men with no faces when Commandant stalked in in her God-Almighty way and ordered her to stop this nonsense immediately, with the result that The Bug wrenched herself free, flew outside, started up her bus, and was off like a rocket into the darkness before one could say knife. Luckily, Tosh caught her up about a mile down the road. She says it was ghastly racing neck and neck on a pitch-black night with The Bug yelling like a raving lunatic, but at last she got ahead, skidded completely round, switched her heads on, and took a chance of The Bug's driving sense making her jam on the brakes—which happened, but it was a nasty chance to take. Dragging The Bug off her bus and getting her back was fairly easy, as The Bug is small and Tosh is hefty, and by the time they returned Commandant had the doctor, who jabbed a hypo into The Bug. She slept through three convoys and awakened, totally oblivious of what had occurred as fresh as a daisy. But did this teach Mrs. Bitch a lesson ? Not at all. Seeing The Bug to outward appearances quite normal, she made her clean the w.c. while we others were resting.

This persecution of The Bug began three weeks ago. The dissatisfaction and unrest in the convoy had at last penetrated to the office and Commandant spoke to us after early roll-call. There were traitors in the camp ; the work was hard, but we had not come to France to slack, but to help our brave soldiers to fight for world freedom—the usual clap-trap, before breakfast too. Were we women of England to be branded by future generations as lead-swingers ?

She then waited for the applause. It did not come.

Oh, that was it, was it ? An evil influence at work—some failure who was returning like the coward she was, trying to undermine the morals of the convoy first, resenting those others who would stay and see their duty through. . . .

" If you mean me," said a " Seeing-Francer," stepping forward, " I am going back before you kill me. And as I return to-night I can speak without being given a senseless punishment duty in addition to working about twenty hours a day. Feed your drivers and treat them like human beings. When

they are trying to snatch a few minutes' rest stop
blowing your whistle. And have some strong
working women brought to France and paid to do
the housework and the cleaning of the ambulances
while the drivers get some sleep. The food is not
fit for pigs to eat. It stinks."

" I eat it," replied Commandant. " If it's good
enough for me it's good enough for you."

" But it still stinks," replied the " Seeing-Francer,"
" and it isn't good enough for *me*. And I intend to
complain to headquarters in London."

" I eat the food," said Commandant stubbornly.
" Don't forget to tell headquarters that."

Which is quite true. She does. The trouble is
we do not all possess iron stomachs like her.

" And do you clean the filth out of your own
ambulance ? " asked the " Seeing-Francer." " No.
If you did we'd hear a different story. As it is,
you deliberately trap girls into petty disobediences
to get it done for you."

We nearly cheered her for this, but Commandant
ignored it absolutely. " Any more complaints ? "
she inquired, and to our astonishment The Bug
spoke up. In her quiet voice she suggested that in
the face of these extra convoys and evacuations
there should be no punishment duties, in order
that the drivers could sleep, that the outside
polishing of ambulances be discontinued and the

7.30 roll-call abolished. To wake drivers who had been out all night and expect them to be neatly dressed for a 7.30 roll-call was rather ridiculous. It was the " rather ridiculous " that got Commandant's back up. Her cold eyes narrowed.

" Christ help The Bug from now on," whispered Tosh.

" I am in charge of this convoy, and while I am in charge the ambulances will reflect credit on it. Punishments will continue when conduct merits them ; and as for the 7.30 roll-call, may I remind the drivers we are on active service with the B.E.F. ? "

So began the persecution of The Bug. She has averaged three hours' sleep a day for the last three weeks and her body is not strong enough to stand the strain. She was in no condition for the shock of the man who had no face. She scrubs and cleans and does Commandant's ambulance every day in addition to her own routine work, running un-necessary errands as well—many happy returns of the day to the matron at Number One, and so on.

When I read the rubbish praising the indomitable pluck and high spirits of " our wonderful war girls " I want to throw things at the writers. Our wonderful war girls—how bored we are with hearing it ! We are not wonderful ; there is nothing wonderful in

134

doing what you've got to, because you've let yourself in for it. It's like having a baby—you're trapped once you've started. How the mob hangs on to a phrase and chews it to shreds ! Like a dog with a bone. That eternal " doing our bit," too. The catch-phrase of the newspapers. It has gone out of fashion here with The B.F.'s exit. There may be an odd few who enlisted in a patriotic spirit—I haven't met any, personally. Girls who were curious, yes ; girls who were bored stiff with home (like myself) and had no idea of what they were coming to, yes ; man-hunters like The B.F. ; man-mad women, semi-nymphomaniacs like Thrumms, who was caught love-making in an ambulance and booted back p.d.q. to England, yes ; megalo-maniacs like Commandant who love " bossing the show " and have seized on this great chance like hungry vultures, yes ; girls to whom danger is the breath of life, yes ; but my observation leads me to the conclusion that all the flag-waggers are comfortably at home and intend to stay there.

Our " indomitable pluck " ! We haven't any left. If we had we'd admit we hate it and crawl home beaten. Our " wonderful high spirits " ! We lost those the first night we arrived. The world seems determined to see nothing but a horrible, high-spirited, perpetual brightness in us. " Our girls love their jobs ; they are always joking and playing schoolgirl pranks on one another." Yes? Here is an example.

A driver developed a dangerous form of measles the other day and four of her friends crept into her hot flea-bag before it was disinfected, hoping to catch the germs and so get into hospital for a few weeks' sleep. That is how full of fun and girlish high spirits we are. There is only one description of life out here, and that is Tosh's and unrepeatable.

Stripped of the pretty-pretty, "gay-lasses-in-khaki" touch, war is a beastly, boring business. Pure, unadulterated hell, and yesterday was the worst dose of all.

The first convoy arrived in at 5.30 a.m. We had been in bed a little over an hour. Fortunately, we were fully dressed—we have not had our clothes off at all for twelve days. It was a sickening affair. Each convoy seemed worse than the last. We got back at 6.30. At 7.30 the whistle went for roll-call, which was interrupted by another convoy, from which we returned at 9 to find that the beast of a cook, knowing we were out on duty, had served breakfast punctually at eight and it was stone-cold. Half-dead, we fell into our beds breakfastless and slept like logs until ambulance-cleaning. Eleven o'clock brought another convoy. Arriving back, we cleaned ambulances again, had a quick inspection, resulting in six of us being given punishments for dirty engines. Dinner stank so badly it was almost impossible to stay in the mess-room. Etta Potato and I made the usual Bovril upstairs, while The Bug lay on the bed. We are not allowed to drive with lights at night now, because of the enemy planes, and that, added to lack of sleep, has made our eyes red and sore. We call ourselves " The Beauty Chorus." The inflammation resembles tropical sand-blight, and The Bug has it badly. Etta Potato forced some Bovril down her neck. She looked awful with her death-white face and red eyelids. Then the whistle went for another convoy and The Bug began to giggle. " Time to collect more men without faces. Hurry, we mustn't be late." She ran out, giggling in a cracked kind of voice. Etta Potato and I rinsed the Bovril cups without a word.

My ambulance was next in line to The Bug's. All the time we were getting away she giggled and talked to herself, but she was quite normal on our return. There was another convoy from 8 till half-past nine, and we had just fallen on our beds utterly exhausted when the whistle blew. Lights out. An air raid. With the first bomb The Bug started to scream. The raiders were not beaten off for an hour, and all the time the bombs were dropping The Bug screamed. We have no shelters built yet, so we stay where we are, but since the raids there has been brown paper nailed over the windows,

137

and there we lay in the darkness listening to The Bug, Tosh holding her down in case she ran outside and was hit. It seemed years before the " All Clear." Then Commandant swooped down on The Bug. Never had she witnessed such a disgraceful exhibition of cowardice on the part of an Englishwoman. The Bug stared at her, dazed, then quietly fainted dead away. I have never seen Tosh so angry. " Get out," she said, and Commandant got out. But it was half an hour before The Bug came round—in time for the signal for the midnight convoy. Tosh ordered The Bug to stay in bed, but Commandant came back and ordered her on duty. We got back and The Bug raved and screamed all night. None of us closed our eyes. She fell asleep just before roll-call and awakened with the whistle, quite normal, not remembering the air-raid or the last convoy. Tosh spoke to Commandant, but she will not believe The Bug is ill ; she says it is a clear case of swinging the lead. The drivers in the adjoining cubicles are going to sign a " Round Robin " insisting on so many hours of sleep, or they will return home in a body.

.   .   .   .   .

Tosh and I have had an adventure. At midday dinner, Commandant, a little subdued by the " Round Robin," announced that as there were no convoys till the evening, those drivers who wished could have the afternoon off for sleep in view of the revolting disturbance of the previous evening— meaning The Bug. Except for emergency duty, she added. The threat of emergency duty settled Tosh and me. We knew who the first victims would be. So we decided to clear out and find a spot in the open air out of earshot of the infernal whistle. Although bitingly cold, the sun was shining, and if we took an extra coat we could sit down. The intrigue was conducted in whispers aside, in case the idea became too popular. The Bug was already in a dead slumber when at half-past one we set forth, ankle deep in mud, but feeling gloriously free. It took us a good half-hour to discover that there was nowhere to sit, unless we wanted a mud bath, so on and on we wandered, talking of this, that and the other, inevitably returning to the War.

We know surprisingly little about the War here, only what we gather from odd out-of-date scraps in the papers, and things the sitters tell. If the sitters have advanced on their small frontage we are winning and there will soon be peace ; if they have retreated we are losing and God knows when it will end. When the great peace comes Tosh is going to retire to bed for a month, but I am hoping Aunt Helen will die and leave me her money, in which case I will take a trip round the world. I was telling Tosh this when we barged clean into two officers round a blind bend.

" Well, I'm blowed ! " exclaimed one of them. " Old Tosh ! "

" Chump ! " Tosh delightedly seized the speaker by the hand and pumped energetically. " What the hell are you doing in this home from home ? "

" I've been here eight weeks."

" I can beat that—I've had eight months."

Tosh then introduced me, and he introduced the other man, a Captain Baynton, who asked where we were going. Tosh airily informed him that we were absent without leave and had no plans. Then, suggested Captain Baynton, why not come with them ; they were bound for a concert in the German Prisoners' Compound. Tosh's friend thought this a tophole brainwave, and Tosh said she was game if I was, though we'd probably be set to rebuild the convoy as punishment if Commandant found out.

" She's pretty bloody, isn't she ? " asked Chump, and Tosh replied that if she said what she thought of Commandant in public she'd be put in clink for a year. So off we ploughed through the mud, laughing.

It was good to laugh again. By the time we reached the Prisoners' Compound I felt quite young. It was quite an imposing affair. The prisoners had built it entirely. There were corrugated tin huts and a big recreation-room—islands in a sea of mud. The outside barricade was quite unnecessary. Any unfortunate prisoner who tried to escape would be wallowing up to the neck in thick greasy mud before he had gone a yard. The planks laid down for us to walk on had sunk a foot deep. One false step and overboard we would have gone. Chump thanked God he was not tight as usual, and proved his assertion by walking the chalk-line for us, holding up the hem of his British warm coyly like a woman with a train and swaying over the mud at a perilous angle. Tosh laughed so much at his antics that she nearly fell in herself.

The officer-in-charge met us at the entrance to the recreation-room. He was a pal of Chump's, so we had no difficulty in being admitted. The concert would begin in five minutes. We were the only visitors ; in fact, Tosh and I were the first women to visit the Compound. Had he had any idea of the honour he would have had some special programmes done ; as it was, he only had these poor things—meant for Chump and Baynton, handing us two postcards most exquisitely inscribed in red and black scroll work, the edges with a fine circle design and at the top a winged head, rather reminiscent of the R.F.C. badge. He was privately very bucked, we could tell, by our admiration, and told us the man responsible was a famous German black-and-white artist.

While they talked on one side, Tosh translated the programme for me. There were German ballads on the piano, a wedding song and a humorous recitation entitled *Heinrich Fliegenbutton*, but mostly the items were choral selections—*Verlassen*, *Verlassen*, and similar things. We then went inside, where I had the shock of my young life. We were seated in a big cage with bars—iron bars—exactly like a cage at the Zoo.

I shall never stare at an animal in a cage again ; I shall feel too sorry for it. If it experiences half the embarrassing sensations I experienced, its life must be one long torture. Five minutes passed before I dared glance up from my programme, to meet hundreds of staring eyes. Brown eyes, blue eyes, small eyes, large eyes—curious eyes all of them, and all hungry and unspeakably filled with longing. I went scarlet. Once I dreamed I was travelling in an Underground carriage minus a stitch of clothing ; I felt exactly now as I did then. Naked and exceedingly ashamed. The prisoners circled round and round the cage whispering and pushing the front ones away when they had stared long enough. It was the first time most of them had ever seen an Englishwoman, and Tosh whispered that their remarks were distinctly uncomplimentary.

She made me see the funny side of it. While they admired my red cheeks, my bust was too small and my legs inches too thin ; and while Tosh's bust and calf measurements met with universal approbation, they did not like her wind-tanned face. Unanimously they decided that Englishwomen were not physically attractive. They were very nice about it, Tosh translated ; the remarks were more in sorrow than in anger, all without a smile and quite impersonal, with none of the cheeky, witty, Cockney atmosphere our own Tommies would have managed to infuse into a similar situation. Most of them would have condescended to sleep with us, however, in lieu of anything more exciting, Tosh translated.

Fortunately neither Chump nor Baynton spoke German, and the officer in charge had no idea Tosh was a fluent conversationalist in that language. As it was, he kept shooting agonized glances in our direction when the whispers became too penetrating. Tosh and I were almost in hysterics with suppressed laughter at his facial expressions. " What's that they are saying ? " Chump kept asking, and he would say : " Oh, they are wondering what kind of uniform the ladies are wearing," or " They are admiring the big fur gloves Miss Smith has and saying how warm they must be in this weather." It was killing, in view of the actual remarks. Finally, just as a young man had glued himself to the cage near Tosh and was treating her to the most passionate glances—a prisoner called Von Someone opened the piano, an order was ripped out, the men took their seats on the benches and the concert started, to my relief. It is something of an ordeal to sit in a cage and be stared at by hundreds of men who haven't seen a woman for months. The iron bars seem less iron-like as the seconds pass. It is not the safest feeling in the world.

The concert was excellent—or we were ready to be amused by anything. The pianist in particular was good, although Chump called the officer-in-charge a liar when he said he was the Paderewski of Germany. In a minute, Chump said, he'd have the Kaiser on the platform doing a song and dance. The officer was furious ; he was very proud of the talents of his prisoners. I wish I could have understood the comic recitation, *Heinrich Fliegenbutton*, which amused Tosh more than the prisoners, who received it much in the resigned manner that Mother adopts when Father tells his pet stories at dinner-parties—whereby I gathered they had heard it on many weary occasions. The elocutionist, said the officer-in-charge, was a former head waiter at the Savoy. " Oh, make him Von Hindenburg," pleaded Chump, but the officer-in-charge ignored him. Queer, one never speculates on a waiter being an enthusiastic amateur reciter off-stage, so to speak, particularly a dignified head waiter in a first-class hotel, but I suppose we all have our little weaknesses.

Baynton kissed me on the way back. It was not a Platonic kiss, either. When I ticked him off he said : " Have a heart, old dear, I'm going up the line to-morrow. I'll probably be dead mutton before I get a chance to kiss another girl."

So I let him kiss me again. I have never looked at it in that light before. " I wish we could spend the night together," he whispered just before we parted. I was just about to ask if he thought the remark worthy of a gentleman when it struck me as being silly. Silly to accuse a man of being ungentlemanly when he is practically sentenced to death. Instead I kissed him of my own free will and wished him a speedy " Blighty." To my astonishment I wasn't in the least shocked by his proposal. How one's outlook changes !

.   .   .   .   .

We arrive back to find tea in full swing. Commandant has not discovered our absence, either. Cheers. Everyone is feeling better after the rest. Tosh and I tell the adventure to our gang in whispers.

" Mentally undressing us," chuckles Tosh. " Poor old Smithy's face—if you'd seen it. Beetroot."

"Poor wretches," sympathizes Chutney; "and I'd like to let Mrs. Bitch loose among them."

We shout with laughter at the idea.

"Tantalise them with your buxom charms, Tosh, if you must, but don't torture them by giving them Commandant. Talk about punishment duty!"

We shout with laughter.

"How disgusting you all are!" says Etta Potato. "I'm sure the prisoners weren't thinking horrid things, Tosh. They've all got sisters of their own."

"I hope they don't look at them in the same way, then. Isn't Etta Potato sweet, girls? The one and only *virgo intacta* in the convoy."

There is a yell of indignation. "Here, what about me?" "And me?" "And me?"

"Children," says Tosh, "you may be *virgo*, but I'm blowed if you're *intacta*."

"Nothing will convince me that all men are so— so animalish," insists Etta Potato.

I think of Baynton. Rather like Roy Evans-Mawnington—the clean English boy type; . . . to look at Baynton you'd never think . . . "I wish we could spend the night together." . . . Oh, damn, why not? Why not? Why not get something out of life before . . . you, Nellie Smith, a virgin, thinking these things, after the sheltered way you've been brought up, after . . . if there had been a chance, would you? . . . I don't know, I don't know—I might be dead and buried to-morrow, killed in an air-raid, smashed up in an ambulance, anything. . . . " I wish we could spend the night together." . . . Oh, damn, what does virtue matter—a little thing like chastity? . . .

" Where are you going, Smithy? " asks Tosh.

" Must see how The Bug is," I tell her.

.   .   .   .   .

The Bug is not in our room. Out on emergency duty, then? I rush back to the board. Her name is on the top of the list, crossed out. My relief is painful. What an idiot I am! I return slowly to the bedroom to carry out the decision it has taken me weeks to make—cut my hair off. I cannot bear the filth and worry any longer. What Mother will say I do not dare contemplate, but as I will probably never get leave it seems futile to worry. I get The Bug's scissors and begin to snip. As I snip I think of Baynton. I feel sorry we are unlikely to meet again. Into the newspaper goes my hair. Would Baynton like me with short hair? What a fool I am! What will happen to Mother's story of me and Trix now?

The deed is done. I burn my hair in the chamber and examine myself in the mirror. Not bad. Makes me look about sixteen. Something quite pleasant about the feel of short hair. Boyish.

Tosh thinks it will become quite a universal fashion, but I don't agree. It isn't feminine enough. Women will never adopt a mode that isn't essentially feminine. I suddenly see three letters on the bed—Mother, Roy, and Trix.

I honestly believe Mother writes one letter, makes several copies and inserts the date when each Tuesday comes round. Every letter is an exact replica of the last. She always has a cold and is always " carrying on," and she is always being appointed to a new committee, and she must always close because she is going to a most important recruiting meeting. Oh, here is something fresh. The new maid Jessie has just gone to a home to have a " war baby " at the expense of the War Baby League. One must help the war babies, mustn't one? I think of poor little Tanny, who was turned out to fend for herself three years ago in a similar situation. There wasn't a war on then. Well, out of evil cometh good, if only temporary good.

Roy—going up the line to-night—no date—why don't people date their letters?—he will write again soon—if anything happens to him good-bye and thanks for the photograph in uniform. . . .

Written at least a week ago. I open Trix's letter slowly.

Not well at all—general depression—trying to get leave—Jerry gone to the trenches again—fed up, every time you get to like anyone off they go to the trenches—trying to get leave. . . .

Trix depressed. Who is Jerry?

The exhilaration caused by the concert and Baynton goes, leaving me empty and with a ghastly feeling of impending beastliness. Something is going to happen. I know it. Where is The Bug? Back in the canteen yet?

The Bug? The drivers stare at one another. Isn't she in? Isn't her ambulance in? Someone rushes out into the yard. The Bug went out at two—the first emergency duty—to Number Three with a parcel. Tosh swears loud and long. Do they mean to say Commandant sent that sick child out, woke her up to take a parcel. . . .

The Bug's ambulance is not in the line.

" Coming, Smithy? I'm going out hunting."

As we circle the convoy on Tosh's ambulance Commandant comes out. " What does this mean, Toshington? "

" Go to hell," says Tosh.

. . . . .

It is an hour before we find The Bug's ambulance on the hill leading to Number Thirteen. The Bug is nowhere to be seen. We search the hill on foot without result. Better get back and report, organize a search party, says Tosh. I drive The Bug's bus back.

Rubbish, insists Commandant, the girl is not lost—somewhere without permission. All the same, I can see she is getting the wind up. Any driver who wishes can search ; mind, Commandant is not ordering anyone—purely a case of volunteers. The whole convoy immediately volunteers for the search-party duty. Very well, says Commandant, everyone report once an hour at the station in case of a convoy.

We report once an hour.

Seven o'clock—nothing.

Eight o'clock.

Nine o'clock.

Ten o'clock.

The search party has grown. Officers and orderlies from the camps have joined in. The district has been scoured thoroughly. There is no sign of The Bug. It is a clear moonlight night with a full moon, and searching is comparatively easy. Sick at heart, not daring to voice our feelings, we start off once more.

Eleven o'clock—nothing. We turn in at the station yard for the fifth time.

And on the stroke of eleven a convoy and an air-raid are signalled simultaneously.

CHAPTER VII

" AMBULANCES ! "

Commandant's whistle blows.

The station rocks about me, up and down, up and down, like a ship coming up on the crest of a wave and sinking again into the hollows. I am sick with cold fright.

" Lights out ! "

Mechanically I sit up straight behind my steering wheel. Mechanically I switch off the lights that I have been using against orders in my efforts to find The Bug. The ambulance rocks up and down. I am watching myself from a distance, suspended in mid-air over the radiator front. Look, that's Nellie Smith sitting there—that white blob of a face with terrified eyes, that's Nellie Smith. Some-one's put her in charge of an ambulance. That white-faced blob is going to drive an ambulance of helpless men through a rain of dropping bombs. . . .

Ploo-oop ? Crash.

The first bomb. A long way off. The convoy rounds the curve. Won't be here for ten minutes, says a voice, a wavy up-and-down voice. It is talking of the aeroplanes, not the convoy, because the convoy is coming in the station now. I watch the white blob called Nellie Smith from the radiator. Quite calm. You wouldn't think she was dying of fear—wondering how long one can live when one's heart has ceased to beat at the thought of having to drive an ambulance of wounded through a rain of dropping bombs.

" I say, what a rag ! "

The girl in the next ambulance said that. She is one of the heroines the papers write about—smoking a cigarette in the face of danger. Talking to Nellie Smith. Nellie Smith begins to laugh hysterically— giggling and laughing hysterically to hide that she is dying of cold fear from the heroine with the cigarette.

Ploo-oop ! Crash !

" It's this sod of a moon," says a stretcher-bearer resentfully.

A round reddish moon, hanging low in the sky. Somewhere where there isn't war lovers are walking beneath it, softly beautified by its rays. A lover's moon, not a moon to enable men in aeroplanes to drop bombs straight and sure. There must be some mistake. That's why Nellie Smith is laughing.

" Here, take a pull at this."

A stretcher-bearer hands Nellie Smith a flask.

Ploo-oop. Bang !

The convoy pulls in, lights out, a dark, creeping, stealthy thing, quietly, as though afraid the enemy will hear the chug-a-chug of the engine.

Ploo-oop. Bang !

Nearer that time. Every time nearer. Why did I drink that brandy ? It was easier when I could watch myself. My lips are dry. I am panting for breath. I can hear myself breathing in loud uneven spasms.

Ploo-oop. Bang !

A shell-shocked man begins to run senselessly up the platform, shouting madly. Three orderlies run after him, overpower him, push him none too gently into the nearest ambulance and lock the doors on him.

Ploo-oop. Bang !

The heroine next door laughs. A pretty tinkling laugh. A lovely flash, wasn't it ? Quite near, too. She is loaded. Still laughing, she drives off. In the moonlight her teeth gleam. The laughing heroine the papers idolise.

The bombs are dropping faster now. Every one a little nearer. Soon they will be over the Hill of the Witch's Hand, then the cemetery, then Number Thirteen. . . .

Up and down, up and down, why are the stretcher bearers waving the wounded up and down ?

It will be my turn to go in a minute. A sitter is being hoisted next to me—not very bad, only a broken arm—jolly, laughing, like the girl who was smoking a cigarette. . . . " They follow me about, mate," the sitter is saying ; " fair love me, do them there bombs, can't leave me in peace. . . ." Up and down, up and down, he is waving up and down. . . .

" Loaded. Six stretchers and four sitters."

Brake off. Clutch out. Gear. Gas. I am not doing it—it's doing itself somehow . . . crawling to the station gate. . . .

Ploo-oop. Crash !

" Gordamighty "—the sergeant is talking—" that was just beyond the Witch's 'And—what load ? "

I cannot answer him—my lips are dry—they are sticking together—I cannot go out of the gate—I cannot go out of the gate towards the dropping bombs——

" Six stretchers and four sitters."

Who said that ? It wasn't my voice, that queer cracked whisper.

" Number Four," says the sergeant.

Number Four. Number Four. Number Four. That is where I have to go with my load of wounded men. Five miles along the open road. First to the right, on past Number One, turn left then, left again and then straight on.   Number Four.

Ploo-oop.   Crash !

" I can see them distinct.   Look."

The sitter can 'see them distinct,' he says.   I cannot look.   Number Four.   Five miles along the open road.   First to the left.   The sitter is counting the enemy planes.   I can hear them now, the whirr of the engines.   The sitter thinks they will discharge their cargo before they get into the camp.   Flash. I saw that one myself; it hit the hillside.   The sitter has never seen the bombs so thick.   Like rain.   Ah, our planes are up now.   No need to get the wind up.   Far safer here than in a trench. If they hit an ambulance it will be a ruddy miracle. He apologises for the adjective.   Once they drop one bomb and miss you, the next will clean pass over, ten to one ; it depends on the speed they're travelling. . . .

The bombs are getting nearer.

A picnic after the trenches . . . the night he was hit . . . he goes into a long description of the bombardment that ended in his broken arm.   Survived an eighteen-hour bombardment to trip over someone's boots head-first into a trench and break his bleedin' arm.   Funny that.   His pal Arthur would have enjoyed the joke if he'd been alive.   But he wasn't.   It was old Arthur's boots he'd tripped over.

155

Not meant to stop one, and that's a dead cert. . . .

The bombs are getting nearer.

What is it I fear? Not death. No, I only wish with all my heart I were dead and safely out of this hell. No, I do not fear death. Then what? I do not know. The dying, perhaps. I have seen men die so dreadfully. Oh, God, if there is a God, let me die swiftly and mercifully. Let me be here one second not thinking of dying, and the next. . . .

Ploo-oop. Crash!

Surely there is no sound anywhere as sickening as the sound of a bomb dropped from the air. A flattening sound, as though the sky were jealous of the earth and was determined to wipe it out of existence. Each time a bomb drops I see myself under it, flat, like the skin of a dead tiger that has been made into a rug with a little nicked half-inch of cloth all round the edges . . . flat, all the flesh and blood and bones knocked flat . . . useless to tell me I would be wiped clean out of existence as though I had never been . . . I still see myself like the skin of a dead tiger that has been made into a rug with a little nicked half-inch of cloth round the edges. . . .

Ploo-oop. Crash!

I laugh. The sitter tells me I have pluck,

laughing like that. He's got four girls himself, the youngest four, the eldest twelve. He would rather have daughters than sons. Fine girls every one of them. His missus makes every stitch they wear; oh, a good woman and a better wife, his missus. . . .

Number Four, Number Four, NUMBER FOUR.

All the time they unload me the bombs are getting nearer. Silence except for the bombs. Nearer every time. Not so many now. All beaten back but one machine, a nurse says. I look up. One solitary plane. Sisters and stretcher-bearers whispering, hastily removing the wounded inside to that thin inadequate shelter of canvas, none of them afraid like me, coward, coward, coward, waiting to be flattened into the skin of a dead tiger that has been made into a rug with a little nicked edging of cloth. . . .

" Right."

Off again.

The bomber is nearly overhead. I can see the bomb leave the carrier. What an age it is dropping ! I am out on the road. Half a mile ahead is another ambulance travelling at top speed towards the station. From Number One. Who is it ? Commandant, of course. She always takes Number One. Yes, it is sure to be Commandant. All this I think while the bomb is dropping.

Ploo-oop.   Crash !

That was near.   Behind me, a few fields away.
The next one will get me . . . the sitter said it would
be a miracle if a bomb hit a moving ambulance . . .
but the next one will get me . . . it cannot help it . . .
they are dropped at regular intervals according to
the speed the aviator is travelling . . . he is right
over my head—his engine is drowning the sound of
mine . . . he'll get me, he'll get me, he doesn't
know me, he doesn't know me . . . he has no personal
grudge against me . . . it doesn't seem fair for him
to flatten me into a tiger skin with a little neat
half-inch of nicked cloth round the edges. . . .

I tear along . . . I must get away, I must get away
before he drops the next bomb on me. . . . Commandant is ahead . . . I am gaining on her. . . . If
he must flatten out someone, let it be Commandant.
. . . Oh, God, if there is a God, let the next bomb
drop in the ambulance ahead . . . let it be Commandant . . . don't let it be me . . . don't let it
be me. . . .

Ploo-oop.   Crash !

A flash of flame.   My ears are deafened, but he
has missed me—he has missed me. . . .

Oh, God, something has happened to the dark
blob that was Commandant's ambulance . . . it
is in the ditch . . . it has swerved into the ditch . . .
the bomber has gone on . . . the next bomb has

158

fallen . . . making for the station—they say the enemy want to wipe the station out . . . but Commandant's ambulance is lying on its side in the ditch. . . .

Where is the driver? Where is Commandant? I cannot find the driver. Someone is groaning . . . Commandant is groaning . . . the ambulance is lying on its side, it is quite intact, the bomb has not caught it . . . she is groaning from somewhere, horrible groans, dying groans, where is she? Where is she?

Another groan. A dark figure thrown a few yards away . . . lying on her face . . . Commandant, blood . . . my hands covered with Commandant's blood as I turn her over. . . .

Tosh!

Tosh, not Commandant.

Tosh lying there covered in blood. Her head is bleeding . . . Tosh.

" Splinter . . . got me . . ." she chokes. I can hardly hear her. " Bomb in field, Smithy. . . ."

Tosh bleeding. Tosh lying there helpless, big brave Tosh with her head hanging childishly on one side . . . Tosh hit by a splinter of bomb dropped by a man who didn't know her, who had no grudge. . . .

" Oh, Christ ! " mutters Tosh, and dies.

Dead. One second lying there trying to laugh

and the next her throat rattling and her head lolling back. Dead. Tosh dead.

" God, if there is a God, let the next bomb drop on the ambulance in front—on Commandant's ambulance. . . ."

Not Tosh.

Commandant. Not Tosh. Not Tosh.

The bombs are raining on the station. Dropping like rain. Ploo-oop. Crash !

" God, if there is a God, let the next bomb. . . ."

Tosh lies in my arms dead, soaking my overcoat with blood. Dead.

Yesterday she compiled a war alphabet : B for Bastard—obsolete term meaning war-baby. . . . I for Illegitimate—(see B). . . . V for Virgin—a term of reproach (ask any second loot). . . .

I should have fainted at hearing that once ; yesterday I laughed till the tears rolled down my cheeks, I was so amused.

They are rolling down my cheeks now . . . I am laughing, laughing, laughing, laughing . . . but I am not amused. It is funnier than Tosh's war alphabet—but I am not amused.

Tosh lies in my arms dead, killed by a splinter of bomb. Tosh the brave, the splendid, the great-hearted. Tosh is dead.

And I, the coward, the funk, the white-livered . . . I am alive.

160

It is funny. It is the funniest joke I have ever heard. Far, far funnier than Tosh's war alphabet.

That is why I am laughing.

I am still laughing when, after roll-call, they come in search of the missing ambulances.

CHAPTER VIII

I AM afraid of going mad . . . of being discovered one morning among the boulders at the foot of a rocky hillside as was The Bug the day following on the air-raid that smashed the station and the convoy train to matchwood . . . a night of smashings, though none so cruelly smashed as The Bug. She had lost her way and missed her footing in the darkness, said the powers-that-be. This on the brightest night in a season of moonlit nights.

An accident. . . . So The Bug rests alongside Tosh in the bleak cemetery in the shadow of the Witch's Hand.

An accident . . . drivers walking about with sullen eyes, and whisperings that are not pleasant listening . . . and I, in the hours after the midnight convoy, sitting thinking things that are best not thought . . . my fingers tight against Commandant's thick, red throat, gloating in the ebbing strength of that squat, healthy body until I am sick and faint with murderous longing.

The impulse has gone . . . but in its place has come something worse. I am haunted now as The Bug was haunted. Whenever I close my aching

red eyes a procession of men passes before me :
maimed men ; men with neither arms nor legs ;
gassed men, coughing, coughing, coughing ; men
with dreadful burning eyes ; men with heads and
faces half shot away ; raw, bleeding men with the
skin burned from their upturned faces ; tortured,
all watching me as I lie in my flea-bag trying to
sleep . . . an endless procession of horror that will
not let me rest. I am afraid. I am afraid of
madness. Are there others in this convoy fear-
obsessed as I am, as The Bug was . . . others who
will not admit it, as I will not, as The Bug did not
. . . others who exist in a daily hell of fear ? For
I fear these maimed men of my imaginings as
I never fear the maimed men I drive from the
hospital trains to the camps. The men in the ambulances scream, but this ghostly procession is ghostly
quiet. I fear them, these silent men, for I am afraid
they will stay with me all my life, shutting out beauty
till the day I die. And not only do I fear them, I
hate them. I hate these maimed men who will not
let me sleep.

Oh, the beauty of men who are whole, who have
straight arms and legs, whose bodies are not cruelly
gashed and torn by shrapnel, whose eyes are not
horror-filled, whose faces are smooth and shapely,
whose mouths smile instead of grinning painfully
. . . oh, the beauty and wonder of men who are

whole. Baynton, young and strong and clean-limbed, are his eyes serene and happy now as they were the afternoon of the concert in the prisoners' compound . . . or are they staring up unseeingly somewhere in No Man's Land, with that fair skin of his dyed an obscene blue by poison gas, his young body shattered and scattered and bleeding ? Roy Evans-Mawnington . . . is he still smiling and eager-faced as on the day he was photographed in his second-lieutenant's uniform . . . or has the smile frozen on his incredulous lips ?

Oh, the beauty of men who are whole and sane. Shall I ever know a lover who is young and strong and untouched by war, who has not gazed on what I have gazed upon ? Shall I ever know a lover whose eyes reflect my image without the shadow of war rising between us ? A lover in whose arms I shall forget the maimed men who pass before me in endless parade in the darkness before the dawn when I think and think and think because the procession will not let me sleep ?

What is to happen to women like me when this war ends . . . if ever it ends. I am twenty-one years of age, yet I know nothing of life but death, fear, blood, and the sentimentality that glorifies these things in the name of patriotism. I watch my own mother stupidly, deliberately, though unthinkingly —for she is a kind woman—encourage the sons of other women to kill their brothers ; I see my own father—a gentle creature who would not willingly harm a fly—applaud the latest scientist to invent a mechanical device guaranteed to crush his fellow-beings to pulp in their thousands. And my generation watches these things and marvels at the blind foolishness of it . . . helpless to make its immature voice heard above the insensate clamour of the old ones who cry : " Kill, Kill, Kill ! " unceasingly.

What is to happen to women like me when the killing is done and peace comes . . . if ever it comes ? What will they expect of us, these elders who have sent us out to fight ? We sheltered young women who smilingly stumbled from the chintz-covered drawing-rooms of the suburbs straight into hell ?

What will they expect of us ?

We, who once blushed at the public mention of childbirth, now discuss such things as casually as once we discussed the latest play ; whispered stories of immorality are of far less importance than a fresh cheese in the canteen ; chastity seems a mere waste of time in an area where youth is blotted out so quickly. What will they expect of us, these elders of ours, when the killing is over and we return ?

Once we were not allowed out after nightfall unchaperoned ; now we can drive the whole night

165

through a deserted countryside with a man—provided he is in khaki and our orders are to drive him. Will these elders try to return us to our conventional pre-war habits? What will they say if we laugh at them, as we are bound?

I see in the years to come old men in their easy chairs fiercely reviling us for lacking the sweetness and softness of our mothers and their mothers before them; chiding us for language that is not the language of gentlewomen; accusing us of barnyard morals when we use love as a drug for forgetfulness because we have acquired the habit of taking what we can from life while we are alive to take . . . clearly do I see all these things. But what I do not see is pity or understanding for the war-shocked woman who sacrificed her youth on the altar of the war that was not of her making, the war made by age and fought by youth while age looked on and applauded and encored. Will they show us mercy, these arm-chair critics, once our uniforms are frayed and the romance of the war woman is no longer a romance? I see much, but this I do not see.

And the next generation . . . our younger brothers and sisters . . . young things raised in a blood-and-hate atmosphere—I see them hard and callous and cold . . . emotionless, unfriendly, cruelly analytical, predatory, resentful of us for stealing the limelight from their childhood, bored by the war and the men and women who fought the war, thanklessly grabbing the freedom for which we paid so dearly . . . all this I see as my procession of torn, dreadful-eyed men passes in the cold dark hours preceding the dawn.

And I see us a race apart, we war products . . . feared by the old ones and resented by the young ones . . . a race of men bodily maimed and of women mentally maimed.

What is to become of us when the killing is over ?

.   .   .   .   .

Commandant is willing that I should go.

A rest—sick leave she calls it—but she avoids my cold glance carefully when speaking the words. She understands. I have finished with the war for good. I will take no more part in it. Why should I, who hate and fear war with all my heart, and would gladly die to end it if that were possible, work to keep it going ? Etta Potato says my logic is unsound, but I am too weary to argue, too eager to be gone from the little communal bedroom where nightly marches my procession of maimed men.

I divide my kit between Etta Potato and Chutney, leaving only my uniform to travel in. My overcoat is deeply stained where Tosh's head rested . . . but I must wear it, for I have no other clothes. There are a few farewells ; Etta Potato drives me to the station . . . I do not see Commandant . . . I am in the train at last . . . Etta Potato waving farewell from the platform. . . .

My war service is ended.

I am going home.

Darkened stations . . . endless cold waits . . . soldiers in khaki . . . wounded soldiers in blue . . . V.A.D.'s . . . nurses . . . grey, uninteresting landscapes . . . bare trees . . . camps, camps, camps . . . tin huts, wooden huts . . . marching troops . . . desolation . . . cemeteries of black crosses . . . hospitals . . . and everywhere mud, mud, mud.

I am going home.

The train stops, starts again, stops ; I change to another, on and on and on. . . .

I am going home.

Why am I so calm about it ?

Boulogne at last. Why do I not shout and laugh and dance ? How often have I pictured this Channel crossing, my wild exhilaration, arriving under the chalk cliffs of England, the white welcoming chalk cliffs of England.

The sweetness of England . . . England, where grass is green and primroses in early springtime patch the earth a timid yellow . . . where trees in bud are ready to leaf on the first day of pale sunshine. . . . England, England, how often have I promised to throw myself flat upon your bosom and kiss the first green blade of grass I saw because it was English grass and I had come home?

But now I am coming home . . . and I do not care.

I have pictured arriving at Charing Cross. Perhaps it would be raining, but it would be English rain and I would hold my face up to its drops. Father and Mother would meet me . . . drive me through familiar places—Piccadilly, Regent Street . . . as it grew dusk lights would reflect warmly on the wet, shiny pavements . . . London and then out through innumerable streets of toy villas towards home. . . .

Home, home . . . and I do not care.

I do not care. I am flat. Old. I am twenty-one and as old as the hills. Emotion-dry. The war has drained me dry of feeling. Something has gone from me that will never return. I do not want to go home.

I am suddenly aware that I cannot bear Mother's prattle-prattle of committees and recruiting-meetings and the war-baby of Jessie, the new maid ; nor can I watch my gentle father gloating over the horrors I have seen, pumping me for good stories to retail at his club to-morrow. I cannot go home to watch a procession of maimed men in my dainty, rose-walled bedroom. It is no place for a company of broken men on parade. . . .

169

I cannot go home. In the morning, perhaps, but not to-night.

What has happened to me?

I am in England and I do not care.

.   .   .   .   .

" You've just come from France, haven't you ? "

I look up from the coffee I am drinking in the hotel lounge. He is a second-lieutenant, very spick and span in his new Sam Browne and well-cut uniform—" Rather a nut," The B.F. would label him. He is so immaculate I feel dirty immediately, despite my pre-dinner hot bath, my shampoo and hair-cut, my manicure and my newly-acquired powder-puff.

He smiles disarmingly. " Awful cheek my coming over, but I embark to-morrow. First time out. Frightful novice."

First time out. I avoid his laughing blue eyes. He is indeed a frightful novice . . . that is why his eyes are still laughing.

" Do let me talk to you," he begs. " I'm lonely and you seem lonely, too. I've been watching you all through dinner, wondering why you stayed in Folkestone instead of going straight through. Do talk to me. I'd love some tips first-hand from some-one who's been out there. . . ."

I agree to talk to him . . . but not of the war.

Anything but the war. My voice hardens. He notices it and his eyes are suddenly grave . . . but I do not want them to be grave. Let them smile while they can still smile, they will be grave soon enough. I make a stupid joke . . . the blue eyes dance again. Blue eyes, dancing like the sea on a breezy summer's day. There is a hop going in the ballroom . . . I hesitate, my uniform is almost in rags . . . he tells me it may be, but I look tophole, and my short hair is the sort of hair a fellow would like to rumple his fingers through if he dared . . . he clasps his hands together in mock penitence. . . .

He is so gay, so audacious, this boy of my own age who is so young and brimming over with life. He invents a wild fandango, and shouts with laughter at an old lady in the corner who stares disapprovingly through lorgnettes. He is clean and young and straight and far removed from the shadow procession I watch night after night, the procession that came to me early this morning and wakened me shrieking in the presence of a compartmentful of shocked strangers. He is so gay, so full of life, this boy who is holding me closely in his arms . . . he could never join that ghostly parade. . . .

Dance, dance, dance, go on dancing . . . press me against your breast . . . talk, talk, talk, go on talking . . . yes, daringly drop a kiss on top of my cropped head in full view of the shocked old lady with the lorgnettes . . . laugh, laugh, laugh, go on laughing . . . yes, I will drink more champagne with you, I will smile when you smile . . . I will press your hand when you press mine under the table . . . yes, I will dance with you again till I forget I have seen you at the end of the ghostly procession that has crossed the Channel with me.

He asks me to call him Robin. I tell him my name is Nell. I wish it were something more charming.

But it is charming, as charming as its owner. Oh, yes, yes, *yes* . . . if I shake my head again he'll kiss me in the middle of the ballroom, and the disapproving old girl with the lorgnettes will pass out completely . . . he loves to see me smile. . . . Not unhappy as I was at dinner now, am I ?

The last dance comes. The last chord crashes. He pulls me to him so roughly that I am left breathless for a second. " The King " is played. He stands rigidly to attention, his eyes clouded for a moment. " The King " finishes. I make a quick joke about Paris leave ; he throws his head back and laughs. Easily and swiftly he laughs, this Robin who is straight and clean and whole.

We walk into the lounge slowly . . . bed now, he supposes, with a side-glance at me . . . hardly worth while undressing, embarking at five . . . filthy, unearthly hour to get a fellow out of bed. . . .

We get into the lift without speaking . . . **our** rooms are on the same floor. . . .

At my door he kisses me, at first gently . . . "**a** good-night kiss " . . . then more ardently . . . how strong and beautiful he is, this Robin who has not been out to hell yet . . . *Dear Nell* . . . he kisses me again . . . *Dear Robin.* . . .

Must he say good-night ? . . . Can't he come in and talk to me after I am in bed ? . . . I don't think him an awful rotter for suggesting it, do I ? . . . How ingenuous he is, this Robin who kisses me so ardently, whose eyes are blue and sane. . . . He'll be good, honestly—well, just as good as I want him to be . . . he kisses me again . . . poor Robin, poor Robin. . . .

.   .   .   .   .

The luminous hands of my watch say four o'clock. It is pitch dark. I switch the bed-lamp on. He is deep in the abyss of sleep. . . . " Time to go, Robin."

He awakens smiling and flushed, like a child. " Nell. . . ."

Then, after a while, " You will write—promise ? " I promise.

" I feel a cad, an absolute . . ."

No, no, no.

" I'm your first lover, aren't I ? Why, Nell ? Were you a bit in love with me, too ? . . ."

I nod. A lie, but it will do. But it was not only

173

because he was whole and strong-limbed, not only because his body was young and beautiful, not only because his laughing blue eyes reflected my image without the shadow of war rising to blot me out . . . but because I saw him between me and the dance orchestra ending a shadow procession of cruelly-maimed men. . . .

Poor Robin, poor baby.

" I shall always treasure this, Nell ; . . . you're the first girl I've loved, decently ; . . . there have been others, but . . ." he stammers boyishly, embarrassed. . . . " When I come on leave we'll dance again, won't we ? . . . We'll have such fun, Nell. . . ."

I kiss him despairingly, the hot tears choking me. . . . We will not dance again, this Robin and I ; it is so pitiful ; he is twenty and I am twenty-one, but he is so young. . . .

Poor Robin, poor baby, poor baby.

He closes the bedroom door softly behind him.

CHAPTER IX

THE ghostly procession at last fades and I sleep, and as I sleep I dream sweetly. I am in my soft low bed at home with its rose satin eiderdown and its fragrant-scented sheets. My head rests on downy pillows. My nightgown is soft and silken.

I awaken gradually, gently. I half open my eyes and close them quickly again. Let the dream continue, the lovely, lovely dream. In a minute Commandant's whistle will blow, and I shall be transformed into Smith, ambulance driver.

Let the dream go on.

"A fine morning, Miss Nellie, a real touch of spring in the air."

That was Sarah. I watch her place the dainty breakfast tray on the little bed-table where I can reach it without effort. She draws the curtains aside, the spring sun floods the room, shining on a china bowl of early daffodils and jonquils. Oh, peaceful, peaceful dream! In a minute she will vanish—fat, comfortable Sarah in her old-fashioned black frock and plain, enveloping apron. None of your flibberty-gibbert modern maids about Sarah.

In a minute she will vanish as she has so often vanished.

The little enamelled clock strikes nine.

" Letters, Miss Nellie.   Wake up."

She thrusts some letters into my hand. The contact rouses me. I am awake. I am not dreaming. I am at home. I am not dreaming. I bury my face thankfully in the soft pillow so that Sarah may not see the tears in my eyes. . . .

It is three weeks since I came home, but every morning I imagine I am dreaming and weep when I am not.

" Now then, Miss Nellie, I boiled that new-laid egg myself ; eat it up like a good girl and get some flesh on your bones."

She goes out fussily, tactful Sarah, without noticing the tears.

Since ever we moved to Wimbledon Common this room has been mine, yet never till now have I loved it and revelled in its luxurious comfort. The ghostly procession still parades for me, yet nightly it is growing less vivid—soon it may fade altogether. Slowly I am becoming normal. France is far away, a foreign land separated by a tract of water wider than the Atlantic, and I am no longer Smith, ambulance driver, but Miss Smith, of Wimbledon Common, although mother is becoming restive about my prolonged sick leave. Wimbledon

NOT SO QUIET . . .

Common does not encourage idleness in war-time.

I open my first letter eagerly. It is from Trix, and Trix has not written since I have been home.

" Glad you've left that dog's hole of a convoy, Cis . . . too tired to write much of a letter . . . fed up, utterly . . . rotten time here . . . dirty dishes get you down after a while . . . wish I could get leave. . . . Is mother still flying the British flag from every pore ? . . . Rotten letter this. . . ."

What is wrong with Trix ? Once she was the brightest thing on earth, now behind the most comic incident in the hospital routine I see a dreadful tiredness.

" Sunny and I nipped into the town without leave with Pip and Squeak, two of the convalescents . . . we all got terribly blotto. Sunny was awfully funny, she's a tophole sort ; you'd like her awfully. . . ."

Not if she takes Trix and gets her blotto I won't.

" I wish the war was over, Cis, and you and I were living peacefully again. . . . Sunday mornings I always think of our long gossips on your bed. . . ."

The second letter, also marked *On Active Service*, from Etta Potato.

Commandant has been promoted, had I heard ? The new Commandant a bit of a madam, but sensible with it ; fixed hours for sleep and French

177

charwomen for the housework. . . . Why don't I have another shot at the convoy ? I'll have to get another war job if I don't go out to France—it's done, isn't it ? . . . Can't slack about when there's a war on, can one ? . . .

A large expensive envelope the third, written in a round affected backhand in green ink—green hand-torn paper with green initials on the flap—B.F.

" DEAREST DARLING SMITHY,

" Etta Potato told me you were home, and, as you gave your kit away, are not likely to go out again. My dear, how *appalling* about darling Tosh, but perhaps you have read the interview I gave the reporter who discovered I had been her *inseparable* friend in the dear old convoy ; so I gave him all the details of our life and how *brave* dear Tosh was, and he took a flashlight picture of me in my new uniform, breeches and leggings and a gorgeous khaki tunic with officers' pockets, terribly smart, dear, and underneath written, ' A Beautiful War Worker '—the dreadful flatterer, although everyone says you could have told it was me any-where. Tosh's uncle, the darling old Earl, came to see me and took me to lunch at the Savoy, and he was terribly cut up about Tosh, and, I must confess, wasn't frightfully patriotic about the war ; said the W.O. would be satisfied when it had killed off its young women as well as butchering its young men. 'Now,' I said to him, 'you know you'd go to-morrow if you were young enough,' and what do you think he said ? 'No, I'm damned if I would if I could get out of it decently '—so like dear blunt Tosh in his manner, but a sweet thing underneath, I feel sure.

" I've fallen into a perfectly adorable job, driving the dearest young Colonel about London, such a lamb of a man and unmarried too. Still doing my bit, as dear Tosh used to say. I'm a despatch rider, but although we work long hours I get dances and dinners innumerable, and I've thousands of adorable men friends. Perhaps I could work you in ; now you're back you'll want to carry on with the good work, won't you ? One must do one's bit ; it's done, isn't it ? Do let us meet and chat about the dear old convoy ; I'm just aching to know the details of poor, dear Tosh's sad death. It must have been too thrilling, though very, very tragic. How I love the memory of the convoy ; such a wonderful privilege to have had the experience. I told the reporter that, but perhaps you read it.

" With fondest love,

" BERTINA FARMER

(Or The B.F., as dear Tosh would call me).

" P.S.—Rather sad about The Bug, too."

" The B.F.'s of the world are to be envied."
. . . Who said that ? The Bug, of course, the night
of The B.F.'s farewell party. " I envy her youth,
beauty and money, but most of all I envy her
genuine love of life's little conventions. . . ."

Etta Potato and The B.F.—both genuine lovers
of life's little conventions, both devotees of the
" It's Done " cult. " Of course you'll go on doing
your bit—it's done, isn't it ? "

" May I come in, darling ? "

Mother bustles in, handsome with her white hair
and expensive morning dress. She is carrying a
sheaf of papers—committee papers, she explains ;
she is so rushed she won't have time for a morsel
of lunch—two committee meetings, a sewing circle,
then canteen work, and this afternoon a *monster*
recruiting meeting. She glances nervously at me
as she chatters. She has come to say something and
lacks the courage.

" A really *monster* meeting, darling," she repeats ;
" and Mother wants her girl to do something special
—Mother wants her girl to wear her uniform and
make a little speech at the recruiting meeting."

I sit up, hard-eyed, the blood draining from my
face.

" No ! "

Why not ? . . . It is three weeks since I came
home and surely I am not going to moon about any

longer . . . people are thinking it's funny . . .
perfectly absurd the way I refuse to go anywhere ;
it isn't as though I was a *wounded soldier*.   I was tired
possibly when I came back, but after *three weeks* . . .
surely a little speech at a recruiting meeting.
After all, when a girl's mother is working at top
pressure, the least her daughter can do is to encourage her and help . . . why, I won't even wear my
badge of honour—my *uniform*.

I laugh.

Why am I laughing ?   Other girls on leave go
out with their mothers in uniform and are proud
to see their mothers are proud of them. . . . I won't
allow my mother to be proud of me.   What's the
matter with me ?   Once I was a sweet girl, happy
and interested in local things, now I'm bitter and
snappy and sarcastic and with a tongue like an
adder, yes, and not above swearing, either, actually
swearing.   Goodness knows where I picked up such
language, certainly not at home. . . . When Roy
Evans-Mawnington came home with his fractured
arm he went everywhere with his mother in uniform
to please her. . . . Why *should* I object to saying
a few words at a recruiting meeting to show an
example to the male and female slackers who are
hanging back and refusing to obey the call of King
and country ?

" I won't do it, mother."

" Why not ? "

" Why should I encourage people to do what I have no intention of doing myself ? "

" You ? You're going back soon. . . ."

" No. I've burnt my uniform and given my kit away. I have finished with the war for good."

There, it is out at last.

Mother rises, the committee papers dropping on the floor, fluttering about her feet like large, dismayed butterflies.

" You have what ? " she gasps.

" I have left the convoy. I am not on leave."

She glares at me, resentful, unbelieving. It is a bitter blow to her pride. For a whole minute she glares, then gathers up her papers slowly.

" What will Mrs. Evans-Mawnington say ? " she bursts forth at last. " What will she say to my daughter taking a cushy job in England ? "

How well up in war-slang is mother !

I might as well get it over.

Not even a cushy job, I tell her, not even a cushy job in England. I have finished ; I am not having anything to do with the war in future. I hate war. I disapprove of the whole principle of licensed killing. I am about to tell her I am afraid, a rank coward, when she bursts into a torrent of words.

182

" Are you mad ? What will Aunt Helen say ? She has just made you her heiress. She is one of our most ardent recruiters. She will never forgive you, never. And your father, chosen to respond to ' Our War Girls ' at his club's annual dinner next week because of you and Trix—what will he say ? "

What will Mrs. Evans-Mawnington say ? What will Aunt Helen say ? What will Father say ? Not what do *I* say ? " Butchered to make a Wimbledon Common holiday." . . .

No, I will not be flippant. Neither will I argue. I have finished. There is no argument.

" I think it's the most disgraceful thing I've ever encountered," says Mother. " You, a young strong woman, determined to slack at home instead of doing your bit, shaming your mother before everybody, your own mother, who is working night and day until she is nearly dropping. Just think of how Mrs. Evans-Mawnington will crow over me now, and Roy with a wound-stripe. And any of these people at the recruiting meetings can stand up and say : ' And what about your own family ? ' That's going to be nice for me, isn't it ? Surely you can at least get a cushy job in England if you won't go back to France ? "

" Neither England nor France."

She tries a touch of pathos.

" We were so proud, Daddy and I, of our two war girls. Every night we used to put your photographs on the dining-table and tears would come to our eyes. . . ."

" Yes, while Trix and I were doing the dirty work you wept comfortably over your comfortable dinner-table." . . . No, I will not say it aloud.

" I don't believe in war. I think it's vile and wrong, mother. It's a chemists' war. There's nothing decent in it. Men are being killed by men, miles away, they've never seen. . . ."

" Wrong ? How can it be wrong ? The freedom of the world was threatened. . . ."

What's the use ? The clap-trap of the recruiting platform. . . .

" I am not arguing, mother. I just don't believe in war."

She gives a cry.

" Nellie, you're not a *pacifist* ! "

" I'm a pacifist if they're against war."

She sneers. " You'll be saying next you're a conscientious objector." (She could not be more contemptuous if she had suggested " streetwalker.")

" I am if they are against war."

She throws up her hands in horror. " To think that I, your mother, should have to stand here and

184

listen to such dreadful things—almost blasphemous things in the face of the splendid deeds our soldiers are doing in France. A pacifist indeed—an excuse for cowardice."

" I am a coward, mother." I lean forward and catch her hand to try to make her understand. " Mother, you don't know what it's like out there driving those ambulances full of torn men—torn to bits with shrapnel—sometimes they die on the way. . . ."

She pulls herself away. " At least they have died doing their duty," she says.

She goes out weeping.

.   .   .   .   .

Aunt Helen is the first to attack me. She refuses to credit anything so utterly absurd as the tale Mother has told her. Mother is rather like a mother in a Lyceum melodrama when her emotions are stirred, says Aunt Helen jovially.

I say nothing.

Firstly, Mother informs her I am opposed to war on principle? Well, quite right; we are all opposed to war on principle, but we must stand by our country just the same.

I say nothing.

As to my being afraid, Mother is a fool. She should have sent me to Aunt Hadow's in Devon for a complete change of air; anyone can see my nerves are all on edge. Very well, I shall go at once ; a few weeks will soon fix me up, get me strong and able to resume war service.

It takes the best part of an hour to convince Aunt Helen there will be no resumption of war service. Then she hurls her last bomb !

" Unless you return to France I alter my will to-morrow."

I smile.

Furious, she rises. " Your conduct is outrageous, degrading." She stalks out, white with anger at her failure. The human sacrifice has gone on strike, and Aunt is unaccustomed to human sacrifices going on strike.

Next comes Father—angry with me, but hating what Mother is making him do. I feel sorry for him. My allowance is to be stopped until I come to my senses. I don't mind. I tell him if the worst comes to the worst I can always be a charwoman— I have had plenty of experience in the convoy. But I will not do any more war service.

In the house Mother treats me as a pariah—but she is cunning. Elaborately she hides my shame from the outside world. If I were having one of the war-babies in which she is so interested she could not be more cunning. The doctor calls every second day. Bulletins of my health are carefully circulated. " Nellie is a trifle better," or " The poor child has gone to pieces again." I can rouse her to the last pitch of fury by facetiously inquiring how am I this morning—blooming or prostrate? And although as the weeks pass into months Mrs. Evans-Mawnington gets more and more suspicious, she can prove nothing.

.   .   .   .   .

Roy has come home on leave unexpectedly. I was not told he was dining with us. I met him by accident in the hall—a tall, grown-up Roy I hardly knew.

" Nell ! "

He told me I'd grown awfully pretty. I hadn't, but I liked him to say so. All through dinner we kept watching one another, he was so inconceivably changed—and I . . .

" He's got seven days," Mrs. Evans-Mawnington kept saying, " but he's dying to get back, bad boy."

I caught Roy's eye understandingly and we both grinned.

" Nellie's got *indefinite* sick leave," said Mother ; " she *hates* it."

Roy and I grinned again.

" I wish you'd do a theatre to-morrow, Nell," said Roy.

I accepted promptly, in spite of Mother's warning glances. Mrs. Evans-Mawnington, too, was

furious. She was determined to keep Roy away
from me, and I was equally determined she should
not, but Mother, seeing my face, swerved round to
my side. A little gaiety, perhaps, would not harm
me. So I am going.

.   .   .   .   .

Roy telephones to make sure I have not forgotten.
Forgotten ? When I have washed my hair and sewn
buckles on my slippers and put fresh shoulder straps
on my satin petticoat.

Queer that I should be so thrilled at the prospect
of going out with Roy, whom I have known all
these years.

Queer sitting in a pink-shaded restaurant alone
with Roy.

Queerer still catching my breath because he looks
at me instead of choosing dinner, to the waiter's
irritation.

Queerer even to have him fussing—can I eat this,
that, and the other ? Am I well enough to have
an ice ? . . .

" I'm not ill, Roy, not physically, anyhow. I'm
war-sick. I'm fed up with the whole business,
scared to death ; Mother's ashamed of me, bitterly,
that's why she's telling people I'm ill."

He understands, as I knew he would. Of course
Roy would be the only one to understand.

" Aren't the parents bloodthirsty ? The way I've

got to pretend I'm the little hero, Nell. I had a month in the trenches before I got that Blighty fracture, and I'd do anything on God's earth rather than go back. The wires I pulled to get this base job, I can tell you. You understand ? . . ."

" I understand, Roy."

" In the home circle I hate being out of things, all that muck—Mother dying for me to get decorations, V.C.'s and things ; sometimes I fancy she'd rather have them than me. The V.C. ? When my stomach turns over with fright every time I hear a shot fired. It's pretty bloody, Nell, when you've got men under you and you've got to be a shining example. Only for my sergeant, I'd have turned and run the first time ; I swear it. ' Steady on, sir,' he said. ' You'll get the hang of it in 'arf a tick '—and I suppose I did. I wanted to thank him afterwards —but we never saw him again. Prisoner, or blown to hell—God only knows ! I can tell you this, Nell, can't I ? "

" You can tell me, Roy."

I tell him something of the convoy ; how good to tell Roy, who understands ! He holds my hand while I am talking. A silence falls between us. He taps a fork abstractedly.

" Would it matter two damns to you if I was not shot to blazes, Nell ? "

The waiter comes back, takes an order, goes again.

" Would it ? "

Would it ? Roy one of my maimed procession—
dear God, no.

.   .   .   .   .

The theatre is jolly—a revue, lights, music, fun,
pretty girls, but to us it's merely a background.
We sit in the shadow of our box and whisper, Roy
with his arm across the back of my chair, now and
again caressing my ears, rubbing his hand up and
down my short hair—" kid's hair," he calls it.

Queer to have Roy, suddenly grown-up, smooth-
ing up and down the back of my head, caressing
my ears, calling my hair " kid's hair."

He asks me something, I hold my face up to reply,
and he kisses me, shyly, half-afraid, gently.

Queer to be kissed by Roy—our lips resting gently
together in the half-light while someone sings a
ragtime song.

" You don't mind, Nell ? I love you ; I expect
I've always loved you, only I didn't know till you
came down the stairs last night in that summery
thing covered with flowers. I wish you loved me,
Nell."

Roy wishing I loved him. . . .

But I do. Of course I do. I've always loved
Roy. Queer that I've just discovered it. Who else
should I love but Roy ? Oh, the infinite peace of
loving Roy, like a ship coming into harbour after

a stormy voyage. Tears roll down my cheeks; he comforts me, puzzled that I cannot tell him why they are there, because I do not know myself.

In the taxi going home he begs me to marry him quickly, but I cannot ; it is all too sudden. After the war, yes, but not now. I will be engaged to him . . .

" Oh, Nell, you do love me, don't you ? "

I do. I do. I love him—Roy I have squabbled with and romped with, Roy, grown up and sun-burned and suddenly a man.

" I do love you, Roy."

He kisses me again, not as he kissed me in the theatre, boyishly and half-shyly, but as a man kisses the woman he is going to marry.

God, how happy I am !

" I'm happy ! I'm happy ! I'm happy ! "

He thinks it's beautiful to hear anyone say that. " How seldom people say ' I'm happy ' ! ' I'm miserable ' or ' I'm ill " or ' I'm lonely ' or ' I'm depressed '—but seldom ' I'm happy ' ! Rottenly ungrateful for happiness, human beings, eh, Nell ? "

How adorable he is, this grown-up Roy ! He holds me protectingly and my head tucks into his khaki shoulder as he paints our peaceful future when this mess of war has been cleared up. A little cottage in the country somewhere—an old-fashioned oak-beamed affair brought up-to-date ; a crazy pavement leading to the little green front door. . . . " It must be green, Nell ; I'll paint it myself—jolly handy with a paint-brush I am " . . . a big brass knocker . . . lupins and roses and sweet peas and high marguerites in the garden . . . a smooth green lawn . . . " I'll roll it myself to keep in condition. Can't you see me on a hot summer afternoon puffing and blowing ? " . . . Inside cool rooms with lattice windows . . . " You'll have the furnishing of those, Nell."

"Green-leafed chintz," I stipulate. "I know the very place they sell it ; only one shop in Town does. And a white piano ; once I saw a white piano in a cottage, and it was just right. I'll build a whole room round that white piano. . . ."

He gives me the white piano. We furnish downstairs, then upstairs, the bedrooms, our bedroom, a big one with a dressing-room each, says Roy.

" This is a cottage, Mr. Evans-Mawnington, not Buckingham Palace. If we each have a dressing-room, where is the nursery going ? I suppose we do have a nursery ? "

We deliberate with mock gravity the important point, then Roy says we must consider the garden. " For what cottage garden is ever complete without a perambulator on the lawn ? " he demands. " But," he adds, " into the kitchen garden he goes quick if he yells."

" He ? You mean she," I argue.

We compromise on one of each. Oh, the fun and peace and cleanness of the life we plan after the war, Roy and I. Oh, the sweetness of the play-mate I have surprisingly found I love. Happy, happy taxi-ride that ends in finding ourselves at Father's doorstep before we realize we have left central London behind.

The scent of the flowers floods our nostrils, the rays of the summer moon bathe us in gold. So they should, we think, on this night of nights. What are scents of flowers and golden moons for if not the exclusive use of lovers ? It is a long parting, this doorstep farewell. Our first. We cannot tear ourselves apart. At last the romance ends on a note of farce. Father comes to the door. It is long after midnight and time all decent people were in bed, he says tersely.

" Just like a comic paper," whispers Roy. " In a minute he'll talk about the gas-bill and introduce me to the toe of his boot."

We go into fits of laughter, to Father's annoyance. Am I or am I not coming in ? I am. What would happen if I refused ?

" Good-night," says Roy formally, " I'll telephone you about that matter we were discussing in the morning."

" Yes, do," I reply. " Good-night."

Father bangs the door—puts up the chain—
I run upstairs.

My face in the mirror is flushed, happy, laughing.

How lovely life has become all of a sudden, how
lovely !

" God, I'm happy ! I'm happy ! "

For the first time my ghostly procession does not
parade in the early hours before the dawn.

CHAPTER X

" You're wanted on the 'phone, Miss Nellie."

I sit up with a jerk. Eight o'clock. Who on earth is indecent enough to telephone at this ungodly hour? Not Roy. . . .

No, not Roy ; Roy went to France last night.

I refuse to think of Roy and France. Eyes half-closed, I stumble out of bed, downstairs—why can't Father have the telephone put in a decent place. . . .

" Hello ? "

" Is Miss Helen Smith speaking ? " A woman's voice, husky and unknown to me.

" Yes, speaking."

" Prepare for a shock and don't say my name at the other end. Ready ? "

" Yes, I'm listening."

" Trix speaking. Quiet now, Cis. I'm in England on leave and I don't want the family to know. Got that ? "

Trix in England. . . .

" Yes."

" Cis, something awful has happened. I must see you at once. Will you take the address ? I'll wait in all the morning for you. You won't fail me, will you ? "

Fail you, Trix. Fail you, the little sister I love ?

" Tell me the address and I'll come."

She tells me.

" I'll be there in an hour or two."

" I shan't go out till you come." She cuts off abruptly.

Trix home on leave. Trix home secretly. " I don't want the family to know."

I go slowly into the bathroom and light the geyser.

.   .   .   .   .

All the noises of the world have stopped except for Trix's voice, sobbing, terrified, rising in hysterical cadences, failing into tear-choked inaudibilities. . . .

" A hundred pounds—you'll get it for me, Cis, somehow. She won't do it for less—Sunny gave me the address—quite safe she says ; she knows lots of girls who've been. . . ."

All the noises of the world faded into uncanny silence—the clang-bang-rattle of the trams, the newsboy's raucous shout—" Latest Cazz-yew-allit-eess," the honk-honk of the taxi-cabs : all hushed as though listening to Trix. . . .

" Rotten mess—just my luck—others can play merry hell and nothing happens. Cis, I swear it isn't dangerous or anything ; you needn't be afraid

of anything happening to me. You're the only
one I've got to turn to ; don't look like that,
Cis. . . ."

All the noises in the world stopped while Trix
weeps helplessly like a forlorn baby, heartbroken,
waiting for me to speak.

What can I say ? What can I do ?

" Cis, you'll get the money for me ? "

" Trix, don't ask me. I haven't anywhere to get
it, and even if I had—girls die—I'd be responsible
if you died ; they do die, you know they do. . . ."

She springs to her feet, her eyes mad, words
tumbling out of her mouth, no longer a forlorn
baby, but a desperate woman.

" Listen. I nearly ended the whole thing crossing
over. I prayed for a torpedo, and when it didn't
come I nearly chucked myself over the side. If
you hadn't been at this end I would have gone
overboard and finished it—you at this end saved me.
' Don't be an ass, Cis'll save you. Don't be an ass,
Cis'll save you,'—I told myself that over and over
again. If you turn me down I'll chuck myself in
the Thames ; it's quite the conventional thing to
do, isn't it ? . . ." She laughs.

" Trix, for God's sake . . ."

" I will, I will. Can't you see I'm nearly off
my head ? For nearly five months I've been slowly
going mad, and one night I plucked up courage and

told Sunny, and she gave me this address. I've
got a chance this way to start all over again. . . ."

" What about the man ?   Won't he marry you ? "

We are both panting like wild animals, glaring
into each other's eyes.

" Marry me ? " she cries defiantly. " I don't
know who it is ; it might be any of three. . . ."

The floor, patterned in faded green squares, rises
up to hit me—Trix, my little sister, my little sister—
any of three. . . .

" Now perhaps you'll talk sense."

I sink to the couch, a red velvet couch with a
worn seat. The springs have gone in two places,
I notice. I feel as though I have been hit by an
icy wave—too numb to recover my breath—floating
out to sea. . . .

" You don't understand what it's like out there
—the atmosphere. You can't call your soul your
own. Nag, nag, nag, from the sisters—all day
bullied about and given the bird by everybody.
The V.A.D.'s were the first to volunteer, and they've
been snubbed and treated like dirt ever since for
it. Make you scrub your washhouse floor in a
clean, starched white apron with a big red cross
on the front and tick you off if they come in and
find you've dirtied it—that's the sort of thing.
My God, it makes me laugh to think I paid to do
it, too, out of my own pocket, I was so keen. Paid

198

for my own uniform, my own training, even paid my own doctor's fee to be signed medically fit. And what do I get out of it. Damn-all. Doing the work of a scullery-maid—only a scullery-maid would be off like a rocket if she was spoken to as I get spoken to. All very well for girls with no guts—insults and things roll off them like water off a duck's back—but for people with a spirit. . . . I'm not blaming Matron ; she's a good old sort ; she can't be expected to have eyes in her behind, but some of those ward sisters want tarring and feathering. Bitches—no other word. I've always stuck up for women when men called them cats— but never again. If you've got any spirit they deliberately set out to break it, and they pass the good word on to their pals. Talk about a trade union ; I've never struck anything like these nurses. And if they can't break your spirit, what happens ? You bottle it all and get keyed up, and when you do get loose you go mad, like me and Sunny and a few others. I wouldn't care if we were paid for it—but we're giving our youth and the good times we ought to be having free of charge ; we're like kids out of school when we get loose—pity our games aren't as harmless. The boredom and the rules, rules, rules . . . no wonder we go a bit mad off duty . . . don't know what you're doing half your time. . . . And the men, making love to you one

day and dead the next. I've been on leave twice
with different subs and they're both dead : Jerry
was one. I liked Jerry awfully, but he died—
they don't think anything rotten of a girl who sleeps
with them nowadays, just that she's a fool if she
doesn't. Cast-iron virgins they call those who won't.
There aren't many of them knocking about by all
accounts ; a lot of them swank they are, but they're
not. Easy for the plain ones, the men don't worry
them much ; but I've got to the stage of wondering
what's wrong with my appearance if a sub doesn't
ask me to sleep with him—that's what the war's
done for me—pretty, isn't it ? Here to-day and
gone to-morrow, that's what they tell you, and it's
true, it's true, people dying all round you. Makes
you determined to get a bit of enjoyment out of
life while you're alive to take it—you're not alive very
long nowadays if you're young, are you ? *Are you ?*"

She begins to laugh again. I take her by the
shoulders. " Someone will hear you, Trix. . . ."

She calms herself in a few minutes, weeping
again, pleading—my little sister whom I have never
seen weeping in my life—my laughing little sister. . . .

" Cis, get it for me, get it for me—all my life I'll
be grateful, get it for me. . . ."

What shall I do ? What am I to do ? Three
or four pounds in the bank at the most. Yesterday
I spent eight guineas on a new coat to see Roy

off to France—last night. Was it only last night Roy went back? Silk stockings another guinea. Yes, no more than three or four pounds in the bank at the most.

" Cis, get it for me—get it for me. . . ."

Aunt Helen cutting me out of her will for refusing to go back to France. Father stopping my allowance. Trix down on her knees to me, oh, no—no. . . .

" Get up, Trix, I can't bear it, darling, get up. When must you have it by ? "

" To-day if you can ; the sooner the better. I've only got seven days' leave. I don't know how long . . . she won't do anything till she gets the money . . . she won't take a cheque in case. . . . Oh, Cis, get it for me, save me——"

" I'll get it, darling ; don't cry any more, I'll get it somehow."

We cling together for a moment, desperately, as two terrified passengers on a sinking ship might cling—then part. She throws herself face downwards on the red velvet couch. Poor little sister. Poor little sister I would willingly die for.

" Oh, Cis, get it for me, save me. . . ."

I close the door quietly.

.   .   .   .   .

Aunt Helen.

Out of the chaos of my mind the name disentangles itself.

Aunt Helen.

It is curious that I can sit in the Corner House and sip coffee quite calmly on this summer morning, when my world is toppling about my ears. Outside in the streets people are leisurely basking in the sunshine or walking in twos and threes, chatting amiably. Who would imagine that such a short distance away guns are thundering, and men are engaged in murder on a mass scale ? France is very near to me this morning. All in a brief hour the Channel has changed from a tract of sea wider than the Atlantic to a narrow neck of water. Despair swamps me like a tidal wave—to recede and leave me petrified with a numbing coldness. I shall never be warm again.

Last night I kissed Roy good-bye at Victoria, but to my surprise there was no tragedy in the parting—a sweet sadness, a gentle melancholy at the temporary severing—nothing more. He would write every day ; so would I. He was safely at the Base. Soon leave would come round again and I should be waiting at home for him. " I want you to smile me out of England," he said. " Say ' I'm happy ! ' " It was not difficult to say.

" I'm happy ! I'm happy ! "—my last words before the train steamed out. " I'm happy ! I'm happy ! " —a magic formula that was not magic enough. " I'm happy ! I'm happy ! "—thankful am I to have whispered it from my heart, for fatalistically I know now I shall never mean the words again. The picture my lover painted for me on the palette of his fancy will be nothing but a dream picture of peaceful colours. " I'm happy ! I'm happy ! . . ." I should have known. There is no lasting happiness for this stricken generation of mine. Happiness past for the old ones, happiness to come for the young ones, but nothing for the race apart from whom youth has been snatched before it learned to play at youth. How sad is the sadness of a sunny summer morning when hope has died !

.   .   .   .   .

Aunt Helen is at the War Workers' Canteen, Sanders the maid tells me. She waits there at table every lunch-time. Sanders is openly disapproving. One gathers that in her opinion a lady of Aunt Helen's position is lowering herself many degrees socially by feeding Government clerks. However, she writes down the address and offers me a glass of sherry and the gratuitous information that I'm looking like death and ought to be lying down, instead of gallivanting over Town in this heat, Miss Nellie.

The canteen is in the basement of a large hotel. I am obliged to tack on the end of an enormous queue of men and women of all ages who are impatiently waiting for the doors to open. They are all grumbling : " Do they think we've got all day ? The doors ought to be open for us—not us waiting for them to open."

Eventually the doors do open and the queue surges rapidly along. " Passes, please. Show passes."

Once through the barriers, the war workers scuttle like rabbits to their favourite tables.

The lady at the turnstile is extremely suspicious of me. Where is my pass ? I haven't any ? I feel criminally guilty. Miss Helen Smith's niece ? Oh, perhaps I'd *better* wait—this in a voice indicating that any attempt to steal the canteen cutlery will be made only over her dead body.

The huge underground room is filled with long trestle tables, each laid with places for forty or fifty people. The tables are covered with clean blue-and-white check cloths, and there are vases of flowers everywhere. A slight difference from the ambulance convoy. A day or two in France would soon cure the war workers of their grouse.

" Perhaps you'd better sit somewhere," suggests the lady at the turnstile. " You look white and you're rather in my way. I've sent word to your aunt."

I thankfully sink into a chair at the nearest table.

" Pardon me," interrupts a cold voice, " but this table is reserved for the *despatch riders*." Had the speaker been referring to royalty she would probably not have been half as reverent. She is a musical comedy attired young woman with waves of golden hair escaping from her khaki cap with careful carelessness. I apologise and wearily remove myself, and the musical comedy young woman comments audibly on the cheek of some of these blasted slackers. All at once I am embraced ecstatically. " Smithy, *darling*. You've come to see me at last."

It is The B.F.

" Let me introduce you, Smithy, to all the despatch riders."

The B.F. is a born showman. She proceeds to tell my life history, or what she knows of it, to the assembled despatch riders. " Smithy was at the convoy and was with dear Tosh when she was killed." The musical comedy young woman appears considerably disconcerted. The other drivers murmur semi-audible " Reallys ! " and The B.F. invites me warmly to luncheon and is *so* disappointed when I explain about Aunt. Oh, dear, and she did *so* want to chat about the dear old convoy, *so* happy— none of these dear girls have ever been to France, *of course*—all very loudly for the benefit of the dear girls who have never been to France, the said dear girls looking as fed up as The B.F. means them to. Whatever have I been doing to my dear self?—all white and drawn, quite old in the face, and, of course, I'm only twenty-one, everyone knows. Oh—catching sight of my engagement ring—a romance ? But how thrilling ! Why are your hands so cold, dear ? Dead and numb they feel. Such luck catching her in, she babbles on—usually she's terribly naughty, lunching at the Savoy or somewhere nice with some nice man. This is *awfully unusual* being here alone. The B.F. is most apologetic at being caught paying for her own lunch. In her eyes it is a confession of inferiority.

Fortunately I spot Aunt Helen staggering under a heavy tray of food and make my escape. The B.F. does not amuse me to-day. My sense of humour has departed.

Aunt Helen is just as pleased to see me as I expected. She cannot imagine my having anything to say of interest to her, and she is too busy to bother now. I can sit at her table and wait—if I must wait.

I seat myself and watch Aunt Helen dispassionately. It takes exactly one minute to discover that as a waitress she is the world's hall-marked washout. The war workers, having deduced from my welcome that I could not possibly know Aunt very intimately, make no effort to conceal their disgust. " Silly old blighter," " Doddering old messer," " One-foot-in-the-grave-Gertie," " Mercury "—I should like Aunt to hear a few of the flattering descriptions.

She certainly is the last word in incompetence.
She mixes up each order systematically, and has to
make return journeys for things she has forgotten
in practically every instance. If roast beef and
baked potatoes are wanted she will bring the roast
beef, and the baked potatoes materialise with luck
any time after the beef is stone cold. Once the
bread basket is emptied it remains empty, despite
frenzied pleas. One girl asks six times for water
and then doesn't get it. It is a pitiful exhibition,
and the war workers have no false ideas of gratitude
towards their voluntary waitress. They are hungry
and in a hurry. Aunt knows she is messing things
up, and the fact that I am a spectator does not help.
She becomes hot and bothered and flustered.
Her grey hair is hanging in wisps from under her
dust-cap—a vivid pink. All females with com-
plexions like my aunt's should be prohibited by
Act of Parliament from wearing crude pink dust-
caps. She flutters aimlessly to and fro like a foolish
hen. If only she used a little method she could save
herself seven-eighths of the trouble. Vague old
fool. Why doesn't she devote herself to the small
jobs of her own home, dusting and filling flower
vases, washing china, answering the telephone—
then she could release one of her competent maids
to wait on the war workers ; but, of course, that
would not be spectacular enough for a red-hot

207

patriot such as Aunt Helen. What a godsend the war is, coming just as Spiritualism was beginning to bore her !

All around I see similar exhibitions of incompetence ; Aunt is one of many.

At last the twelve o'clock batch is fed and the doors closed while the tables are put in order for the " one-o'clocks." Aunt ungraciously permits me to fill her water jugs and bread baskets.

" Well ? " she barks at last.

" Do you still want me to go to France ? " I am as curt as she.

" Do you imagine it pleases me to see a niece of mine slacking about Town ? " she counters.

" I'll go back if you give me a hundred pounds."

Her eyes light up with an unholy light, but she is still suspicious. " A hundred ? Whatever for ? It's a lot of money."

" I must have a hundred." I repeat doggedly. " Father's cut my allowance off and the last time it cost a hundred for my outfit. . . ."

" Oh ! M-m-m-m." She tries to be casual. " When do you propose enlisting ? "

" To-day. As soon as I cash the cheque."

" M-m-m-m." Suspicious again. " Your Mother isn't influencing you, by any chance ? " She is not paying for Mother's fun.

" No, Aunt, as a matter of fact, I've been thinking of the things you said. . . . "

Ah, I have hit the right nail on the head. She smiles. A wintry smile ; she must not thaw too soon, that would not be dignified ; but still a smile.

" I'm glad the seed did not fall on stony ground." She smiles again, a real smile this time, a positively arch smile—oh, very arch is Aunt Helen now that she has won a smashing victory. " No stopping you once you've made up your mind, eh, Helen ? Ha, ha, ha ! " A rippling laugh. " Well, come along, impatient girl, into our office. . . ."

All eagerness now is Aunt Helen, almost running in case the prey may escape even now. She opens her cheque-book with a flourish.

" Shall I cross it, Helen ? "

" She won't take a cheque in case. . . ."

" No, leave it open, Aunt," I reply.

.   .   .   .   .

Trix has gone with the hundred pounds—where I do not know. She will telephone me as soon as— or if—she can. I must wait. Useless arguing. I must wait. I will not have to wait long one way or the other. What do a few days matter ? I am strangely apathetic. Useless struggling. I was never a strong swimmer, and now I must float along with the current until it casts me high and dry or carries me further and further out of my depth. My one

209

big effort to get back to dry land has been a failure. Caught up like a piece of driftwood, all the struggles in the world are futile. I have no fight left in me.

I cross slowly into Trafalgar Square, along Haymarket into Piccadilly, past Hyde Park . . . on and on until I reach my objective. I find myself at last in the entrance hall of a solid-looking house. Someone directs me to a big room on the ground floor.

Two women are sitting at a large desk ; girls in khaki are bustling about. There are printed bills tacked neatly on the walls—

WANTED

WOMEN FOR THE DURATION OF THE WAR
W.A.A.C.

One of the girls in khaki approaches me. " I hope you've come to enlist. Good pay, uniform found, no expense. . . ."

" Yes."

They are galvanized into immediate action. The elder of the two women pulls a business-like form towards her, the other importantly dips a pen in the ink, one of the uniformed girls bustles about encouraging me, until I tell her, to save her breath, I have every intention of enlisting. I've come specially to do it. She looks offended, but relapses into silence. Service abroad, I stipulate, that is

the only condition under which I am enlisting.
They put it in writing at my request.

" Name and address ? "

I give them.

" What are you enlisting as ? Driver, Cook, Clerk,
Domestic Worker. . . ."

Aunt Helen's smug face rises before me, Mother's
ladylike voice : " My eldest daughter, Helen, an
ambulance driver in France ; oh, a most exclusive
class of girl, most exclusive, all *ladies*—they stipulate
that, you know. Most exclusive ; Georgina Toshington is out with her, you know, the niece of the
Earl of . . ."

" Domestic worker, please."

The last claw of the cat before it is put in the sack
and drowned !

" Domestic worker. Probably a cook's assistant.
That all correct ? Sign here."

Domestic worker. If I had a laugh left in me I
would split my sides with vulgar mirth. " My
daughter a common W.A.A.C., a domestic worker,
mixing with dreadful people out of the slums,
some of them really *are*, you know. And I've even
heard some of them are immoral—babies and all
that kind of thing. My daughter not even an
officer, and she could have enlisted with the very best
people. . . ."

Domestic worker.

Put that on your needles and knit it, my patriotic aunt.

Tell that to the titled ladies on your committee, my snobbish mother.

" You'll get your calling-up papers in a day or so."

I turn on my heel.

.   .   .   .   .

It is five days before Trix telephones. Everything has gone according to schedule. I see her off by the leave-train. She is miserably thin and white, and there are lines about her mouth that are not good to see in a girl of nineteen. For a minute we hold one another closely. " Cis, I'll never forget to my dying day. . . ."

After that we say little. I ask for no details, nor does she offer any ; neither do I tell of my sleepless hours waiting for the telephone to ring. She knows.

She is apologetic about her abstraction. Her mind is a blank . . . she has nothing to talk about— nothing seems to matter . . . she doesn't know whether I understand. . . .

I understand, but I say nothing.

Instead, I break the news that I am returning to France. Her comment is brief : " Bit of a damn fool, aren't you ? "

As the train goes out of the station my last emotion

goes with it. Nothing will ever stir me again. I am dry. Worn out. Finished.

.   .   .   .   .

Evidently there is no preliminary training necessary for a cook's assistant. They are needed too urgently.

Two weeks later I entrain with my draft for France. No one of my family sees me off this time.

CHAPTER XI

THE months pass, each day a replica of the last, time on and time off, work and rest and recreation. I have had no leave, at my own request. It was early autumn when I came out and now spring is here—nearly seven months since I started peeling potatoes and onions at the trestle table outside the camp kitchen alongside Misery, Cheery, and Blimey. We are known as " the Four Whys," our nicknames all ending in the same letter—for, of course, I am again Smithy, the inevitable fate of all Smiths in the Army since ever there was an Army.

I have become accustomed to being a machine, to living by the clock, to having my amusements and my religion set before me in carefully-measured doses, to sleeping certain hours, to working certain hours, to exercising certain hours, to taking aperients on certain days whether they are necessary or not, and to donning the cheery indomitable personality of a member of the women's army each morning with my uniform, and discarding it only when the bugle signals " Lights Out."

I am a slot machine that never goes out of order. Put so much rations into the slot and I will work so long, play so long, and sleep so long. The administration is perfect. Everything is regulated. Even my emotions. I am serious at given moments, such as church parade ; I laugh at given moments, when there is a visiting commission, or at any entertainment where the programme tells me the item is comic in order that I may not register incorrectly. I am not unduly happy, neither am I noticeably unhappy . . . I would not dare be either. If I were over-happy I should be sent for—as Cheery is often sent for—and be kindly chided for lack of dignity and control. If I were noticeably unhappy the Unit Administrator would tactfully put me through the third degree and, if unable to trace the cause of my state of mind, would make a determined effort to restore me to a standardised state of mental elation. Amusing books would be selected for me. I should be invited to tea and talks —a pleasant form of confession with a chocolate biscuit accompaniment that is highly popular ; or I should attend special concerts and be roped in for a course of vigorous Morris dancing, as Misery is. But I am neither over-happy nor noticeably unhappy. I am the most equable disposition in the unit. The Administrator says so. My companions like me because I am " always the same." There is no hanky-panky about me, I am told ; you can neither shock nor surprise, please nor displease. I

NOT SO QUIET . . .

never complain, I have no grievances, and I never
argue. The Unit Administrator is fond of upholding me as an example. I never request a pass.
There has never been one black mark against my
conduct or my work. I have never even broken a
rule. I do not tell her I am not interested enough
in the rules to break them . . . for she would not
believe it. She is determinedly kind and tactful,
and takes a personal interest in every member of
her unit, whom individually she knows by name.
She calls herself our " Mother Confessor." I have
heard her privately described as " Nosey Parker,"
but not often, for my comrades revel in pouring
confidences into her willing ear. Besides, they like
the chocolate biscuits that go with the maternal
advice. She tells our mothers, with whom she is
fond of corresponding, that the minds of her girls
are as open books to her. Naturally, the Rabe-
laisian pages are reserved for the dormitories.

I live in a Nissen hut, with a number of companions. Once this communal life would have
stifled me, but now I am quite content that the
details of my body, my personal habits, and my
underclothing should be common knowledge. Outwardly I am Smithy, assistant cook ; inwardly I am
nothing. I have no feelings that are not physical.
I dislike being too hot or too cold. My body is
healthy, my mind negative. I have no love or

hate for anyone. Long ago I ceased to love Roy ; long ago I ceased to hate my mother. Both processes were gradual. I am content to drift along in the present. The past has gone ; I have no future ... I want no future. With this mental atrophy my physical fear has vanished, for fear cannot exist when one is indifferent to life. The droning of the enemy planes that make the nights noisier than the days leaves me unmoved, where once it petrified me with a senseless horror ; the ceaseless pounding of the guns has no more effect on me than the hidden drums of an orchestra ... for I have no nerves. Automatically I bathe my body, automatically I converse with my fellow-workers, automatically I write letters, obey orders, eat and sleep ... a flesh and blood case containing nothing save the machinery that keeps Smith, assistant cook, alive.

Spring. ... Cheery and Blimey singing over the vegetables as though they were primroses and daffodils. Even Misery not grousing for once. And I do not care.

Spring. ... Soft breezes on our wet hands instead of cutting winds that chap and crack our skins. Tender sun forcing its way through white, impudent clouds ... slits of blue widening and widening. And I do not care.

" 'Ark at that soppy little bird," says Blimey,

217

" singin' its guts out over there. Makes yer feel like a new 'at some'ow."

" Wisht I 'ad a new chap," says Cheery. " Blow the new 'at."

" I've finished the third corner of my crochay bedspread," says Misery. " Turned the corner last night."

.   .   .   .   .

Cheery and Blimey are sprucing up. Blimey has discarded the issue hat which has never suited her little sharp face, and has become the proud possessor of a softer, more becoming shape.

Cheery and Blimey argue about most things . . . but on one point they agree emphatically . . . it's a jolly good war, and they hope it goes on for ever. They will probably get their wish. They both derive from large families living in two small rooms in a crowded slum district, and they still revel in the luxury of a bed to themselves. At first they mistrusted the long rows of bathrooms, but now they are immersed at every available opportunity. Blimey has developed into a " Reg'ler K-Nut." She has cut her hair in imitation of mine, her skirt is a fraction shorter than the others', and her Burberry a few shades lighter. At church parade she wears yellow wash-leather gloves with the cuffs turned back from the wrists and a yellow *crêpe de Chine* handkerchief tucked coyly into her sleeve.

Her stockings are well-fitting and her shoes as highly polished as those of the girl in a well-known boot-polish advertisement. Her teeth protrude slightly, but they are even and white. Until she became a W.A.A.C., she had never cleaned them, but now she does it several times daily. It is her staple topic of conversation.

This personal cleanliness and extravagance of dress is not for mere show. It is a commercial proposition—the capital, so to speak, that Blimey is putting into her business . . . the business of marrying the first suitable Tommy she can ensnare. For, as Blimey shrewdly says, you get it all ways. . . . "If 'e comes through the war 'e works and keeps yer; if 'e won't work an' keep yer 'e gets sued for maintenance; if 'e gets wounded 'e gets pensioned; an' if 'e's killed there's yer widow's allowance . . . yer can't go wrong."

Which is why Blimey enlisted. At home she had no wages to buy clothes. Her father took every penny she earned. She is refreshingly frank about it . . . unlike most of the others who joined up in the sacred name of patriotism. "Dirty lot o' liars," Blimey calls them, and takes a fiendish delight in winning the confidence of the flag-waggers until she unearths their real motive, which she then discloses without the slightest compunction to the world. . . . "Joined up to

219

help win the wa-wer me foot ! . . . joined up to
do it on 'er ma for wallopin' 'er for comin' 'ome at
midnight with a soldier. Patriotic me belly ! "
. . . Or when she hears someone boasting, " 'Ere,
is yer trumpeter dead ? "

My sister W.A.A.C.'s are certainly not backward
in blowing their own trumpets. The newspapers,
the recruiting officers, and the Army out here have
told them they are noble creatures, and they resent
not being patted on the back all the time. The
band must go on playing for the Mutual Admiration
Society. When the music fades to a *pianissimo*
passage they help it out with a concerted chorus
of self-praise. " We're each releasing men to fight,
don't forget . . . each of us doing her bit for the
country. . . . The slackers at home ought to see
us. . . . Good job they've started tribunals for
the men hanging back . . . pity they haven't
got them for the women too. . . ."

Some of them don't even know what the war is
about. I met a canteen waitress the other day who
thought the Huns were black and came from Africa
and were on the side of the Allies. She knew
the Germans as Fritz and was astounded that the
Huns were the same. She had joined up to see
Paris, and although she wasn't exactly seeing Paris
she was having the time of her life. The truth is,
the greater percentage enlisted because of the pay,

NOT SO QUIET . . .

which was good, considering they are rationed and uniformed free. Incidentally, the change from home life is not to be despised. They had no idea there would be personal danger, but once in they stick it because they're here for the duration. There is just as much danger from the air in England now, by all accounts, and the munition girls on high explosives are taking far greater chances. Incompetence or lack of discipline will always get you a free ticket Blightywards, of course.

Cheery joined up in a fit of pique because her regular young man was billeted in a French village where there were " Mamselles." " I told him two could play at that game," says Cheery. She is a born flirt. Her motto is " Familiar to all, courteous to none "—a reversal of the routine order, " Courteous to all, familiar to none." She is pretty and has a roving eye. Cheery off duty without her Tommy would be as strange as a meal without Maconochie. Her favourite recreation is " leading the boys up the garden." Blimey openly questions this and accuses her of occasionally " lettin' them into the summer-'ouse." Cheery does not deny this. " I'm a grown woman an' I can enjoy meself if I like an' 'ow I like ! "

But Blimey does not hold with this view. " No bloke wants a girl wot ain't pure," is her contention. " A bloke likes to be first, don't 'e ? If

NOT SO QUIET . . .

'e can get wot 'e wants without marriage, why marry ? "

That is why Blimey is as chaste as a nun. She is the most rigidly virtuous woman I have ever met. Not even a kiss on the lips, says Blimey, till the ring is on her finger and the lines tucked in her bosom. A terrifying chastity, that of Blimey.

Misery is engaged to be married to a young man in England exempt from military service on the grounds of " indispensable." She comes from a good home with a piano in the parlour and lace curtains at the front windows. She's not used to this sort of rough life. She came out to save money for the wedding. Her grouse is as permanent and perpetual as her catarrh. She crochets fiercely on every opportunity at a crochet bedspread destined to cover herself and Fred at some remote date.

" Garn, yer'll be too busy blowin' yer nose to need a bed," gibes Blimey. " In between sneezes. I 'ope Fred's nippy."

.   .   .   .   .

The Unit Administrator wants me in her private office. I have only had this special summons once before . . . when Mother wrote to her the month I arrived with a request that I should be recommended for a commission on account of my previous war service at the convoy. The Unit Administrator

222

reminded me forcibly of Aunt Helen in her manner. She was breezy, she was jovial, she was energetic, she was determined and dreadfully, overwhelmingly charming. The interview might be described as a succession of surprises. On her part, that is. She was *surprised* I had not spoken of my excellent record. She was *surprised* I had not confessed to being the driver who was with the well-known Georgina Toshington on the occasion of her sad death on active service. She was *surprised* I had not tried for a commission in the W.A.A.C.'s. She was *surprised* that if I had not tried for a commission in the W.A.A.C.'s I had not joined up as an ambulance driver. All these things surprised her. But not to the extent that my refusal to budge from my assistant cook's job surprised her.

I knock on her door and enter indifferently in reply to her invitation. She has a letter in her hand. I recognise the hand-writing instantly. Mother. I have not answered her last half-dozen letters.

" You wanted me, ma'am ? "

" Sit down, Smith."

I obey. It is an uncommon request. The Unit Administrator does not usually request the rank and file to be seated in her presence.

" Smith, I have an unpleasant task before me. I want you to prepare yourself for some rather sad news. Your mother thinks it would be better for

me to break it to you than have you open a letter
and receive a shock."

I wait patiently.

" It has to do with your *fiancé*, Captain Evans-
Mawnington."

Roy? Killed, I suppose? I am not surprised.
Everyone else is killed. Trix was wiped out in an
air-raid on the hospital five months ago, Etta
Potato was torpedoed crossing the Channel within
the last three weeks . . . everyone is killed. If the
submarines, the aerial torpedoes, the poison gas,
the liquid fire, the long-distance guns, the hand
grenades, the trench mortars, and all the other
things injure without killing them, they are sent
back again and again after being patched up until
they are killed. It is only a question of time.
Why should Roy expect to escape? He is better
dead. I am glad he is dead—because once he
brought romance into my life and I loved him for
a little while.

" He has been wounded, badly wounded."

Roy is not dead. He is wounded. Well, that
is nothing. He has been wounded before. This
will be his third wound-stripe. He will be patched
up and perhaps next time he may have more luck
and be killed and out of it for good.

" Your mother writes . . . I hate having to
tell you this, Smith, it is *so* unfortunate . . . she

writes that he is blinded and has had a leg amputated from the hip."

I watch her stolidly.

" But he behaved with conspicuous bravery and is to have the M.C. Smith, let that console you. The M.C. It helps, doesn't it ? The M.C."

" *Sometimes I think Mother would rather have a decoration than me.*" *Roy said that the night we became engaged, the night we dined together in the little restaurant with the pink lights. The night I was so happy I kept on saying it aloud—" I'm happy ! I'm happy ! I'm happy ! "*

" The M.C., Smith. A great, great honour. If you want to weep, Smith, weep. I understand, my dear."

She waits for me to do something. She expects me to speak, I think.

" His mother will be pleased about the M.C., ma'am," I say quietly.

The Unit Administrator looks disappointed. She expected a big emotional scene and feels cheated. She would have fussed over me with a smelling bottle and personally supervised my removal to the sick bay. She prides herself on the personal touch she introduces into the love affairs of her girls.

" Perhaps you would like me to arrange urgent leave, Smith ? "

" No, thank you, ma'am. I'd rather carry on."

225

She smiles. " Devotion to duty, Smith. Private griefs must be set aside when duty calls, mustn't they? I am proud of you. You have set a fine example to the Unit."

She shakes my hand emotionally.

I go back to my trestle table where the onions and carrots are waiting.

CHAPTER XII

WHEN the air-raids come, as they do every night when the moon shines, a whistle blows, we collect our blankets and mattresses and are marched about a mile out of camp to the trenches that have been built since the time a bomb fell on a wing of the camp hospital and crumpled it to powder. Now the weather has improved the raids are increasing in number and violence. Each becomes more daring than its predecessor.

The rumour is flying around that we are losing the war, and our army is recoiling before the big advance of the enemy. Every day we are losing ground, they say. Soon we expect to strike camp and retreat. It is a curious feeling, as though a terrific landslide were sweeping down and we, in the valley, were doomed to be engulfed unless we run. Daily the guns grow nearer, more menacing, almost deafening. We can distinguish between the different ones now . . . we know the lines must have dropped back if only for that reason. A queer tenseness is in the air. And nightly the raiding aeroplanes grow in numbers and daring.

.   .   .   .   .

Three letters lie open on my bed before me . . .
Mother's, Mrs. Evans-Mawnington's, and Roy's.

" MY DEAREST GIRLIE,

" Isn't it wonderful that Roy has had the
M.C. ? Wonderful and sad. Our poor blinded
hero. And my little girlie is to marry him and be
his eyes. I am proud of him. I gave my youngest
girl to England, my little Trix, whose medals I
always wear on official occasions. But, in the midst
of my grief, I can still smile and thank God she
died in the service of her country—a country that
will never forget. The brave boy is in hospital in
Brighton, and his poor mother is with him. She
is grieved at his affliction, but, as she says, how
much worse if he hadn't been recommended for
an M.C. It really is a *great compensation*. I'm sure
the dear boy thinks so too. Dear boy, I feel already
that he is my own son.

" I think a quiet wedding, don't you ? as soon
as he is strong enough. Just a few relations and
friends by the hospital bedside. Perhaps a reporter,
for your example ought to do a few of these appalling
creatures good who have refused to marry their
wounded heroes.

" And, darling, you really must give up that
absurd W.A.A.C. job. The wife of a Captain and

M.C. can hardly go on peeling vegetables, can she ? I have written to your Unit Administrator and suggested it. What a charming woman she seems ; she wrote me the sweetest letter *re* Roy. Mrs. Evans-Mawnington said it was a *great comfort*.

" Darling, what an inestimable privilege you have, marrying one of England's disabled heroes, devoting your life to his service !

" No orange blossoms or anything like that—I think it would be bad form—but a smart grey frock and hat ; and I think Father *might* be persuaded to give you a nice squirrel coat for a wedding gift . . . such a pretty fur, I think, so soft and suitable for young girls.

" Your ever-loving,
" MOTHER."

" MY DEAR NELLIE,

" I am grief-stricken, but I feel I must write to tell you of Roy's splendid achievement—how he got his M.C. He held a trench under machine-gun fire when three-quarters of his men were dead, although one of his legs was blown off. Just as relief came a piece of shrapnel caught his face, and his eyesight was ruined for ever. My poor brave son. But they gave him an M.C. As soon as he is strong enough he goes to Buckingham Palace for the investiture—a great honour—and the King will personally thank him for his bravery. You and I will go—his mother and his wife, for I hope by then you will be his wife ; the doctor says he needs an incentive to get well, and that should do it. He is, of course, a trifle depressed, but that will wear off once he is out of hospital and has been decorated.

"It is a terrible calamity, but I refuse to weep for my son. I gave him to his country, my only son, he was all I had to give—the widow's mite—but I would give him again if the call arose. I am proud of his blindness and his disability. The sight of him will be an object lesson to the men who have allowed others to fight their battles for them. If the sight of his blindness shames one of the cowards then he has not suffered vainly. As Shakespeare puts it :—

> " ' And gentlemen in England now abed,
> Shall call themselves accursed they were not here,
> And hold their manhood cheap whiles any speaks
> That fought with us,' etc.

"No, Nellie, I hold my head proudly, as befits the English mother of an English soldier, and I thank God for blessing me among all women for

NOT SO QUIET . . .

mothering a hero, an M.C. My brave, brave boy.

> " With love,
>> " ETHEL EVANS-MAWNINGTON."

" DEAR NELL,

" The nurse is writing this for obvious reasons. Mother will have told you about my eyes and my leg, but there is something she hasn't told you because she doesn't know. There will never be any perambulator on that lawn of ours, Nell. You understand ? I couldn't expect you to marry me. You're brick enough to stand the blindness and the limp, but the other is too much to ask any woman. So I release you from your promise.

" I suppose they've told you of the M.C. If I was writing this myself I'd tell you what they could do with it.

" Don't worry about me, Nell ; I don't really care. I haven't cared about anything for a long time. I only wish to Christ they'd left me another five minutes in the trench.

> " Yours,
>> " ROY."

I pick up my pen slowly.

"DEAR ROY,

"Don't be a silly ass. I hate kids, anyway. Yours in haste to catch the post,

"NELL."

   •   •   •   •   •

"Air raid!"

I collect my blankets and mattress methodically as usual and don my coat and hat and muffler. It is the ninth raid in succession since the moon came this month. From a pale crescent she has grown into a rakish silver ball. She is the most aggressively radiant moon I have ever seen. The night is clear and cold and cloudless, without a breath of wind. An ideal night for a raid. Outside the girls are hastily falling in, ready for roll-call. Cheery, Misery and Blimey fall in beside me. They are laughing and chattering. We are so accustomed to this sort of thing that we regard it merely as an infernal nuisance. Familiarity breeds contempt. Our shelter is lined with sandbags and earth, and unless the man in the machine scores a bull's-eye nothing can harm us. We know it is difficult to make a direct hit from the air. So let's make the best of life. Cheery has a tin of toffee, Blimey and I have some biscuits and chocolate, while Misery has the inevitable crochet work which she can do as ably in the dark as in the light.

"March!"

We stagger forth, stumbling and giggling with our cumbersome loads. A mile is not a long distance, but Army biscuit mattresses are no joke to carry for any length of time. We arrive gasping. There is no sign of the enemy planes as yet . . . the warning has been given in excellent time. We settle ourselves comfortably. I find a cosy corner, and Cheery, Misery and Blimey drape themselves comfortably round me. They like being near me during raids because I am " always the same."

Misery immediately starts a frenzied assault on the bedspread, while Cheery and Blimey, *sotto voce*, in case a forewoman hears, begin to chi-ack her about the wedding night with Fred. They accuse her of " knowing all about it," of having already had intimate relations with Fred. She ignores this. To their chagrin she is not to be drawn to-night.

" I betcher Fred's 'avin' a good old 'ot time in the ole town to-night with some of them munition girls," says Blimey, slyly digging me in the calf. " 'Ot stuff, them munitioners. I betcher old Fred's 'ot stuff w'en 'e gets loose, too."

This annoys Misery, as it invariably does.

" Ere, you leave my Fred be," she retorts. " 'E's never 'ad nout to do with no woman yet, 'as my Fred. 'E's a pure man."

" Blimey ! A 'e-virgin," teases Blimey. " Fancy

233

marryin' a feller 'oo's goin' to practise on yer, Misery. I . . ."

" Hark ! " interrupts Misery. " Hark ! "

The enemy planes have come within earshot. Buzz, buzz, buzz . . . like a giant hive of giant bees.

" Bigger fleet than ever to-night."

The gossip and the laughter die down to a murmur, then gradually fade away altogether. We sit there in the semi-darkness waiting. It is not the most pleasant sensation in the world sitting in a shelter waiting for bombs to drop. Even though the odds are a hundred to one against a direct hit, it is a nasty feeling . . . like anticipating a dentist's drill, or making a speech in public, or hearing a burglar trying an insecure window-catch . . . apprehensive, uncertain what may happen next.

Now the picnic has started. The bombs are falling thick and fast, each explosion nearer. Worse to-night than they have ever been, we whisper. We whisper the same thing every night. In the half-light I can see Misery's fingers working rapidly . . . in and out she wriggles the crochet hook, her voice murmuring . . . " Two chain, three treble, two double crochet, four treble, turn, two chain. . . ." Her plain, gaunt, absorbed face bends over the work as though she can see the pattern plainly. She has been working on the bedspread for eighteen months . . . another six months and it will be ready for her and Fred. "*If* the war ends then, but wot 'ope?" says Misery, always the perfect pessimist.

There is a terrific explosion, startling in its unexpectedness, like a frightful peal of thunder, followed by a rain of shots. We know what that is . . . machine guns aimed from the air at some target after the bomb has scored a hit. We sit up. Hardly have we recovered from the shock than there is another ear-splitting explosion . . . nearer. More machine-gun fire follows it. Now we see the machines overhead, outlined black against the clear sky. The bombs are dropping all round the trench. Our ears are ringing. We are all deathly quiet now, watching . . . all but Misery, who crochets for dear life. Another bomb and another hail of machine-gun fire. We stare at one another, not daring to ask what we are all thinking.

Have they found our trench? Are they aiming at us? They seem to be concentrating dead on us. Usually they make for the soldiers' encampment to the right or the woods to the left, but to-night is different. Another ear-splitting explosion. A flash of flame. That was very near. The noise of the engines is near, too. They are flying very low to-night.

235

Ploo-oop. Crash ! Through the half-light our eyes seek one another, startled. We listen. Four engines. We can count them distinctly. Four bombers flying low over our trench. Someone asks what our own planes are doing to let the raiders through like this, dropping their bombs like rain, deafening us until our heads are pounding and our ear-drums throbbing.

" Put that blarsted crochay away," whispers Blimey harshly. " Fair get on my nerves you do, crochayin' as though they was playin' marbles up there with them bombs ; gettin' on everybody's nerves you are with yer rotten crochay. . . ."

Ploo-op. Crash !

The end of the trench suddenly collapses with a roar. There is a flash of flame outside. The sand-bags cave in slowly as though coming to a mighty decision before falling. The bomb has caught the end of the trench. Five feet to the left and the airman would have scored a direct hit. One of the girls is hit—bleeding. The others begin to panic and huddle together at the other end. The plane comes down in a swoop, lower, lower . . . engine roaring. We can see his bombs hanging below the wings. Lower, lower . . . another bomb is unleashed. It falls in the middle of the trench. There is a mighty explosion, a flash of flame, an ear-splitting percussion that knocks me flat on the ground. Something falls on me. I lose consciousness. When I come to girls are screaming all round me . . . the air is filled with the groans of the dying. Something heavy is lying across my legs. With difficulty I remove it. It is a sandbag. I stand up. My mouth is full of dirt, but I am not hurt. Beside me lies Cheery . . . she is quite dead. The top of her head is blown off and one of her hands is missing. She looks as though she has tried to shield her face. Blimey is bleeding from a wound in the arm . . . the blood is pouring from it. " Now see wot's 'appened to me new Burberry, all covered in blood. Now see wot's 'appened to me new Burberry, all covered in blood," she keeps muttering, holding her arm out to divert the stream from her clothing to the ground. I cannot see Misery anywhere. There is a pile of earth and wood where she has been sitting. Madly I begin to dig, with bare hands. I find an edge of the crochet work—she is not far from it. I manage to get her out. I raise her head. She is alive . . . just. She cannot speak. Her lips open and shut soundlessly. She wants something. I hand her the crochet work. A look of content comes over her plain face. The crochet bedspread will never be finished by Misery. She dies as I watch her.

The trench is like a slaughterhouse. All round me girls are lying dead or dying. Some are wounded.

The wounded are trying to staunch one another's blood. A few are shell-shocked. One scales the side of the shelter frantically, scrabbling and digging her toes into the earth like a maddened animal, then runs shrieking into the night. In the distance the buzz of the planes grows fainter and fainter. The raiders have been beaten off at last.

I tie Blimey's arm. She nearly fights me as I tear strips from her petticoat to bind the artery. At last voices are heard. Soldiers from the camp rush on the scene, cursing and blaspheming at the sight of the mangled women.

The roll is called. The casualties are heavy. Ten dead, two missing, twenty-four injured. Four are unhurt, and of these three are shell-shocked. I am the only woman out of forty to escape.

The ambulances are coming. The dead are lying neatly in a row. The wounded lie beside them. Soldiers are trying to dress their wounds. Blimey is unconscious from loss of blood. Her Burberry will never be any use again. Misery and Cheery lie at my feet. Misery is clasping her unfinished crochet bedspread. Cheery looks curiously naked without her right hand. The stump of her arm is still shielding her face.

A soldier comes over to where I am sitting on the side of the trench.

"Well, you wasn't meant to die to-night," he says.

I turn my head in his direction and begin to laugh softly. He is alarmed.

"Can't get you a drink, can I? You're not hysterical nor nothing?"

I tell him no. I have never felt less hysterical in my life.

. . . . .

Her soul died under a radiant silver moon in the spring of 1918 on the side of a blood-spattered trench. Around her lay the mangled dead and the dying. Her body was untouched, her heart beat calmly, the blood coursed as ever through her veins. But looking deep into those emotionless eyes one wondered if they had suffered much before the soul had left them. Her face held an expression of resignation, as though she had ceased to hope that the end might come.

239

AFTERWORD
CORPUS/CORPS/CORPSE: WRITING THE
BODY IN/AT WAR

A declaration of war should be a kind of popular festival with entrance-tickets and bands, like a bull fight. Then in the arena the ministers and generals of the two countries, dressed in bathing-drawers and armed with clubs, can have it out among themselves. Whoever survives, his country wins. That would be much simpler and more just than this arrangement, where the wrong people do the fighting.

Erich Maria Remarque
All Quiet on the Western Front

Any day and in every way this can be seen, eating and vomiting and war.

Gertrude Stein
Wars I Have Seen

1. *La Zone Interdite*

The body itself. The body of writing about the body. The body of writing about war. The body of men's writing about the war. The

241

body of women's writing about the war. The body under stress. The body in duress. The sleepless body. The hungry body. The body in uniform. The body under fire. Bodies maimed, wounded, and killed. Bodies sexed and unsexed by war. . . . The Corps. The body of fighting men . . . or women. Bodies of bodies. Dying bodies. Dead bodies. Bodies without faces. Arms without bodies. Cannon fodder. Dead mutton. Bodies with dysentery. Abortion. War babies. The body of the Kaiser. The War Office as a body. The body of a comrade. Foreign bodies. The body of the enemy. The ludicrous body of the Commandant. A lover's sweet body. The jaundiced body of the lesbian. The cancerous body of the mother. The shuddering body of shell shock. Artificial limbs and prosthetic devices. The frozen body. The body with chilblains. The dream of the body at home in bed. The mustard-gassed body vomiting out its lungs. The body transporting other bodies. The body mending the broken body. The body numb. The body abject and the body erect, killing and being killed. Half-dead bodies of prisoners of war. The gangrenous body. Mad bodies. Bodies in blood, shit, and vomit.

The purpose of this essay is to change the subject of critical focus on the erotics of war to the un/gendered body in pain. I do not simply valorize the feminine over the masculine war narrative, but rather wish to recover the lost voices, the cultural "music," as Gertrude Stein says, of a noisy war.

Helen Zenna Smith's *Not So Quiet . . .* (1930) is a book about the body. Specifically, it chronicles the experience of a corps of six English gentlewomen, whose average age is twenty-one, as they drive field ambulances of wounded men picked up by trains at the Front to hospitals set up just behind the fighting lines in what Mary Borden has also memorialized as "the forbidden zone" in France in 1918.[1] Their war is not a popular festival, like Erich Maria

242

Remarque's in *All Quiet on the Western Front*.[2] It is a grotesque parody of the "brotherhood" felt by the German men, an inversion of "sisterhood." Helen and her companions are volunteer ambulance drivers. They, like V.A.D. (Volunteer Aid Detachment) nurses, have actually paid for the privilege of serving at the Front, their patriotic upper-class families proud to sacrifice daughters as well as sons for the war effort, providing their passage money and their uniforms, sending packages of cocoa and carbolic body belts to keep off the lice.

These body belts, personal disinfectants, always fighting a losing battle against the invasion of delicately bred female bodies by lice and fleas, worn between skin and rough clothing, suggest a "forbidden zone" on the body, dividing upper and lower, the spiritual and the physical. They remind us of chastity belts with which men of an earlier age "protected" the bodies of their womenfolk from invasion by other men when they went off to war, an age when women's bodies were clearly defined as the property of men. Like the forbidden zone itself, marked neutral by signs and barbed wire, an unholy territory of dead and dying men, the wounded and their hospitals, the ambulance drivers and V.A.D. nurses were marked out for the most polluted of war work. Like gravediggers in peacetime they were shunned by the society whose dirty work they did. They were neither the "ladies" they had been brought up to be, nor were they paid professionals like working-class nurses in the Women's Army Auxiliary Corps (W.A.A.C.s) or Women's Royal Naval Service (W.R.E.N.s), respected and rewarded for their labor. They were both terrorized and scorned by women in the regular armed services, precisely because they were volunteers but also because they were ladies exposed to the most acute

243

physical horrors, suffering themselves under severe hardships, for which a comfortable life at home with servants had hardly prepared them. They made everyone except their patriotic parents at home feel ashamed.

Like a company of Wagnerian Valkyries (though, of course, they would not have made such a Germanic comparison themselves) the ambulance drivers resembled Amazon goddesses, carrying slain soldiers from the battlefield to glory in Valhalla or to hospitals where they could recover to fight again. European intellectuals welcomed the war as a mystical purification of decadence, a revolution against greed and materialism. Women would, as usual, clean up the mess. The ambulances were the mythical horses of the modern Valkyries, and the women drivers cared for their engines as if they were horses. Transporting the dead or dying is a dangerous job, but it has also always been invested with mythological significance. The ferryman who guards the borders of life and death is a ghostly figure in our cultural myths. This corps of ferrywomen seems unreal as well, ghosts whose bodies had disappeared from history until revived by the reprinting of *Not So Quiet . . . .* (For photographs of women engaged in various kinds of war work see Diana Condell and Jean Liddiard's *Working for Victory?: Images of Women in the First World War,* London: Routledge and Kegan Paul, 1987.) All motor vehicles were rare and glamorous creatures at this time and driving itself a male and upper-class activity. In stiff-upper-lipped long-suffering bravery, the women had to be superhuman, driving for weeks on three hours of sleep a night, eating spoiled food, and very little of that (no decent Army rations for volunteers). They became experts at the geography of hell, driving at night with their lights off in the freezing cold and snow (the cabs were open to the elements, the backs of the lorries covered with canvas) with their loads of screaming and moaning wounded.

One assumes that the War Office counted on class codes of honor to keep the women from telling or writing what they had seen or heard. *Not So Quiet . . .* brilliantly broke the sound barrier about what "Our Splendid Women" had really seen and heard and done in the war, offending all of those who had blocked their ears. When *Not So Quiet . . .* was published, one English reviewer suggested that it be burned (but the French gave it the Prix Severigne as "the novel most calculated to promote international peace"). Young, healthy, well-educated women became the charwomen of the battlefield, the cleaners of the worst human waste we produce, the symbolic bearers of all its pollution and disease. Like the mythological ferryman, their bodies became *La Zone Interdite,* for themselves as well as for those who sent them to the battlefields, forbidden, dangerous, polluted carriers of a terrible knowledge. This knowledge effectively separated them from the complacent, jingoist Home Front and the mobile battle fronts, which left these polluted zones behind as they moved on.

Because women's role in World War I and women's writing about that war is just beginning to receive attention, I want to begin with a discussion of the issues surrounding historical and literary revaluation. In particular, because *Not So Quiet . . .* is not in any sense an example of *écriture feminine* but a textual deconstruction of gender stereotypes in writing, it is important to place it in relation to other women's war writing.

In 1929, the American V.A.D. nurse, Mary Borden, published poems and sketches written during 1914–18 when she was with the French Army, along with five stories

245

written after the war: "I have called the collection of
fragments 'The Forbidden Zone' because the strip of land
immediately behind the zone of fire where I was stationed
went by that name in the French Army. We were moved up
and down inside it; our hospital unit was shifted from
Flanders to the Somme, then to Champagne, and then
back again to Belgium, but we never left 'La Zone
Interdite.' "[2] The horrors of the forbidden territories also
extended to an unspoken ban on writing about it—Enid
Bagnold was dismissed from her V.A.D. post after publish-
ing *A Diary without Dates* in 1918.[3] Both of these collections
of fragments document women's wartime experience in
essentially "feminine" voices. Serious literary achievements, the books are marked by the fragmentation and
dislocation of poignant love/war battles and the romantic
and chivalric, almost religious, ethos of self-sacrifice. Enid
Bagnold is proud that her nursing ability brings order and
tranquillity to a hospital full of wounded men. Like a nun,
she domesticates devastation. She writes:

> I lay my spoons and forks. Sixty-five trays. It takes an hour
> to do. Thirteen pieces on each tray. Thirteen times sixty-
> five . . . eight hundred and forty-five things to collect, lay,
> square up symmetrically. I make little absurd reflections
> and arrangements—taking a dislike to the knives because
> they will not lie still on the polished metal of the tray, but
> pivot on their shafts, and swing out at angles after my
> fingers have left them.[4]

Her pride in gleaming trays and scrubbed corridors is
obviously a small human success after the failure to bring
such healing graces to the suffering soldiers. (The knives
will truly never lie still.) The women drivers in her later *The
Happy Foreigner* are as attentive to the material objects in
246

their charge—the cars they drive for the French Army—
and the heroine puts a whole village to work making a
dress for her to wear to a dance with a French officer.

Mary Borden's book is equally interesting on an aesthetic level. While Bagnold's voice is lyrically nostalgic and
romantic, despite the chronicle of hardship for volunteer
nurses, Borden is a modernist, obviously influenced by
Gertrude Stein. She carried Stein and Flaubert to the
Front with her, and *The Forbidden Zone* speaks in her flat
Chicago accent. It is hallucinatory and yet detached. The
voice seems submerged in the unconscious like a nightmare that numbs with repetition. She, too, turns to
material objects for solace at the sight of maimed men:

I had received by post that same morning a dozen beautiful
new platinum needles. I was very pleased with them. I said
to one of the dressers as I fixed a needle on my syringe and
held it up, squirting the liquid through it: "Look. I've got
some lovely new needles." He said: "Come and help me a
moment. Just cut this bandage, please." I went over to his
dressing table. He darted off to a voice that was shrieking
somewhere. There was a man stretched on the table. His
brain came off in my hands when I lifted the bandage from
his head. When the dresser came back I said: "His brain
came off on the bandage." "Where have you put it?" "I put
it in the pail under the table." "It's only one half of his
brain," he said, looking into the man's skull. "The rest is
here." I left him to finish the dressing and went about my
own business. I had much to do. It was my business to sort
out the wounded as they were brought in from the
ambulances and to keep them from dying before they got to
the operating rooms: It was my business to sort out the
nearly dying from the dying. I was there to sort them and
tell how fast life was ebbing in them. Life was leaking away
from all of them; but with some there was no hurry, with

247

others it was a case of minutes. It was my business to create a counter-wave of life, to create the flow against the ebb. It was like a tug of war with the tide.[5]

The repetition of the word "business" in such circumstances and the brief emotionless descriptive sentences mark a detachment that has a calculated effect on the reader. We understand her pleasure in her new needles. Borden simply cannot bear the burden of womanhood and continue to work with wounded men: "It is impossible to be a woman here. One must be dead."

There are no men here, so why should I be a woman? There are heads and knees and mangled testicles. There are chests with holes as big as your fist, and pulpy thighs, shapeless; and stumps where legs once were fastened. There are eyes—eyes of sick dogs, sick cats, blind eyes, eyes of delirium; and mouths that cannot articulate; and parts of faces—the nose gone, or the jaw. There are these things, but no men . . .[6]

The fragmented bodies of men are reproduced in the fragmented parts of women's war texts, the texts themselves a "forbidden zone" long ignored by historians and literary critics. Writers of war produce pieces of texts, like parts of a body that will never be whole. The texts are specific to World War I and the kinds of warfare specific to that particularly horrible war and its mutilation of millions of bodies. They wrote the body of war, the wounded soldier's body and their own newly sexualized (only to be numbed) bodies as well as the effect of war on the body politic. The textual fragmentation marks the pages of their books as the forbidden zone of writing what hasn't been written before, and their books actually look like battlefields where the body of Mother Earth has been torn apart by shells and bombs. The works of Mary Borden and Enid Bagnold cited above are not exceptional. There are many important women war writers. A materialist analysis of the fragmented texts would look immediately to the passage in Irene Rathbone's *We That Were Young* (1932) that excruciatingly details the step-by-step process by which a nurse removes fragments of shrapnel from a soldier's wound. (*We That Were Young* has also been reprinted by The Feminist Press, 1989.) One might then observe that the fragmentation described as typical of modernist texts has an origin in the writing practice of women nurses and ambulance drivers. The recent discovery and reprinting of many "lost" examples of women's war writing by Virago and The Feminist Press may be linked to the work of feminist scholars in many disciplines over the last fifteen years. This work ranges from psychological studies of gender and aggression; to new historical studies of pacifism; to philosophical treatises, such as Nancy Huston's provocative essay on the relation between war and motherhood, which argues that men make war *because* women make babies.[7]

The study of World War I and its effect on women in England begins with the acknowledgment that all wars destroy women's culture, returning women to the restricted roles of childbearing and nursing and only that work that helps the war effort. The struggle for women's own political equality becomes almost treasonous in wartime. World War I practically destroyed the women's movement in England, a struggle of nearly fifty years in education, for the vote, marriage, and divorce and child custody legislation, in labor laws—an extraordinary mass movement of women demanding political justice and equality. Any

249

account of women's wartime energetic and responsible performance of social labor must recognize that that performance in the public sphere came from the previous struggle against an immensely hostile state to win the elements of education, knowledge, and skills that any democracy today customarily grants its citizens, but which, in Edwardian England, were systematically denied to half the population. The self-education in political organization, public speaking, social work, and other areas that thousands of English women *provided for themselves*, in opposition to the ruthless repression of the Liberal government, as they worked tirelessly in the suffrage movement is the source of such strengths commonly attributed by historians to a mythical "natural" female ethic of heroic self-sacrifice.[8]

In the *Daily Chronicle* in 1916, Rebecca West reminded her readers that it was "the rough and tumble" of the suffrage movement that hardened women for their wartime tasks:

> The story of the Scottish Suffrage Societies' Hospital in Serbia and Rumania is immortal. The biggest factory in France which supplies an article most necessary to our armies is under the sole charge of a woman under thirty, who was formerly a suffrage organiser. One could cite many such cases. And one doubts that women would have gone into the dangerous high explosive factories, the engineering shops and the fields, and worked with quite such fidelity and enthusiasm if it had not been so vigorously affirmed by the suffragists in the last few years that women ought to be independent and courageous and capable.[9]

We cannot assume that it was easy for this newly transformed feminist consciousness, on the collective level, to give up the struggle for freedom, despite the alacrity with which Emmeline Pankhurst and her daughter, Christabel, the militant suffrage leaders, began to harrass conscientious objectors, or the fact that many women did identify with the ethic of self-sacrifice and produced books urging nursing and ambulance driving as opportunities for the full expression of the female need to suffer. But Rebecca West and other (especially left wing) feminist theorists had already punched holes before the war in the idea of self-sacrifice as natural to women, and there is no reason to suppose that these brilliant deflations of the reigning ideology were so easily forgotten. And yet, even feminists "forgot." One agrees with Rebecca West's assessment of May Sinclair's *Journal of Impressions in Belgium* as "one of the few books of permanent value produced by the war." It should be read as a companion volume to *Not So Quiet* . . . . But her novel, *The Romantic,* mocks the unmanly man as viciously as scandalized old ladies wrote to the papers about "She-men" in uniforms.

Certainly F. Tennyson Jesse's *The Sword of Deborah* (1919) is sheer propaganda for recruiting V.A.D.s and W.A.A.C.s: "How could we bear to do nothing when the men are doing the most wonderful thing in the world?" And Charlotte Redhead in May Sinclair's *The Romantic* (1920) seems to support Sandra Gilbert's thesis that women rose at the expense of man's fall when she rejects John Conway, her lover, because of his cowardice (and her own fear-lessness) as they drive field ambulances in Belgium. It seems just as logical to suppose that women who had fought in the streets to protect and demand votes for women should be ready for action at the Front. Obviously, war values dispensed horrifying shame to men who were deemed cowards. Early in the war Rose Macaulay wrote

251

"Oh, it's you that have the luck, out there in the blood and muck/. . . . In a trench you are sitting, while I am knitting/ A hopeless sock that never gets done."[10]

But May Sinclair in *The Romantic* created a realistically revengeful portrait of the weak male from the point of view of the strong female. Why did gender distinctions keep her from action? Charlotte's psychoanalyst condemns Conway. A more human analysis would allow more room for men lacking in the brutal, aggressive qualities required for war:

> Conway was an out and out degenerate. He couldn't help *that*. He suffered from some physical disability. It went through everything. It made him so that he couldn't live a man's life. He was afraid to enter a profession. He was afraid of women . . . the balance had to be righted somehow. His whole life must have been a struggle to right it. Unconscious, of course. Instinctive. His platonics were just a glorifying of his disability. All that romancing was a gorgeous transformation of his funk . . . so that his very lying was a sort of truth. I mean it was part of the whole desperate effort after completion. He jumped at everything that helped him to get compensation, to get power. He jumped at your feeling for him because it gave him power. He sucked manhood out of you. He sucked it out of everything—out of blood and wound.[11]

There it is. In wartime, the impotent male is a vampire. The language of popular psychology joins the discourse of martial valor—degenerate, disability, funk, jumped, sucked—to condemn those who don't fit the most polarized gender categories. Men must be potent. Women must be maternal. Sinclair's voicing of the popular fear of male weakness in war also reveals the unspoken truth that men were just as terrified of war as women. Virginia Woolf valorizes the impotent suicidal Septimus Smith in *Mrs.*

Dalloway. And Sylvia Townsend Warner brilliantly mocks the enforced rigidity of wartime sex roles in her splendid poem, "Cottage Mantleshelf," which celebrates the "uncomely" portrait of "young Osbert who died at the war," a "nancy boy" with enormous ears, whose "beseeching swagger" endears him to the reader. The poem is an English "red and black" tribute to a victim of the ideology, "Keep the home fires burning."[12]

Joan Scott's introductory essay in *Behind the Lines* is the most sophisticated guide to date to a methodology for feminist historiography in the service of a cultural critique. She warns against facile reversals of established theories, the projection of present concerns onto the past, and the simple search for heroines. Women's literature of World War I runs the gamut from patriotic propaganda to pacifist protest. For all those who jeered at conscientious objectors and handed them white feathers, there were also the founders of the Women's International League for Peace and Freedom. Artistic standards will have to acknowledge the greatness of "Cottage Mantleshelf" as well as much other writing by women about the war, now that patriotism no longer dictates that the combatant's writing is superior to that of the noncombatant. We need to examine the war ministries' posters and propaganda images of men and women for all the countries involved in the war, to contextualize German and French writing with British fiction and the autobiographies of American volunteer nurses.

The effort to expand the literary canon is greatly aided by publishers such as The Feminist Press and Virago Press in reprinting lost texts. The reprinting of Katharine Burdekin's *Swastika Night,* a feminist dystopia from the thirties, for example, allows for fresh and interesting ways to read George Orwell's classic *1984* and to view Nazi ideology from the perspective of its misogyny, a neglected area since historians have concentrated particularly on anti-Semitism. While I intend here to propose a reading of Helen Zenna Smith's *Not So Quiet . . .* in conjunction with Erich Maria Remarque's classic *All Quiet on the Western Front,* on which it was based, a more thorough examination of the issues raised would have to take into account the French and Belgian women's experiences of invasion and bombardment. Dorothy Canfield's *Home Fires in France* (1919), a collection of short stories, might be analyzed, as well as Colette's wartime newspaper articles.

Women's history asks that we look not only at war texts but at those particular fictions where suffrage and war overlap and intermix. There are some excellent examples: Cecily Hamilton's *William, An Englishman,* May Sinclair's *The Tree of Heaven,* and Ford Maddox Ford's *Some Do Not* and *No More Parades,* the Tietjens novels, which tell the same events from different characters' viewpoints, wonderfully deconstructing the meanings of feminism, patriotism, marriage, war, religion, and all the social issues of the period. These novels are perhaps the best literary representations of all the issues under discussion here. Ford himself seems to have been anything but an admirable character, but his brilliant modernist fictional techniques, in particular the undermining of narrative authority, schooling his readers in the unreliability of all narratives, evoke the instability of an age of conflicting values more powerfully than the more valorized work of T. S. Eliot or Ezra Pound. In addition, these novels, like Irene Rathbone's *We That Were Young,* allow the reader to escape from the standard historical confines of wartime and peacetime. Rathbone's later *They Call It Peace* (1936) in fact decon-
254

structs this convenient historical fiction, showing that the government continued to wage war against women and the working class "between the wars."

William, An Englishman is another story. Cecily Hamilton had certainly earned her credentials as an active suffragette and had written plays and polemics for the cause. Yet its "feminism" is disturbing, despite the fact that it won the Femina Prize in 1919. "Neither William nor Griselda had ever entertained the idea of a European War; it was not entertained by any of their friends or their pamphlets." William and Griselda are socialists and activists in the suffrage campaign. He, a clerk, inherits a small amount of money from his mother and throws himself into political action and public speaking, "a ferment of protestation and grievance." Griselda, a suburban suffragette, is attracted to him because of the pleasure they share in denouncing the enemies of their cause. Hamilton's ruthless satire of political activists is amusing, for we all know the type— "cocksure, contemptuous, intolerant, self-sacrificing after the manner of their kind." Their punishment for not knowing the war has begun when they go off to honeymoon in Belgium is a little excessive. Moved to leave their woodland retreat because Griselda "missed the weekly temper into which she worked herself in sympathy with her weekly *Suffragette*," they are devastated by seeing the Germans shoot innocent villagers. She is raped and he is put in a work camp. Escaping to find her again, William is horrified by her silence; then, melodramatically, "she died very quietly in the straw at the bottom of the cart."

Hamilton rather overdoes the death of Griselda as "real" suffering compared to her previous choice to hunger strike and be forcibly fed in Holloway Gaol for the cause of suffrage. The newly patriotic William is rejected

255

by the British Army and dies unheroically in a bombing raid. This novel is a shameless example of the ideological repression of both socialism and feminism that was one of the major social achievements of World War I. Certainly in England, the war was a stunning setback to the struggle for liberty at home. Arthur Marwick's *The Deluge: British Society and the First World War* (Norton, 1970) is the honorable exception to histories of the war that ignore "the forbidden zone" of the class struggle and the repression of women. His *Women at War* (Fontana, 1977), along with Gail Braybon's *Women Workers in the First World War* (Croom Helm, 1981) and Anne Wiltsher's *Most Dangerous Women: Feminist Peace Campaigners of the Great War* (Pandora, 1986), have trespassed quite firmly on the forbidden zone of World War I history. For other examples of how quickly the European intellectuals rallied around their respective flags, see Roland N. Stromberg's *Redemption by War: The Intellectuals and 1914* (The Regents Press of Kansas, 1982), though he doesn't include women among the "intellectuals."

Like Hamilton's *William, An Englishman,* the insularity of the ordinary English folk is also the point of H. G. Wells's *Mr. Britling Sees It Through,* but suffrage again becomes the scapegoat in May Sinclair's *The Tree of Heaven* (1917). Frances and Anthony refuse to face up to the Boer War, but they and their children eventually reject suffrage and pacifism and movements for political justice at home for an almost evangelical devotion to "the Great War of Redemption." All the authors cited here (male and female) were active in the suffrage campaign. Their fiction is the field on which we may see a great ideological battle fought, where the struggle for sexual freedom becomes "silly" and the leaders, like the Pankhursts, are called proto-fascists as the war mentality condones militarism, nationalism, and patriotism. On the pages of these obscure novels we see how quickly the intellectuals come to the aid of their country, embracing violence and war as a mystical cleansing, rejecting the feminist, pacifist, and socialist reforms needed at home to agree to internationalist slaughter of a whole generation in the name of democracy. Stromberg documents the ideology of destruction as spiritual and idealistic renewal. The authoritarian nature of the ideological powers to which this generation submitted is then displaced onto a critique of authoritarianism within the suffrage movement (perhaps out of guilt for their joy in war (?) and abandonment of the struggle for real social change at home).

This is not to argue that there was not some justice in the earlier claim by Mrs. Charlotte Despard and the Women's Freedom League that the Women's Social and Political Union (W.S.P.U.) was an autocratic paramilitary organization. In many ways it was. But those young women who had pledged total commitment to the suffrage cause and obedience to its leaders, who had learned to speak in public, to defy their families and the law to march in the streets, who had been attacked by hecklers and ruffians, gone on hunger strikes in prison, and been forcibly fed were the perfect recruits for war work. They were disciplined and self-controlled. It has always seemed to me very curious that historians do not mention the suffrage campaign as the training ground for ambulance drivers and V.A.D. nurses in World War I. Bravery, physical courage, chivalry, group solidarity, strategic planning, honor—women learned these skills in the streets and gaols of London, the *first* "forbidden zone" they entered. The spiritual and sacramental aspects of the suffrage movement

257

as a "holy war" were exploited by idealist figurations of the war as a purge of bourgeois materialism.

Then again, historians also neglect to mention that the work of these women—glamorous heroines to younger generations—was for a long time rejected by the British government. "My good lady, go home and sit still" was what the War Office told the distinguished Dr. Elsie Inglis when she offered them a fully staffed medical unit with women doctors and nurses![13] The French government hired her to take this staff to Serbia. Cecily Hamilton remarked in her autobiography that the British were so opposed to hospitals *run* by women that all the women's hospital units were employed by the Allies, France and Russia, and operated in France, in the Balkans, and in Russia. These fully trained groups of women doctors and nurses were far less popular than volunteer upper-class girls who could be shown in uniform in the picture papers, glamorous, pretty, and clearly unprofessional. The "Balkanization" of British women doctors and nurses in Serbia and Russia may be seen as part of the larger historical repression of the Eastern Front in favor of the story of Western Europe in histories of the war. The Eastern Front is the female "other" of World War I history. Where all is *really* quiet is on the Eastern Front, perhaps because attention to the other Front would mean attention to the other back—that is, the background of capitalism and imperialism and colonialism that were behind the curtain of the European theatre of war. This is echoed in *Mrs. Dalloway* when Lady Bruton espouses the cause of the Armenians and, fearing that she will not be taken seriously as a woman, convinces Richard Dalloway and other important men to help her frame her letter to the London *Times*.

258

These oppositions—Western Front/Eastern Front, manly/womanly, professional/volunteer, patriot/feminist—need to be undone along with others that reinforce them—male/female, killer/coward, martyr/traitor—as we recover the history of women in this period along with the class and gender biases that intersect with them. Looking back, we can see the message in May Sinclair's 1917 satire on Christabel Pankhurst—the hysterical man-hating Miss Dorothy Blackadder in *The Tree of Heaven*—as sheer propaganda for the authority of the nation, party, and government that had oppressed women. Dorothy "was afraid of the Feminist Vortex. . . . She was afraid of the herded women. She disliked the excited faces, and the high voices skirling their battle-cries, and the silly business of committees, and the platform slang. She was sick and shy before the tremor and surge of collective feeling; she loathed the gestures and the movements of the collective soul, the swaying and heaving forward of the many as one."[14] There is nothing like an appeal to individualism and personal freedom to sway the reader. Examine the skillful rhetoric of this passage, as a "feminist" discredits her own movement. The class bias against the masses, human beings in the collective, is unabashed. What else was service in the war but joining a similar "herd," swirling in a far more destructive "vortex"? It was "women in the collective," struggling for their own freedom, who were now marked as Public Enemy No. 1. This propaganda was so effective that another ex-suffragette, Amber Blanco White, was able to argue later in the thirties that the suffragettes had actually brought dangerous fascist (read "foreign") political techniques to "democratic" England. (Blame the victim. Name the freedom-fighter as a fascist. Re-inscribe the mass hysteria of war as individual heroism.)[15]

259

From a literary perspective, the reprinting of women's wartime writing will also allow us to contextualize the canon, reading *A Farewell to Arms* along with the experience of an American nurse, Ellen La Motte, whose powerful *The Backwash of War: The Human Wreckage of the Battlefield as Witnessed by an American Nurse* (1916) was banned during the war and not reprinted until 1934.[16] La Motte's prose style stands up to Ernest Hemingway's, drained of emotion and restrained before the bodies of wounded men:

> From the operating room they are brought into the wards, these bandaged heaps from the operating tables, these heaps that once were men. The clean beds of the ward are turned back to receive them, to receive the motionless, bandaged heaps that are lifted, shoved or rolled from the stretchers to the beds.[17]

We could also read Richard Aldington's *Death of a Hero* with H. D.'s *Bid Me to Live* or Irene Rathbone's *We That Were Young* (which Aldington supposedly got published), H. G. Wells's *Mr. Britling Sees It Through* with Amber Reeves's *Give and Take* or E. M. Delafield's *The War Workers*, Robert Graves's *Goodbye to All That* with Laura Riding's *A Trojan Ending*, Siegfried Sassoon's *Memoirs of a Fox-Hunting Man* with Sylvia Thompson's *The Hounds of Spring*. Virginia Woolf's *Mrs. Dalloway* and *Jacob's Room* and Rebecca West's *The Return of the Soldier* are already being read as classic feminist anti-war novels. Their distinguishing feature is the insertion of class into the narrative of war and gender. It is the class critique that also distinguishes Helen Zenna Smith's *Not So Quiet . . .* from much other women's war fiction, as a relentlessly realistic document in brutally masculinized prose of what war does to women at the Front. Not only does this brilliant novel overturn the stereotypes of "male" writing and "female" writing by writing from the subject position of the masculinized woman (as Erich Remarque writes from the subject position of the feminized soldier in *All Quiet on the Western Front*), it unforgettably inscribes better than any other fiction I know the female body in/at war. The hero of *A Farewell to Arms* (1925) is embarrassed by the words "sacred," "glorious," and "sacrifice." The heroine of *Not So Quiet . . .* is also driven mad by patriotic words. The corruption of language is war's first casualty. Hemingway writes *"There were many words that you could not stand to hear* [italics added] and finally only the names of places had dignity."[18]

2. *Ears Only*

Governments stamp their secret documents "Eyes Only." I call this section "Ears Only" to mark the experience of war in *Not So Quiet . . .* as a violation of the ear drums and Helen Zenna Smith's writing as a bombardment of the reader's ears in a text pock-marked with ellipses of silence and rushes of noisy belligerent words. Despite Mary Cadogan and Patricia Craig's dismissal of this novel and its sequels as "crude" socialist realism and "emotional melodrama," the genius of *Not So Quiet . . .* lies in its unswervingly truthful reportage of a war that was both crude and emotionally melodramatic, its prose style revealing the death of the feminine sentence, or at least exposing the myth that writing comes from gender rather than experience. I mean these remarks about the assault on the ears as a compliment, of course. In *Paris France* (1940) Gertrude Stein characterized the experience of World War I as "Music in the Air": "War naturally does

AFTERWORD

make music but certainly this war with really everybody listening to the radio, there is nothing but music."[19]

My section title, "Ears Only," is not only meant to convey the urgency and secrecy of messages sent in wartime. It suggests that as Freud interprets blinding or the assault on the eyes in dreams as a figure of castration, we might consider the ear as an image of female sexuality, with its outer folds and inner labyrinthine passages where balance and equilibrium are lodged. If we experience noise as rape, what does it mean if the woman writer writes a noisy text? To use Julia Kristeva's terms, it is a "semiotic" rather than a symbolic text. But by her criteria, the semiotic text is in touch with the child's experience of learning sounds from the mother before it is initiated into masculine or symbolic language. Yet the whole force of this novel on the level of content is rage against the mother, refusal to deal with the fathers as makers of war. The heroine of this novel is truly "up to her ears" in war; it disorients and unbalances her. As an ambulance driver at the Front, she is not only overwhelmed by the noise of battle, she is a noise-maker herself. By taking over a man's job, she both experiences the rape of the ear and she "ears" herself, in the Old English sense of the word meaning to plough, an apt term for driving an ambulance across no man's land.

Helen Zenna Smith was the pseudonym of Evadne Price. The National Union Catalogue lists her birthdate as 1896, but Kenneth Attiwill, her second husband (of 54 years), claims she was born in 1901. (The narrator of *Not So Quiet . . .* would have been born in 1896 or 1897.)[20] When Angela Ingram and I began to work on these novels [*Not So Quiet . . .* and its sequels, *Women of the Aftermath* (1931), *Shadow Women* (1932), *Luxury Ladies* (1933), and *They Lived*

262

with Me (1934)], information on the author was hard to come by. Zenna was spelled Zennor in some places, but Evadne Price was revived by Cadogan and Craig in *You're a Brick, Angela,* a popular account of the history of English girls' books, and *Women and Children First: The Fiction of the Two World Wars.*[21] Evadne Price was a very successful freelance journalist, and her career includes everything from children's books to romances, serious stage parts to acting and writing for several films, as well as playwriting. Her Helen Zenna Smith books were serialized in *The People,* and she was their war correspondent from 1943, covering the Allied invasion and all the major war stories through the Nuremberg Trials. Her husband was a POW in Japan, and for two years she believed he was dead. She wrote a great deal of popular fiction with titles like *Society Girl, Glamour Girl, Escape to Marriage,* and *Air Hostess in Love.* Her play *Big Ben,* written for the Malvern Festival in 1939, was successful (the *Times* called it "a large, comfortable play with a soul to call its own"). *The Phantom Light* (1937) was a stage version of her novel, *The Haunted Light,* and it was also made into a film starring Gordon Harker. *Once a Crook,* on which Kenneth Attiwill collaborated (1939), was also both a play and a film.

The author of several hundred paperback romances first serialized in *Novel Magazine,* Evadne Price had another career when television began, as a broadcast storyteller. An afternoon horoscope show called "Fun with the Stars" led to a long-running evening horoscope program. Price was "our new astrologer extraordinaire" for twenty-five years for *SHE* magazine and published a successful collection of these columns as *SHE Stargazes.* When she and her husband retired to Australia in 1976, Evadne Price wrote the monthly horoscope column for Australian *Vogue.*

263

Before she died in April 1985, she had begun work on an autobiography to be called *Mother Painted Nudes.*

As I write, the press is having a field day over the revelation that Nancy and Ronald Reagan consult astrologers. What is the feminist scholar to make of a talent that spans social realism and pulp fiction, a talent that composed sensational reports of World War II battlefronts and also concocted horoscopes for fashion magazines? Can we include in our feminist project the magnetic, feminine "little" personality with "raven black hair," a "cultivated" accent, and "English rose complexion," the born performer who longed to be in the public eye, and said:

> I was a real little show-off. . . . I loved reciting, singing, dancing, telling make-believe stories, making people laugh or cry, anything to be the center of attention. And when they took me to my first ever theatre—it was a pantomime—I *knew* that I wanted to be an actress and have my name up in electric lights. . . . I wanted to be a star and shine.[22]

Evadne Price's popularity is a challenge for feminist criticism. Would unacknowledged snobbery about "high" and "low" culture dismiss Evadne Price as a commercial opportunist? Is our reading of the Helen Zenna Smith books contaminated by the astrological charts? Is *Not So Quiet . . .* diminished by the fact that its author adored housekeeping and gardening in Sussex and prided herself on being a very good cook? We claim that aesthetic judgments are no longer based on such considerations. Critical theory insists that the "author" is dead. But what if the dead author is not Shakespeare or Virginia Woolf, but Evadne Price?

Evadne Price's career is a twentieth-century woman's

success story. She had enormous mimetic gifts; she was, as feminist psychologists document in many women's lives, extraordinarily *adaptive.* Evadne Price was a genuinely popular writer. She knew what the public wanted and she gave it to them. Readers of thirties novels of socialist realism will have no trouble recognizing the genre of *Not So Quiet . . .* and its sequels, the lost heroines of the later books, bored and weary mistresses and kept women, enacting the general social malaise of the Depression in a female "depression" at being culturally deprived of *work.* Like Jean Rhys's miserable heroines, "Nello," as she is called in the later novels, is downwardly mobile and ends up sleeping on the Embankment when what prostitutes now call "sex work" is no longer available. Helen Zenna Smith does not write as lyrically as Jean Rhys. There are almost no figures of speech in her brutal, tense, angry narrative. But the technique of dramatic monologue, of inner and outer soliloquy and mental scene-making are superb examples of what Bakhtin calls "dialogism" in fiction. (The recently revived and translated work of the Russian critic, Mikhail Bakhtin, has proved especially useful for analyzing the way that history works in the novel. Gender was not an important category for him, but his ideas are easily translated for feminist readings. His idea of the "carnivalesque" has proved useful for discussing black literature and relates directly to the macabre humor of war novels as well as the latrine scenes of male bonding in Remarque's *All Quiet on the Western Front.*)

Evadne Price here shapes a new form of cinematic, dialogic, and dramatic interior monologue for modernism, a very tightly controlled but daring form, very different from James Joyce, Dorothy Richardson, or Virginia Woolf. One consciousness, Helen's, is a kind of mistress of ceremonies of the *carnival* of voices in her imagination. She jerks the puppet strings and they all "act out." Furious with her mother and Mrs. Evans-Mawnington (her mother's rival in war work and village recruiting) for their pious, smug inability to conceive of the terrors of trench life for soldiers or the unspeakable conditions in which the women drive ambulances, she hallucinates them onto the scene, wanting to imagine their response: "Shut your ears, Mother and Mrs. Evans-Mawnington, lest their groans and heart-rending cries linger in your memory as in the memory of the daughter you sent out to help win the War."

Erich Maria Remarque's *All Quiet on the Western Front* appeared in 1929 to instant international acclaim. It remains a classic anti-war novel, a touching, comic, life-affirming first-person narrative of a young German soldier's experience. Albert Marriott, the publisher, approached Evadne Price with a free-lance project to write a spoof from a woman's point of view ("All Quaint on the Western Front"). She read Remarque and found "quaint" an unsuitable response to its power. She herself had never been at the Front, so she convinced Winifred Young, who had kept diaries of her experience as an ambulance driver, to let Price write a novel faithful to Young's experience of actual life at the Front. We do not have those diaries to compare to *Not So Quiet . . . .* We know that Evadne Price locked herself up with them for six weeks and wrote a novel fit to put on the shelf next to Erich Maria Remarque's. The question of its origins as a work of art, its originality or creativity in the face of Evadne Price's deliberate mimesis of *All Quiet on the Western Front,* and her use of Winifred Young's diaries are fascinating.

Not So Quiet . . . is a multi-authored text, like the King

James Bible, which was written by a committee, and it seems to demonstrate Virginia Woolf's thesis in *A Room of One's Own* that "masterpieces are not single and solitary births. They are the product of thinking by the body of the people . . . ." *Not So Quiet . . .*'s "heteroglossia," in Bakhtin's terms, its multi-voicedness, comes from Evadne Price's extraordinary ability to hear and read the popular experience of the horror of this particular war, popular revulsion at the destruction of a whole generation of European youth, male and female alike.[23] Socialist feminists should be interested in a fiction which makes no pretense at "individual genius" and enacts as well a female literary class demobilization in the narrative of Helen's move from volunteer ambulance driving, a breakdown, and home leave to the deliberate rejection of class privilege and her return to the Front as a cook's assistant with working-class W.A.A.C.s.

Virginia Woolf, in "Professions for Women" (1931), imagined that women would be able to tell the truth about the body in fifty years' time. She meant, of course, female sexual experience. But if she read popular fiction, she would have seen that Evadne Price (and other women war novelists) could tell the truth about the body in/at war. Some subjects remain taboo. Helen never tells us, except in veiled allusion, what happens to the menstruating body at the Front. Did the harsh conditions stop the menstrual flow? Did women connect menstrual blood with the blood of wounded soldiers? Some anthropologists have argued that men's wars are a form of menstruation envy. Did death-blood, flowing so ceaselessly from men's bodies, affect women's perceptions of their own life-blood? Menstruation may still have been in *la zone interdite* for women's fiction in 1929, but the body covered with lice

267

was an arresting and shocking substitute. May I warn the gentle reader to cut her fingernails before reading *Not So Quiet . . .* ? Even on the second and third readings this novel will send you into a fit of itching and scratching, so graphic is its description of the horrors of lice in the hair and sleeping bags, called "flea bags." *Not So Quiet . . .* sends the reader rushing to the bath, wondering whether Army and Navy stores still offer carbolic body belts for squeamish readers of war novels.

The disorder and disorientation of the body at war are evoked immediately by the narrative voice in the modernist "continuous present" of Gertrude Stein (though more familiar to readers in the work of Hemingway and Remarque). The first-person speaker seems to be unreeling a black and white cinematic series of graphic images in the flat (but ominous) monotone of an old newsreel. The personal, reportorial "I" deliberately suppresses emotion, but extends the I-narrative with more private forms—the diary, the letter, the waking dream—so that she creates the illusion of multiple voices, trying to speak, as if over the static of a field radio and the continual rumble and whine of guns and bombs, the screaming and moaning of the wounded. This "background noise," the deafening roar of the engines of death, is the source of the title, as well as a reversal of Remarque.

The word "quiet" in both titles indicates war's insistence on gender reversal. Man, the noise-making animal, is forced to lie still in the trenches, while the silent woman, used to domestic peace, must participate in the incessant noise of warfare. She must take and give orders, run machines, think and act quickly during the infernal din of shelling attacks, rev up her engines. Remarque's Paul Baumer and his comrades must leave the male world of

268

active speaking and noisy work for the eerie *longuers* and passive, silent waiting for attack, which fills them with fear and makes them into "women." The ambulance drivers are equally made into "men" by the requirements of their jobs. They must overcome their fear of open spaces and the dark and drive long distances in the night with their cargo of maimed men. Self-reliance, courage, nerve, and bravery must be summoned.

Each experiences war through the body of the other. Paul is feminized by war; Helen is masculinized. Both novels write the body in distress, as much for gender reversal as for fatigue, sleep deprivation, hunger, rotten food, the invasion of fleas and rats, cold. Remarque writes the claustrophobia of the falsely domestic trench/hearth and Price writes the agoraphobia of the mine-trapped open space, blinding snow and wind, bombs falling from the sky. Unhoused, she must learn to operate Outside. Housed in holes of trenches, the German soldiers must learn containment, self-control, and all the female virtues of the aware and alert Inside. Woman makes noise; man maintains silence. The en-trenched and the un-trenched warfare experience profound gender traumas. The speaker becomes the listener; the listener becomes the speaker. The war/peace, front/back gender oppositions must be negotiated for survival.

Gender identity must be maintained despite the experience of living in the body of the other sex (Helen imagines strenuously the preparations for her coming-out party while driving a particularly stressful ambulance run, and Paul and his friends risk court-martial to make love to some French women). The first opposition in the dialogic experience of reading the two novels together is in the meaning of the word "quiet." For the woman, the new meaning in war of her speech or silence is all the more disconcerting because of the accumulated cultural associations of female virtue with silence in a cultural script which asserts (against reality) that women talk too much. In addition, the new subject position of the woman at war undoes her ordinary sexual role. Heightened sexuality is part of her active role. In contrast, the men in *All Quiet on the Western Front* mostly masturbate. Helen casually sleeps with the first man she meets as she gets off the boat for leave in England, an action unthinkable for a girl of her class before the war. Sandra Gilbert's argument about gender warfare seems inappropriate to those for whom gender identity remains a serious test of endurance and new respect for the *Other*. Paul, on home leave, feels a tender respect for his mother, a respect born of his own feminization in the trenches. He can now empathize with her body, which is dying of cancer, when all of civilian life enrages and disgusts him. Helen falls in love with Roy Evans-Mawnington because she knows in her body's stress what he has experienced as a soldier. The notion of woman's "potency" deriving from men's "impotence" is a far too simple interpretation of gender roles in World War I. The most silent soldier in Remarque's novel, the one who hears and smells, can find food, and "read" the world around him (like a woman), is the most revered. And Tosh is the heroine of *Not So Quiet . . .* , with her foul mouth, continual banter, singing, joking, cursing, and clowning. Helen and her comrades cannot tell their families what they suffer. They write lying, cheerful letters and fantasize about telling the truth as they would have "before the world turned khaki and blood-coloured":

Tell them that all the ideals and beliefs you ever had have crashed about your gun-deafened ears—that you don't

270

believe in God or them or the infallibility of England or anything but bloody war and wounds and foul smells and smutty stories and smoke and bombs and lice and filth and noise, noise, noise—that you live in a world of cold sick fear, a dirty world of darkness and despair . . .[24]

Psychically speaking, what both sexes experience in these novels is a Freudian version of "the uncanny." Though Freud associates the fear of castration with deprivation of sight, in the war experience it is hearing, noise or silence, which indicates the desexualization of the characters. (Feminist critics like Luce Irigaray have written about specularity and touch in female experience and writing as very different from the male. We might think of analyzing whether the woman's experience of hearing and her relation to her own ears is different.) Paul Baumer associates silence with the mass murder of a battle, the final impotence of passive endurance of enemy assault.[25] Helen fixates on one particular noise as the cause of her suffering, the "loathly arrogant summons" of the Commandant's police whistle. Rousing her to roll-call at 7:30 A.M. when she went to bed at 5, the whistle focuses her hatred:

> . . . ruining my pre-War disposition entirely. It rouses everything vile within me. Not long ago I was a gentle pliable creature of no particular virtues or vices, my temper was even, my nature amiable and my emotions practically non-existent. Now I am a sullen, smouldering thing, liable to burst Vesuvius fashion into a flaming fire of rage without the slightest warning. Commandant's police whistle. . . .
>
> If I am bathing or attending my body with carbolic ointment or soothing lotion . . . it orders me to stop. If I am writing a hasty letter, or glancing at a newspaper . . . it shrieks its mocking summons. Whatever I am doing it gives

271

> me no peace. But worst of all, whenever I am asleep . . . it wakens me, and gloats and glories in the action. If only I could ram it down the Commandant's throat, I could die happy in the knowledge that I had not lived in vain. (47)

Later Helen's sadistic fantasies again enact the invasion of the deep throat of the Commandant: "I wonder what she would do if I suddenly sprang at her and dug my fingers into her throat, her strong, red, thick throat that is never sore, that laughs scornfully at germs, that needs no wrapping up even when the snow is whirling, blinding and smothering . . . "(57).

Note, first of all, that these passages are marked heavily by ellipses. In the first-person narrative dramatic monologue or soliloquy, the ellipses indicate self-interruption and the repression of even more rage than is on the page. *Not So Quiet . . .* is punctuated by these elliptical absences throughout. The text looks like letters received and sent during wartime, stamped and opened by the censor with marked-out passages (read by other eyes). The reader is reading as much silence as text, constantly filling in the blanks, supplying the left-out words, decoding the coded wartime message. The ellipses, like the censor's black lines crossing out sentences, sometimes blacking out paragraphs, indicate Helen's self-censorship, but also the utter lack of truthful communication possible in war. Partial messages, missent and misread, propaganda, rumor, lies, the reports of spies, secret codes—these are the messages of war. *Not So Quiet . . . ,* because of its multiple authorship in its imitation of Remarque and its pseudonymous rendering of Winifred Young's diaries in fictional form, is a particularly rich document in which to examine gender and war issues in World War I England. The punctuation asks the reader to read between the lines, to guess at the

272

unsaid and the unsayable. The reading experience is a reproduction of the ambulance driver's route, swerving to avoid obstacles and holes, zig-zagging with Helen Z. Smith. Passages from letters, bits of remembered newspaper articles, phrases like "Our Splendid Women" are rendered in italics, further marking the text as an intertext with all the other cultural productions of war, as well as Remarque's novel. We seem to read secretly, behind the editorial blackout curtain of censorship in conspiracy with Helen Zenna Smith. Her textual practice is a version of the Kristevan "semiotic," those human noises excluded from "symbolic" discourse, marking a repression, which marks another repression. This opens the novel to deconstructive feminism and other modes of contemporary critical discourse.

But it is interesting to note that Evadne Price's writing practice here is not the feminine "writing the body" of Helene Cixous and some French feminist theory. It is not in the least erotic. The words on the page, so full of stops and starts and diacritical messages in italic and so many sentences framed as questions and requiring an answer from the reader are a textual version of *La Zone Interdite,* fragmented like the bodies that litter this forbidden territory with arms and legs and headless trunks. The body of the text is "not whole"; it is a war casualty. The diacritical marks make the text look like noise. It crackles across the page. The rapt reader also feels drowned by noise, the noise in Helen's head and the battle noises around her. This is a remarkable literary achievement and clearly related to Evadne Price's brilliance as a reporter. She reproduces the minefield of the forbidden zone as a dotted landscape on the body of the text, setting up disquieting relations between text and white space on the book's pages, the sight of which invades the reader's ears as well as her eyes. Our eye contact with the fragmented text makes us feel the disorientation of the body at war, and it activates the reading "ear" as if a silent newsreel suddenly connected with its sound track, but faded in and out, as such reports continue to do, keeping the viewer on edge about the physical safety of the reporter.[26]

The content of the quoted passages is also significant. The Commandant is the Phallic Mother, the whistle her phallus, the very voice of violence and war. In the male masquerade that is required of the young women who shoulder these abhorrent wartime duties, Helen's hatred is directed exactly onto the object the Propaganda Office has chosen for its posters, the fearful huge matriarch who points the way to the Front, the enormous maternal nurse who cradles the wounded. She is the Home Front, the Mother Country, the one who gives birth and also kills. It would never do to blame the old men who make war, the kings and kaisers and their counsellors. The Commandant's whistle is, of course, a convenient disguise for the male voice of nationalist authority, the patriarchs in whose interest the war is fought. When Helen figures war as an invasion of her ears, the phallic mother is the rapist. She is the one who is "not so quiet," the literal *disturber of the peace*. She is War.

The repression of the male authority figures and displacement of their roles as killers onto the militant and militaristic mother figure is a precise reading of the cultural needs of the warmongers, and Helen Zenna Smith constructs a plot in which the bad mother is the villain. Edwards recognizes the real enemy, "the politicians"; "the men are failures," women should "refuse to bring children into the world to be maimed and murdered," "let the
274

people who make the wars fight them."(55) As Angela Ingram so carefully and wittily demonstrates in "Un/Reproductions," the ideology of war insists on a primitive call to women to construct themselves socially as mothers first and then argues that the war is being fought to protect those mothers and, by extension, that it is their fault that men are dying.

But Helen's war is fought with the Commandant, known as "Mrs. Bitch," who "would have made a good wife for Napoleon." She can't understand how Mrs. Bitch could be a mother: "No woman who has suffered the pangs of childbirth could have so little understanding of pain in other women's daughters."(49) She is a "hungry vulture" who loves "bossing the show"; "Why is it that women in authority almost invariably fall victims to megalomania?" she asks. This cultural and social displacement of the drive for power onto the mother rather than the father and women's internalization of it as enacted in this fiction may be a clue to the problem of why humanity is unable to stop war. The portrait of the Commandant recalls, of course, Mrs. Breakspeare, "the very maternal general" of *The Well of Loneliness.*

Not So Quiet . . . is subtitled "Stepdaughters of War." In this drama, which problematizes the relation of the family to martial values, war is not the father but the mother, and not a real mother, but a wicked stepmother. The step-daughter is a Cinderella of the battlefront, sweeping up the ashes and cinders, the blood and vomit of her wounded prince. But no fairy godmother comes to rescue her. Bello transvests into Bella, ferocious goddess of war. We might call the "stepdaughter" of war Bellona, as Evadne Price chronicles the transformation of her heroine from "Helen" to "Nell" to "Nello." Virginia Woolf obviously recalls the

275

figure of the stepdaughter of war in a footnote in *Three Guineas:* "Englishwomen were much criticized for using force in the battle for the franchise" she writes in 1938.

> The vote indeed was given to women largely because of the help they gave to Englishmen in using force in that war. . . . This raises the difficult question whether those who did not aid in the prosecution of the war, but did what they could to hinder the prosecution of the war, ought to use the vote to which they are entitled chiefly because others "aided in the prosecution of the war"? That they are stepdaughters, not full daughters, of England, is shown by the fact that they change nationality on marriage. A woman, whether or not she helped to beat the Germans, becomes a German if she marries a German. Her political views must then be entirely reversed, and her filial piety transferred.[27]

Woolf's logic exposes the ideological reversals by which patriarchy and militarism manipulate women in wartime as ruthlessly as does Evadne Price's anti-logical narrative.

There are only two figurative passages in this novel. One is the description of "an ancient tree that never buds into leaf nor yet rots," which is called the "Witch's Hand" for its gnarled trunk that looks like a gigantic palm and "five malformed branches that stretch like fingers into the valley below,"(114) where Helen and her companions drive the dead in their ambulances to the military cemetery. The Witch's Hand is evil, sinister, greedy, demanding, never denied. Helen and the men struggle with the coffins in the mud. The snow, a "white glove that has so graciously hidden" the "claw-like and avaricious" hand, has disappeared, leaving the tree to grab ghoulishly at the dead. "It reaches down evilly, the claws snatching at us as we stand defenceless, as though to squeeze the youth from us until

276

we are dry and lifeless"(119). The Witch's Hand is part of the enormous ideological effort of the novel to mask the paternity of war and its complicity with patriarchy and to blame the mothers. In a massive reversal of reality Helen Zenna Smith makes the life-giving body of the mother the source of death and war in the same way that the insidious propaganda campaign enacted a popular transformation of the bombs of the munitions factories into breasts and wombs as Claire Culleton documents in the popular culture of the period. (Evadne Price is supposed to have worked for the War Ministry during the war, where doubtless such brilliant propagandistic tricks were hatched. There might be a connection with her astrology columns after all. *Not So Quiet . . .* could be read as the propagandist's star turn, if it did not so forcefully turn the reader against the war.)

It is a common characteristic of the literature of this war to figure the Home Front as a phallic mother, especially in the homoerotic poetry of the lost brother. But Helen Zenna Smith doubles the "Terrible Mother" with a classic pair of belligerents who outdo even Woolf's Lady Bruton and Lady Bradshaw in matriarchal militarism—her mother and Mrs. Evans-Mawnington. The two matrons, competing with one another over who can recruit more young men and how many of their own they can sacrifice for the war, make a grotesque twin-headed statue of Bella-Bello, capitalism, imperialism, and jingoism shoring up their flag-waving patriotism. War will always exist "as long as we breed women like my mother and Mrs. Evans-Mawnington"(90). The dialogic structure of the novel is most apparent in the use of the letters from her mother and her aunt in fragments separated by ellipses. Helen dramatizes the letters in her head as reading them enrages her. She

277

creates their voices, mocks and mimics them (Mother "has
seventeen more recruits than Mrs. Evans-Mawnington up
to date"). The Front becomes a *theatre of war* where Helen
acts out all the roles. The letters are dialogized into short
plays with stage directions, indications of "Curtain," as the
war itself is imagined as scenes in a drama whose most
important aspect is that it will end. Helen hallucinates that
her mother and Mrs. Evans-Mawnington join her on her
nightly ambulance run:

Oh, come with me, Mother and Mrs. Evans-Mawnington.
Let me show you the exhibits straight from the battlefield.
This will be something original to tell your committees,
while they knit their endless miles of khaki scarves, . . .
something to spout from the platform at your recruiting
meetings. Come with me. Stand just there.(90)

See the stretcher-bearers lifting the trays one by one,
slotting them deftly into my ambulance. Out of the way
quickly, Mother and Mrs. Evans-Mawnington—lift your
silken skirts aside . . . a man is spewing blood, the moving
has upset him, finished him. . . . He will die on the way to
hospital if he doesn't die before the ambulance is loaded.(91)

See the man they are fitting into the bottom slot. He is
coughing badly. No, not pneumonia. Not tuberculosis.
Nothing so picturesque.Gently, gently, stretcher-bearers . . .
he is about done. He is coughing up clots of pinky-green
filth. Only his lungs, Mother and Mrs. Evans-Mawnington.
He is coughing well tonight. That is gas. You've heard of
gas, haven't you? It burns and shrivels the lungs to . . . to
the mess you see on the ambulance floor there. He's about
the age of Bertie, Mother. . . . The son you are so eager to
send out to the trenches, in case Mrs. Evans-Mawnington
scores over you at the next recruiting meeting. . . . "I have
given my only son."

Cough, cough, little fair-haired boy. Perhaps somewhere
your mother is thinking of you . . . boasting of the life she
has so nobly given . . . the life you thought was your own,
but which is hers to squander as she thinks fit.(92-93)

Such brutal writing might be understandable in the
description of the enemy, but it is clear that for these
young women the real enemy is Mother. When we
compare this murderous prose with the gentle, pacifist
tone of *All Quiet on the Western Front,* we can make the
argument that, because of the gender reversals demanded
by war, Erich Maria Remarque has produced a *woman's
novel* and Helen Zenna Smith a *man's novel.* The *subject
positions* of the experience of the writers, not their *gender,*
produce different forms of *écriture feminine* and *écriture
masculine.* Remarque and Price are important as war
novelists because, more than other writers, they have
marked their prose and their narratives with the profound
experience of gender reversal and the battle to recover the
lost gendered subject position which was the real experience of male and female bodies in World War I.

The gloved and ungloved (mailed fist?) hand formed by
the bent tree, which Smith calls the Witch's Hand, seems a
deliberate answer to the exquisite flowering cherry tree in
All Quiet on the Western Front, which so overpowers Detering,
a man in Paul's company, that he deserts out of a desperate
desire for home. Home is a death-dealing monster to the
British woman, an orchard full of promise to the German
peasant. When Paul kills a Frenchman in hand-to-hand
combat, he is overcome with remorse, reads his identity
card, sees the photo of wife and child, and vows to replace
him—he becomes a writer; the dead man was a printer,
Gerard Duval, compositor.

Helen's experience of the enemy, when for her the real

279

enemy is the wicked stepmother (her own mother, the Commandant, England as her mother country), is a puzzled woman's experience of the male gaze when the German POWs assess her body parts. (She is puzzled because part of her masculine role as a driver is to be the gazer, not the object of men's gaze.) Paul's knowledge of the patriarchal authority that makes war fills him with sorrow and pity. He is feminized and civilized by the humiliations and submissions required by the army, whereas Helen is brutalized and numbed. Paul and his friends play schoolboy pranks on their officer and keep their difference and distance from authoritarian values. Much as Helen, Tosh, and their companions hate Mrs. Bitch, they *become* her, or junior versions of her matriarchal militarism, when they scapegoat, torture, and expel the lesbian in their midst.

One of the most moving scenes in *All Quiet on the Western Front* is a tender and comic story of Lewandowski's Polish wife's visit to the hospital. He hasn't seen her for two years and is almost recovered from a severe abdominal wound. The men on the ward insist that the little woman with the black mantilla get into bed with her husband. They stand guard, hold the baby and play cards so the couple can make love, "like one big family," and then eat sausage with the "sweating and beaming" Lewandowski. Having been feminized by the trenches, the men experience an almost communal desire to be reinvested in the social roles of husband and father, rather than killer or shivering victim (264–268). This is a story of what we now think of as "female" behavior. It is interesting to compare the men's struggle to return to male life-giving rather than death-dealing roles in a man's novel with Rebecca West's portrait of Chris Baldry regressing to a youthful self due to shell shock before he became a husband and father in *The Return of the Soldier*. His name, Bal/dry, clues the reader to a kind of pacifism of the body, the refusal to engender. This is also why the psychiatrists are so enraged with Septimus Smith in Virginia Woolf's *Mrs. Dalloway*. His body has become a pacifist and refuses to sleep with Rezia and give her the child she wants.

In *Not So Quiet . . .* Helen's one night stand with Robin when she returns to England seems to spring from her acquired "masculinity," to be an act done out of fear of loss of sexual identity. But it is clear that the fear of a lesbian in the women's barracks comes from a deeper fear of the pacifist body. It is not so much deviance that frightens them as the body that enacts its pacifism by refusing to bear children. The "carnivalesque" in this scene is a dreadful ritualized eating and speech-making ceremony, which ends, like some tribal ritual, by expelling the scapegoat. The carnivalesque in Remarque's novel enacts bonding by erasing shame. The battlefield has no privileged toilet of one's own. Both novels are mired in the body, as their narrators' own bodies are mired in muddy battlefields. The communal latrines in *All Quiet on the Western Front* relax the boundaries between the men, and they become as close as women. Their bodies, humiliated in *evacuation* and emission, are weak and humanized. The woman ambulance drivers are also deep in others' excrement, but suffer more from *invasion* by fleas. They become brutalized and individualized, acting out their own hatred of authority by sacrificing one of their members rather than sticking together.[28]

There is an extraordinary scene at the opening of *Not So Quiet . . .* when the gallant heroine Tosh cuts her gorgeous red hair and burns the fleas and lice. This sordid ritual scene with its descriptions of filth and food that resembles shit does not unite the women but separates the sadistic Tosh, burning one louse at a time, as the "heroine," different from the other girls who don't dare to cut their hair for fear it would "put the helmet on the womanliness" they desperately need to maintain. It is only because she is an aristocrat that Tosh doesn't fear being "unsexed" by short hair. "Unsexed? Me? With the breasts of a nursing mother?" (17) Tosh winks to Bertina Farmer (called The B.F. for Bloody Fool).

The scene emphasizes the class distinctions among the women: Tosh, The B.F., The Bug, Skinny, Etta Potato (Etta Potter), and Smithy, the narrator. The class distinctions are erased for the German soldiers, but since the women are in a volunteer outfit, they range in class from being, like Tosh, the niece of an earl, to upper-middle-class debutantes like The B.F., daughters of government administrators, like Skinny, whose father is important in the War Office, to Nell, whose father made jam and then settled in Wimbledon Common—"We sheltered young women who smilingly stumbled from the chintz-covered drawing-rooms of the suburbs straight into hell"(165). Tosh calls them *mes petits harlots;* she's their leader and spokesperson. She even compiles a war alphabet for them: "B for Bastard—obsolete term meaning war-baby. . . . I for Illegitimate—(see B). . . . V for Virgin—a term of reproach" (160). Tosh's alphabet inscribes the complicity of motherhood and war. She is, in reality, a budding "Mrs. Bitch," a candidate for the role of Helen's mother or Mrs. Evans-Mawnington, the British matriarch in the making. She both writes and embodies the gender reversal of women at war. Helen thinks that the War Office sends only upper-class girls to the Front because they will obey a code

282

of honor and remain silent and stiff-upper-lipped about the horror. But their "voice" is Tosh's noisy swaggering fearlessness, a voice in training to blow the Commandant's whistle:

> She is wandering around in the flickering candlelight dressed in a soiled woolen undervest and a voluminous pair of navy blue bloomers, chain-smoking yellow perils at a furious rate. There is something vaguely comforting in the Amazonian height and breadth of Tosh. She has the hips of a matron—intensified by the four pairs of thick combinations she always wears for warmth, a mind like a sewer (her own definition), the courage of a giant, the vocabulary of a Smithfield butcher, and the round, wind-reddened face of a dairymaid.(11)

Georgina Toshington, who posthumously becomes a storybook heroine in England after she has been killed by a bomb while driving Commandant's ambulance (Smithy wishes the bomb would kill Mrs. Bitch, but it kills Tosh instead), is the Edwardian version of England as Victoria, a large, imperialist, terrifying maternal figure. When Smithy is driving under the bombs, she is terrified by the "flattening sound, as though the sky were jealous of the earth and was determined to wipe it out of existence. Each time a bomb drops I see myself under it, flat, like the skin of a dead tiger that has been made into a rug with a little nicked half-inch of cloth all round the edges . . . flat, all the flesh and blood and bones knocked flat . . ."(156). This is the second figurative passage in *Not So Quiet . . .* , and it is repeated during the scene in which the bomb fragment kills Tosh. Its meaning is more deeply repressed than the figure of the dead tree as the Witch's Hand. Nellie Smith's *own* fear of annihilation (rather than her disgust at the

283

maimed men whose bodies she ferries to hospital or the grave) is at issue here. While she talks about being a sacrificial victim to Home Front patriotism, her fear connects her own body, flattened like the tiger skin, to those earlier trophies of imperialistic adventures in India and Africa that grace English hearths. She, too, might become a hearth rug for safe warm (not gangrenous or frozen) feet, to lay before the Home Fires that have been kept burning by the sacrifice of so many colonial lives. (This vivid image of Home Front trophies should be compared to Sylvia Townsend Warner's description of the photo of young Osbert in "Cottage Mantleshelf," in which the picture is isolated and "un-paired" when everything else on the shelf is locked into a couple or "married." The image of the female body at war as a flattened rug made out of her hide recalls Barbara Comyns' splendid novel *The Skin Chairs,* 1962, Penguin, 1987.) Actually, Helen does not die like the hero-narrator of *All Quiet on the Western Front.* It is the intrepid Tosh who dies—though not before she has performed her role as keeper of the heterosexual flame.

Margaret Higonnet has argued that the fiction of nationalist wars equates heterosexuality with political correctness, that the linear narrative enforces gender stability.[29] Civil War novels break from linear narrative, often invoking Kristeva's "women's time," allowing more complicated temporal inversions, memories, and incestuous plots. The perfect example, for me, of this argument, is Marguerite Yourçenar's *Coup de Grâce* (Farrar, Straus, 1957), set in the Baltic states just after the First World War, and one of the most disturbing versions of the interconnections between gender and war because the author has inserted an authoritarian preface in the reprint, cautioning the reader against reading for the woman's text and arguing that Eric, her proto-fascist narrator, is not as "unreliable" as we had supposed. Yourçenar is the most stunning example of the woman writing from the male subject position, not in struggle with literary masculinizing as Helen Zenna Smith is in *Not So Quiet . . .*, but valorizing that very "valor" which Evadne Price and Erich Maria Remarque call into question.

Not So Quiet . . . runs on a present-tense time frame, which we might call "fast forward," while *All Quiet on the Western Front* moves in a slow, nostalgic present toward the silence at the end of the war. The fact that *Not So Quiet . . .* does not end, but continues in sequels, with the life of the war-damaged narrator getting worse and worse, indicates Price's realization that, for women, the effects of war last a lifetime and can never be forgotten. Vera Brittain's memoirs indicate that she never got over the loss of lover and brother. The war is not over when it's over in historical time. Irene Rathbone's *We That Were Young* and *They Call It Peace* also demonstrate that patriarchal, capitalist, and imperialist "peacetimes" are still wartimes for the exploited.

The politics of *Not So Quiet . . .* are another matter. The portrait of Tosh, though it's meant to be complimentary, reminds me of the concentration camp commandant in Lina Wertmüller's film *Seven Beauties*. If *Not So Quiet . . .* was intended as a "politically correct" version of English ambulance drivers' experiences, specifically to counter the effects of Radclyffe Hall's *The Well of Loneliness,* which appeared in 1928 and was banned in a sensational censorship trial (and I believe it was), Helen Zenna Smith is writing to clear the volunteers of the charge of lesbianism. Hall's version of the war is very different—romantic, heroic, and she celebrates the hotbed of lesbian lovers in the Ambulance Corps.[30] Tosh is the "Niece of an Earl." One of the most well-known heroines among the ambulance drivers was Radclyffe Hall's friend, "Toupie" Lowther. She was actually the *daughter* of an earl and, as Barbara, Lady Lowther, ran a unit operating in Compeigne from 1917 on and also headed the London Branch of Relief for Belgian Prisoners in Germany. "Toupie" is described as "a bulky tall woman of extremely masculine appearance who had a considerable reputation as a fencer and tennis player."[31] She and four of the women in her unit won the Croix de Guerre. The scandal of *The Well of Loneliness* and its revelations that there were "inverts" among "Our Splendid Women" also made a specific link between the upper classes and lesbianism. Hence, Evadne Price has Tosh leading the sadistic purge of the lesbian figure, Skinny, in *Not So Quiet . . . .* Skinny is described as "yellow," thin (and she is the only member of the company to have dysentery—a "male" form of pollution?). Virginia Woolf's description of Radclyffe Hall when she attended the censorship trial for *The Well of Loneliness* calls her "stringy" and "yellow." The word yellow, of course, indicates both cowardice and jaundice. Her skinniness is a deliberate opposition to Tosh's maternal Amazon's body. Evadne Price effectively rewrites the lesbian body at war to rob it of the healthy romantic glow with which Radclyffe Hall had surrounded it in *The Well of Loneliness*.

Tosh sees that Skinny is separated from her "particular friend," Frost, (another naming of the nonmaternal) as soon as they arrive. At the party (which is a strange counterpart to the grand eating scenes in *All Quiet on the Western Front* when the German soldiers steal pigs and geese, roast and eat them with Paul making potato pancakes as the bombs fall around them, a wonderful

286

Bakhtinian carnivalization of war) Tosh ignores, insults, and taunts Skinny, who has a hysterical fit. Skinny and Frost get sent home for "refusing to obey orders," in an unspoken agreement between Tosh and the Commandant that allows Tosh to retain her "honor" and makes clear to the reader that perversion has been routed and heterosexuality holds sway. The scene is a perfect example of Mary Douglas's arguments in *Purity and Danger* about scapegoating the "polluted" victim. The drivers are polluted in their role as the charwomen of the battlefield, and they sacrifice Skinny to purify themselves. This "purity" is not virginity but the flaunting of credentials of heterosexual experience. The female body at war must announce that it is made for motherhood. In his biography of Radclyffe Hall, Lovat Dickson implies that lesbianism caused an English defeat in the war, deftly reversing Una Troubridge's claim that her husband, the admiral, who refused to pursue the German fleet in an Eastern engagement, had syphilis, and blaming the admiral's "cowardice" on his wife's relationship with Radclyffe Hall.[32]

Helen's mother tolerates a pregnant servant when she had fired one in a similar situation before the war. Yet Nell's sister Trix, who washes dishes in a V.A.D. nursing unit, gets pregnant and has an abortion. Class values are stronger than the need to reproduce cannon fodder. Helen, who has refused to return to the Front, much to the shame of her family, gets the money for the abortion from another patriotic matriarch, her Aunt Helen, and enlists in the W.A.A.C.s as an assistant cook, infuriating her family by rejecting the class glamour of the ambulance unit for the drudgery of peeling vegetables with working-class women, for whom the war salary is a great boost in status. Deliberately suppressing her experience, which would

287

have given her an officer's commission, Helen *chooses* to be declassed, to do women's traditional dirty work, preparing food rather than cleaning the remains of killing. This textual swerve in the rejection of her own class and its complicity in the war is what makes *Not So Quiet . . .* so interesting and problematic a text. While it has followed the narrative of gender normality in its lesbian-bashing (as May Sinclair's *The Romantics* creates the cowardly soldier—read "homosexual"—as a vampire), *Not So Quiet . . .* figures a kind of freedom for Helen in the break from her family and class. She trades the "khaki and red" world of ambulance-driving at the Front for the (relatively) "green" world of preparing food for the W.A.A.C.s.

A feminist reader recognizes that this is a refusal of the glorification of death-work and a connection made to the eternal round of woman's work in the kitchen, life-work. The new class alliance is a move to another *Zone Interdite,* the repressed but always present class divisions of English society, which remain in force in wartime segregation. This suggests to me that Evadne Price had read Virginia Woolf's essay, "The Niece of an Earl," which was published in *Life and Letters* in 1928, and set out to prove that Woolf was wrong in asserting that there is no communication between classes—"We are enclosed, and separate, and cut off." This is the great "disability" of the English novelist—"a gulf yawns before us; on the other side are the working classes," who become "objects of pity, examples of curiosity."[33] Did Evadne Price, the journalist, have any ambitions that might have caused her to meet the challenge of Woolf's statement? I think so. Her pseudonym, Helen Zenna Smith, is a case in point. "Helen" is the figure man has created to name the cause of war as female. Male war novelists are always finding "another Troy for her to burn," and women are always revising, contending with, repudiating, or exonerating their own versions of the classical Helen. Smith is the most common English name, Everywoman. She writes, "How jealously I preserve the secret of that Z., that ludicrous Z. bestowed on me by my mother. Z. was the heroine of a book mother read the month before I arrived on earth. She wanted me to grow up like Z. Z. was the paragon of beauty, virtue, and womanliness" (15–16).

The textual Z is, of course, a semiotic signal for sleep, which is the ambulance drivers' lost luxury. It is also the sign for noise, a textual buzz addressed to the reader's ear. As the letter at the end of the alphabet, it signifies the end of writing, perhaps the end of a certain kind of writing. As Zenna, on the title page, the mysterious name looks like a diminutive for Zenobia. There were two Zenobias, one who died a Christian martyr, the other the great queen of Palmyra, who refused to be subjugated to Roman rule, famous for her love and support of literature (Longinus wrote at her court) and as a military strategist. The letter Z, like King Lear's "thou whoreson Zed, thou unnecessary letter," marks the "third sex," the masculinized woman or the "war baby," as Z in mathematics is the third symbol for the unknown, after X and Y. Evadne Price is the third person in the writing triangle of Remarque/Winifred Young/Helen Z. Smith. She is the "Z-woman," as a "Z-man" was an army reservist and a "Z-gun" an anti-aircraft rocket, a secret weapon. "Zenna" also suggests the word for an Indian and Persian harem, *zenana,* a code for the position of all women during war. Zenobia is also the heroine of Nathaniel Hawthorne's *The Blithedale Romance,* a story-teller of the "Veiled Lady" in a text which also concerns itself with the problem of "authorship" and the

289

relation between history and fiction. The person who invented the name Helen Zenna Smith wanted to write the great feminist war book.

The most brutally realistic scenes in *Not So Quiet . . .* are not so much the night horrors of driving the wounded but the day-time, stomach-churning job of cleaning out the ambulances of the material wastes of the men, blood, shit, and vomit, hosing and scrubbing with chilblained hands, disinfecting the vans in below-freezing weather. The drivers actually *become* their ambulances. Helen says "all the time they unload *me* the bombs are getting nearer." Mary Borden uses images of ambulances as wombs/tombs, pregnant, polluted bodies—"the motor lorries crouch in the square ashamed, deformed, very weary; their unspeakable burdens bulge under canvas coverings"; the men lie "on their backs in the dark canvas bellies of the ambulances staring at death."[34] The drivers feel as if they are undergoing abortions, birth has gone horribly wrong. Accepting this role, they act the pollution of a distorted ideology that implicates motherhood with war, the female body with dirt and death. They are war's charwomen, and Smith returns again and again to this theme—the drivers must do all their own dirty work with their machines, but in addition they have to clean their own latrines and quarters, are served rotten and spoiled food by a filthy and lazy cook, bearing both men's and women's roles. Both *Not So Quiet . . .* and *All Quiet on the Western Front* fetishize food, because, of course, getting enough to eat is everyone's primary concern in wartime. This is why the breasts of the phallic mother (Tosh, the Commandant, the matriarchal figures on the posters) become such important propagandistic signifiers in the literature of war. Everyone is hungry. Bare-breasted pin-ups in soldiers' bunks probably had more meaning in relation to hunger than to sex. Smithy's Aunt Helen, an incompetent waitress in the War Workers' Canteen in London, observes that it would be more productive if she stayed home and did the housework and let one of her competent maids serve the workers.

When Helen enlists in the W.A.A.C.s as a domestic worker, it is for revenge on her class: "Put that on your needles and knit it, my patriotic aunt"(212). But she soon becomes attached to the other young women, Misery, Cheery, and Blimey, who, along with Smithy, make up "the Four Whys" who peel potatoes and onions together. We wonder about the X. Army uniforms are their first experience of good clothes. They have never brushed their teeth nor bathed very often, so the war does improve their circumstances. Helen alone survives the bombing raid that kills these spirited young women, under an "aggressively radiant" she-moon, another matriarchal figure, to return home to marry her impotent wounded fiance—"I hate kids, anyway"(232). "The trench is like a slaughterhouse"; Blimey's new Burberry trench coat is covered with blood. It is this image one takes away from the novel, the dirty, blood-spattered trench coat, the sign of women's transvestism into soldiers in World War I, still worn and called "trench coats" after their original role. The Burberry recalls the scene where Tosh dies in Helen's arms, her blood soaking the coat. The dirty trench coat worn by Miss Kilman enrages Woolf's Mrs. Dalloway, and it marks the class of the hero's first beloved in Rebecca West's *Return of the Soldier*. The trench coat is a class and gender mark covering the body of women at/in this war. Jenny Gould's essay in *Behind the Lines* examines the profound discomfort aroused by the sight of women in khaki uniforms recorded by the Marchioness of Londonderry, founder of the

Women's Legion in *Retrospect* (1938). Amazons who aped men frightened people, who, of course, wrote letters to the papers demanding that women not be allowed to wear khaki, and the militarism was connected to lesbianism. In an anonymous letter of outrage to *The Morning Post* in 1915, a woman complained of the cropped hair of the "She-men": "I noticed that these women assumed mannish attitudes, stood with legs apart while they smote their riding whips, and looked like self-conscious and not very attractive boys."

> Near these ridiculous "poseuses" stood the real thing—a British Officer in mufti. He had lost his left arm and right leg . . . if these women had a spark of shame left they should have blushed to be seen wearing a parody of the uniform which this officer and thousands like him have made a symbol of honour and glory by their deeds. I do not know the corps to which these ladies belong, but if they cannot become nurses or ward maids in hospital, let them put on sunbonnets and print frocks and go and make hay or pick fruit or make jam. . . .[35]

Some of these blood-soaked (and gender-marked) coats are exhibited in the museum of World War I at Le Linge in Alsace, where trenches dating from the war are still in place, the German concrete bunkers a vivid contrast to the flimsy French earthworks. Signs tell visitors not to stray from the path, as mines may still be active. The pathetic and moving personal belongings of soldiers are on view, along with strategic maps of every battle in the war. The propaganda posters and literature of both sides is equally bloody-minded. I am writing this essay in Strasbourg, where Gutenberg invented the printing press and where Rouget de Lisle sang the Marseillaise for the first time in
292

1792, where Drivier's unique sculpture (1936) in the Place de la Republique shows a mother with two sons, one dead for Germany and the other dead for France. The other night there was a small demonstration by Alsatian socialists in the Cathedral Square to commemorate the anniversary of the Paris Commune. A group of young women sang in high, sweet voices, surrounded by votive candles, as others carried signs supporting the current struggles in New Caledonia and South Africa. It rains here all the time. I am never out of my trench coat.

Jane Marcus
Strasbourg
May 1988

Notes

1. Mary Borden. *The Forbidden Zone* (London: Heinemann, 1929).

2. *The Forbidden Zone,* preface.

3. Enid Bagnold. *A Diary without Dates* (London: Heinemann, 1918), reprinted by Virago, 1978. Virago has also reprinted *The Happy Foreigner* (1920), Bagnold's novel about driving for the French Army just after the war ended. Both books are brilliant and beautifully written. But Enid Bagnold's most disturbing novel is *The Squire* (1938), which makes clear how devastating war values are in domestic society. *The Squire* is about the militarization of motherhood as an institution between the wars.

4. *A Diary without Dates,* p. 5.

5. *The Forbidden Zone,* p. 142. See also Susan Millar Williams's "Mary Borden's Experimental Fiction: Female Sexuality and the Language of War," presented at the 1987 MLA session on Women's Writing in World War I, which argues that Borden portrays war as a seductive rapist, airplanes and motor lorries as rakish, teasing "creatures of pleasure" even as they are the bearers of death.

6. *The Forbidden Zone,* p. 60.

7. Nancy Huston. "The Matrix of War: Mothers and Heroes," in *The Female Body in Western Culture,* ed. Susan Suleiman (Cambridge: Harvard University Press, 1986), pp. 119–136. For recent studies of the history and literature, see Margaret Higonnet (and Jane Jensen, Sonya Michel, and Margaret Weitz). *Behind the Lines: Gender and the Two World Wars* (New Haven: Yale University Press, 1987); Helen Cooper, Adrienne Munich, and Susan Squier. *Arms and the Woman: War, Gender and Literary Representation,* (Chapel Hill, N.C.: University of North Carolina Press, 1989). Note the work of a group of scholars working on the World War I archives at the University of Tulsa. The Tulsa group includes Jan Calloway, Claire Culleton, George Otte, Linda Palumbo, Susan Millar Williams, and Angela Ingram. They presented their work at the 1987 MLA meeting. Claire Culleton's study of the popular

representations of women munitions workers in England in World War I was presented at the International Feminist meeting in Dublin in 1987 and appears in *Women's Studies International Forum* 11, #2, 1988, 109–116. Angela Ingram's essay on the banning of women's writing, " 'Unutterable Putrefaction' and 'Foul Stuff': Two Obscene Novels of the 1920s" appears in *Women's Studies International Forum* 9, #4, 1986, 341–354. Her "Un/Reproductions: States of Banishment in Some English Novels after the Great War" appears in *Women's Writing in Exile,* ed. M. L. Broe and Angela Ingram (Chapel Hill, N.C.: University of North Carolina Press, 1988). Claire Tylee's "Maleness Run Riot—The Great War and Women's Resistance to Militarism" appears in *Women's Studies International Forum* 11, #3, 1988, 199–210. Tylee's essay takes issue with a provocative article by Sandra Gilbert, which presents the basic thesis of her new three-volume study (with Susan Gubar), *No Man's Land* (New Haven: Yale University Press, 1988); the original essay is called "Soldier's Heart: Literary Men, Literary Women and the Great War," *SIGNS* 8: 422–450, reprinted in *Behind the Lines.* Claire Tylee's rebuttal of Gilbert's thesis (that British women were empowered, psychologically, economically, and erotically) by World War I, is an important corrective to misleading arguments and quotations taken out of context. Gilbert's argument is also interrogated by the Tulsa group, in Laura Mayhall's "The Indescribable Barrier: English Women and the Effect of the First World War" (unpublished, and my "The Asylums of Antaeus; Women, War and Madness: Is There a Feminist Fetishism?" in *Feminism and Critical Theory: The Differences Within,* ed. Elizabeth Meese and Alice Parker (Amsterdam and Philadelphia: John Benjamins, 1988), pp. 49–81. Another version of "Asylums" appears in Harold Veeser's *The New Historicism* (New York: Methuen, 1988). See Joanne Glasgow's review of Gilbert and Gubar's first volume in *New Directions for Women,* Jan./Feb., 1988, p. 16; and Susan Stanford Friedman's review in *The Women's Review of Books,* July, 1988. Gilbert's "sex war" construct is a limited paradigm, which succeeds in reinforcing the male canon because women writers of the period are only quoted to support the claim that they hated men. This technique appears to be a "feminist" version of the New Historicism, searching texts for evidence to support the argument rather than letting the history emerge with as much force as the literature. "The battle of the sexes" paradigm was outlined many years ago in Samuel Hynes's *The Edwardian Turn of Mind*, based on an argument made by historian George Dangerfield in *The Strange Death of Liberal England*, which, in turn, was taken directly from Sylvia Pankhurst's *The Suffragette Movement*. For an analysis of the rhetoric and ideology provided by Sylvia Pankhurst to future historians, see my essay in *Suffrage and the Pankhursts* (London and New York: Routledge and Kegan Paul, 1988).

8. See *The Young Rebecca West: 1911–1917*, ed. Jane Marcus (New York: Viking, 1978). The most useful feminist history of English women's struggle is Martha Vicinus's *Independent Women* (Chicago: University of Chicago Press, 1985). Other contemporary socialist feminist theory is to be found in Cecily Hamilton's *Marriage as a Trade* (1909). Cecily Hamilton in *Life Errant* (London: J.M. Dent, 1935) regarded birth control as the most important woman's issue, arguing that there would be no advances for women "except under a system of voluntary motherhood" (p. 65). Her rebellion was directed against "the dependence implied in the idea of 'destined' marriage, 'destined' motherhood—the identification of success with marriage, of failure with spinsterhood, the artificial concentration of the hopes of girlhood on sexual attraction and maternity." Nicola Beauman in *A Very Great Profession: The Women's Novel 1914–1939* (London: Virago, 1983) regards Hamilton's *William, An Englishman* (1919) as the best of the women's novels about World War I, "a masterpiece," "incomparable," though her praise enforces an ideological design in the text which prefers a privatized "feminism" to the collective political action of the suffragettes. See also the chapter on the impact of the war on the Suffrage Movement in Sandra Holton's *Feminism and Democracy* (New York: Cambridge University Press, 1986). Holton argues that this "was not a time

of dormancy, defeatism, or depression among suffragists" (p. 116). They "remained intact" by organizing relief work.

9. *The Young Rebecca West,* p. 392.

10. Rose Macaulay's "Many Sisters to Many Brothers" is reprinted in *Scars Upon My Heart: Women's Poetry and Verse of the First World War,* ed. Judith Kazantis and Catherine Reilly (London: Virago, 1981). On Rose Macaulay see Jeanette Passty, *Eros and Androgyny: The Legacy of Rose Macaulay* (Cranbury, N.J.: Fairleigh Dickinson University Press, 1988). F. Tennyson Jesse's *The Sword of Deborah* was published by Heinemann in 1919. May Sinclair's *The Romantic* (London: Collin, 1920) is as much a novel about psychoanalysis as it is about the war. Katherine Mansfield despised its "cheap psychoanalysis," "turning life into a *case.* " Rebecca West's review of Sinclair's report on Belgium describes the effectiveness of the writing as due to its narrative as a record of "humiliations" and praises her "gallant humiliated book." Does that experience of humiliation relate to her humiliation of the "unmanly" man in the novel?

11. *The Romantic,* p. 245.

12. Sylvia Townsend Warner. *Collected Poems,* ed. Claire Harman (New York: Viking, 1982), pp. 21–22.

13. Frances Balfour (Lady). *Dr. Elsie Inglis* (London: Hodder and Stoughton, 1918), p. 144. See also May Wedderburn Cannan, *Grey Ghosts and Voices* (Roundwood Press, 1976) and Cecily Hamilton's *Life Errant* (London: J.M. Dent, 1935), p. 98. Claire Tylee also cites Mrs. St. Clair Stobart's *The Flaming Sword in Serbia and Elsewhere* (London: Hodder, 1916), whose memoir was a release from the anger, "cursing in my heart," she felt as a pacifist, easily transferring her feminism to "votes for life, justice for humankind" after the horrors she had seen in the Women's Convoy Corps, which she headed in the Balkan War, and in hospital units in Antwerp, Cherbourg, and Serbia.

14. *The Tree of Heaven* (New York: Macmillan, 1918), p. 104.

15. See "Asylums of Antaeus" for a discussion of these ideas.

16. New York: Putnam's, 1916, reprinted 1934. For the

banning of books during the war, see Angela Ingram's "Un/Reproductions," cited above.

17. *The Backwash of War*, p. 10.

18. Quoted in Roland N. Stromberg's *Redemption by War: Intellectuals and 1914* (Lawrence, Kans.: The Regents Press of Kansas, 1982), p. 235.

19. Gertrude Stein. *Paris France* (New York: Liveright, 1970), p. 38.

20. Evadne Price died in Australia in 1985. These autobiographical materials were supplied to Virago Press by Kenneth Attiwill. She married him in 1929 but told him little of her past except that she had been born of English parents off the coast of New South Wales in 1901. When her father died she went on stage to support herself. She was understudy to Dorothy Dix in *The Bird of Paradise* and played Princess Angelica in *The Rose and the Ring*. In 1918 she began work as a journalist with a column in *The Sunday Chronicle*, which also published Rebecca West and George Bernard Shaw, called "As a Woman Sees It." From there she went to *The Sunday Chronicle* and *The Daily Sketch* and began to write for serialization in *Novel Magazine* in the late 1920s the Jane Turpin children's books, which were very popular.

21. Mary Cadogan and Patricia Craig, *Women and Children First: The Fiction of the Two World Wars* (London: Victor Gollancz, 1978).

22. Quoted in Kenneth Attiwill's notes.

23. The concepts of "carnival," "heteroglossia," and "dialogism" I use here were developed by Mikhail Bakhtin in his *Rabelais* and *The Dialogic Imagination*. Gender was not a serious category for Bakhtin, but a feminist revision of his theories is useful, particularly for the intertextual reading of *All Quiet on the Western Front* and *Not So Quiet . . . ,* which is my project here, as well as for the carnivalistic aspects of eating, bleeding, defecating, and vomiting in the bodily experience of war which characterize the two texts.

24. Page numbers in the text refer to the Albert E. Marriott edition of *Not So Quiet . . . ,* London, 1930, and reprinted here by The Feminist Press, p. 30.

25. I am using the Fawcett/Crest edition of *All Quiet on the Western Front* by Erich Maria Remarque (1929), trans. A. W. Wheen. The passages on silence are on pp. 120–121: "the soundless apparitions that speak to me." For a similar procession of silent maimed men, see p. 163 of *Not So Quiet . . . .*

26. Cadogan and Craig write in *Women and Children First* "the method is blunt, brutal and ferociously expository. Subjective indignation has a corrosive effect, however, and the pile-up of disasters tends toward farce" p. 42. They find the series of novels "strangely crude and offensive in tone," "a violent, unconsidered reaction to an extreme social condition." Helen's husband Roy commits suicide in the sequel, and she is blamed for it. *Women of the Aftermath* deals with the problem of joblessness after the war and the anger of the excluded women. However, Arnold Bennett reviewed *Not So Quiet . . .* in *The Evening Standard:* "Documentary detail about the war is still thousands of miles from being completed. One might have assumed that everything had been said about the Front—until Miss Helen Zenna Smith published her affrighting book . . . which portrays minutely the daily existence of women—chauffeurs and other women workers just behind the Front. This work too may well become a prime source for historians. I am glad I read it. But no war book has appalled me more . . ."; *Arnold Bennett: The Evening Standard Years. 'Books and Persons' 1926–1931,* ed. and with intro. by Andrew Mylett (London: Chatto and Windus/Archon, 1974). My thanks to Angela Ingram for this reference as well as her invaluable help on all aspects of this essay.

27. Virginia Woolf, *Three Guineas* (New York: Harcourt, Brace, Jovanovich, 1939), p. 148.

28. In *All Quiet on the Western Front,* the bowels are the most important part of the body, as in Bakhtinian carnivalesque. There are lavatory jokes in *Not So Quiet . . . ,* but they are not so blatant. The macabre humor of war novels in relation to gender is also worth study. It is clear that Remarque's novel changed the subject of war fictions roughly from epic invocations of individual

heroism to initiation into brotherhood, and this influence can be felt in *Catch-22* and *M.A.S.H.*

29. Margaret Higonnet, "Civil Wars and Sexual Territories," paper delivered at the Second International Dubrovnik Conference on Feminist Theory, May, 1988 and included in *Arms and the Woman.*

30. For further discussion of *The Well of Loneliness* (Garden City, N.Y.: Blue Ribbon Books, 1928), see Angela Ingram's " 'Unutterable Putrefaction' and 'Foul Stuff '," and "Narration as Lesbian Seduction in *A Room of One's Own*," in my *Virginia Woolf and the Languages of Patriarchy* (Bloomington: Indiana University Press, 1987.) See also the scene in *The Well of Loneliness* in which the "general" cautions Stephen about her "emotional friendship" with Mary Llewellyn (pp. 330–331).

31. My thanks to Angela Ingram for pointing out the references to Toupie Lowther. The quotations are from Michael Baker, *Our Three Selves* (London: Hamish Hamilton, 1985), p. 125. The Hackett-Lowther papers are in the Imperial War Museum and deserve further study.

32. Lovat Dickson, *Radclyffe Hall at the Well of Loneliness: A Sapphic Chronicle* (New York: Scribners, 1975).

33. Virginia Woolf, "The Niece of an Earl," in the *Second Common Reader* (New York: Harcourt, Brace, Jovanovich, 1932), pp. 193–197.

34. Quoted in Susan Millar Williams, "Mary Borden's Experimental Fiction."

35. *Behind the Lines,* p. 119.

About the Author

Helen Zenna Smith is the pseudonym of Evadne Price (1896-1985), a novelist, journalist, playwright, and children's author. First published in London in 1930, *Not So Quiet . . .* was awarded the Prix Severigne in France as "the novel most calculated to promote international peace." Following the success of *Not So Quiet . . .,* Price wrote four other Helen Zenna Smith novels: *Women of the Aftermath* (1931); *Shadow Women* (1932); *Luxury Ladies* (1933); and *They Lived with Me* (1934).

Jane Marcus is Professor of English at The City College of New York and CUNY Graduate Center. She is author of *Virginia Woolf and the Languages of Patriarchy* (1987) and *Art and Anger: Reading Like a Woman* (1988), and editor of three collections of feminist essays on Virginia Woolf, *The Young Rebecca West*, and *Suffrage and the Pankhursts*.

REDISCOVERED CLASSICS OF WOMEN'S WRITING
from the Feminist Press at The City University of New York

A Brighter Coming Day: A Frances Ellen Watkins Harper Reader. Edited by Frances Smith Foster. $14.95 paper.

Brown Girl, Brownstones (1959), by Paule Marshall. $10.95 paper.

The Chinese Garden (1962), by Rosemary Manning. $12.95 paper. $29.00 cloth.

Daddy Was a Number Runner (1970), by Louise Meriwether. $10.95 paper.

Daughter of Earth (1929), by Agnes Smedley. $14.95 paper.

The Daughters of Danaus (1894), by Mona Caird. $13.95 paper, $35.00 cloth.

Doctor Zay (1882), by Elizabeth Stuart Phelps. $8.95 paper.

Fettered for Life (1874), by Lillie Devereux Blake. $18.95 paper, $45.00 cloth.

The Little Locksmith: A Memoir (1943) by Katharine Butler Hathaway. $14.95 paper. $35.00 cloth.

I Love Myself When I Am Laughing . . . and Then Again When I Am Looking Mean and Impressive: A Zora Neale Hurston Reader, edited by Alice Walker. $14.95 paper.

Life in the Iron Mills and Other Stories (1861), by Rebecca Harding Davis. $10.95 paper.

The Living Is Easy (1948), by Dorothy West. $14.95 paper.

Not So Quiet . . . Stepdaughters of War (1930), by Helen Zenna Smith. $11.95 paper, $35.00 cloth.

Now in November (1934), by Josephine W. Johnson. $10.95 paper, $29.95 cloth.

This Child's Gonna Live (1969), by Sarah E. Wright. $10.95 paper.

The Unpossessed (1934), by Tess Slesinger. $16.95 paper.

Unpunished: A Mystery (1929), by Charlotte Perkins Gilman. $10.95 paper, $18.95 jacketed hardcover.

Weeds (1923), by Edith Summers Kelley. $15.95 paper.

We That Were Young (1932), by Irene Rathbone. $10.95 paper. $35.00 cloth.

The Wide, Wide World (1850), by Susan Warner. $19.95 paper, $35.00 cloth.

The Yellow Wall-Paper (1892), by Charlotte Perkins Gilman, $5.95 paper.

To receive a free catalog of The Feminist Press's 180 titles, call or write The Feminist Press at The City University of New York, 365 Fifth Avenue, New York, NY 10016; phone: (212) 817-7920; fax: (212) 987-4008; www.feministpress.org. Feminist Press books are available at bookstores or can be ordered directly. Send check or money order (in U.S. dollars drawn on a U.S. bank) payable to The Feminist Press. Please add $4.00 shipping and handling for the first book and $1.00 for each additional book. VISA, Mastercard, and American Express are accepted for telephone orders. Prices subject to change.